The Sweet Hereafter

"It's pretty obvious that the cause of death was a knife wound. And on the edge of the hole in the blouse, Calvin found cake frosting," Mike said.

Phyllis stared at the knife. She and Carolyn had used it quite a bit during the carnival to cut samples for people. She saw some of that frosting dried on the blade. "Oh, my God," she said softly. "My God. You mean we used it to cut . . ." She suddenly felt sick to her stomach. "Thank goodness you got here when you did."

The idea that she could have used the knife to cut a piece of cake for the murdered woman's daughter was grotesque.

"The paramedics said it looked like a stab wound to the chest. Probably got the heart. Mrs. Dunston wouldn't have lived long after that," said Sam.

A little voice piped up.

"Mrs. Dunston? You mean Becca's mama?"

Phyllis looked around in horror and saw that a small boy had come up to the table without any of them noticing.

He went on. "You said you were gonna get us somethin' to eat." Then he turned his head and shouted, "Hey, Becca, did you know your mama got stabbed in the heart?"

MURDER BY THE SLICE

A Fresh-Baked Mystery

Livia J. Washburn

AN OBSIDIAN MYSTERY

OBSIDIAN
Published by New American Library, a division of
Penguin Group (USA) Inc., 375 Hudson Street,
New York, New York 10014, USA
Penguin Group (Canada), 90 Eglinton Avenue East, Suite 700, Toronto,
Ontario M4P 2Y3, Canada (a division of Pearson Penguin Canada Inc.)
Penguin Books Ltd., 80 Strand, London WC2R 0RL, England
Penguin Ireland, 25 St. Stephen's Green, Dublin 2,
Ireland (a division of Penguin Books Ltd.)
Penguin Group (Australia), 250 Camberwell Road, Camberwell, Victoria 3124,
Australia (a division of Pearson Australia Group Pty. Ltd.)
Penguin Books India Pvt. Ltd., 11 Community Centre, Panchsheel Park,
New Delhi - 110 017, India
Penguin Group (NZ), 67 Apollo Drive, Rosedale, North Shore 0745,
Auckland, New Zealand (a division of Pearson New Zealand Ltd.)
Penguin Books (South Africa) (Pty.) Ltd., 24 Sturdee Avenue,
Rosebank, Johannesburg 2196, South Africa

Penguin Books Ltd., Registered Offices:
80 Strand, London WC2R 0RL, England

First published by Obsidian, an imprint of New American Library,
a division of Penguin Group (USA) Inc.

First Printing, October 2007
10 9 8 7 6 5 4

Copyright © Livia Reasoner, 2007
All rights reserved

OBSIDIAN and logo are trademarks of Penguin Group (USA) Inc.

Printed in the United States of America

This book is dedicated to all PTO and PTA volunteers, with a special thanks to the ladies I worked with at Azle Elementary—Joan Faulkner, Lynne Hall, Janet Merck, Rene Heerwagen, Teresa Dyer, Naomi Washburn, Jennifer Lauderdale, Karen Propp, Tracy Williams, Cynthia Robertson, Barb Karbo, Jeri Geary, Lori Bearfield, Marla Grant, Karen Campbell, Tammy McCraven, Lisette Edgar—and the only guy on the board, my husband, James Reasoner.

Chapter 1

The sun blazed down on the sidewalk in front of the Wal-Mart located in Weatherford, Texas. Phyllis Newsom was glad she had worn a hat to shade her head. Unfortunately, that didn't help the part of her sitting on the uncomfortable metal folding chair.

According to the calendar autumn had started, but that didn't mean the weather had begun to cool off. That was still a month away, maybe even longer. For now, it was still hot—Texas hot.

From the chair beside Phyllis's, Eve Turner waved at someone she knew and called, "Hello there, dear. Would you like to buy a cake or some cookies and help out the Retired Teachers Association Scholarship Fund?"

The man she had spoken to looked a little uncomfortable, as well he might since his wife was with him. Eve had probably had one or more of their children in her English class when she was still teaching, and knowing Eve, she had flirted shamelessly with the man at every school function the parents attended. As she smiled brightly at the man, he said, "Ah, maybe when we come out."

His wife just tightened her grip on his arm and kept walking.

Phyllis wasn't surprised by Eve's failure to sell anything. She had been out here for nearly an hour with Eve, Carolyn Wilbarger, and Sam Fletcher, the four of them sitting behind a folding table filled with cakes and plates of cookies, and they'd sold very little. The cookies were holding up fine, but the icing on the cakes was starting to melt against the clear plastic wrap that covered them.

Phyllis glanced up at the sun. It would move around the building so that they would be in the shade in another hour or so, but it was going to be a long hour until then.

She was as enthusiastic a member of the Retired Teachers Association as anyone—she had spent almost her entire adult life teaching, after all—but she wished she hadn't let herself be talked into helping man this bake sale table.

It was awfully difficult to say no to Dolly Williamson, the retired superintendent of the school district and the head of the RTA. Besides, the scholarship fund needed to be built up again. Each year the association awarded college scholarships to two deserving students who were the children of educators. The amount of those scholarships depended entirely on how much money the association could raise during the year.

The fall bake sale was the first major fund-raiser each year. Dolly had persuaded Carolyn to help with it, and from there it was inevitable that Phyllis, Eve, and Sam would be drawn in, as well. The four of them shared the big house that Phyllis had lived in for years with her late husband, Kenny, and they were good friends.

One thing you could say about Wal-Mart: The place didn't lack for customers, especially on a sunny Saturday afternoon. A steady stream of people had gone in and out of the store since Phyllis and the others had set up their table and chairs and hung the signs Phyllis had printed on the computer announcing what the bake sale was for. A few of them stopped and bought cookies on their way back to their cars. Phyllis didn't think they had sold a single cake.

In a way, she could understand why. It cost so much to live these days that most folks really had to watch what they spent. But it was for a good cause, and the prices weren't really that bad.

A pickup drove by with country music blasting through its open windows. It was followed a few minutes later by another pickup with loud rap music coming from it. Phyllis was always a little amused by the sight of young white men in snap-button shirts and cowboy hats listening to rap, but it was becoming more common.

She saw an attractive woman in her thirties emerge from the store and start toward the bake sale table with a couple of elementary-aged children in tow, a boy and a girl. The woman had shoulder-length light brown hair and wore blue jeans and a T-shirt with LOVING ELEMENTARY printed on it. Phyllis knew that wasn't a declaration of affection but rather a reference to Oliver Loving Elementary School, one of several elementary schools in the Weatherford School District. It was named for the famous rancher and cattleman who had been the inspiration for one of the characters in *Lonesome Dove,* either Gus or Call; Phyllis never could remember which. Loving was buried here in Weatherford.

The woman had a somewhat harried look about her— shopping at Wal-Mart with a couple of kids would do that— but she smiled pleasantly as she came up to the table and said, "Hello, Carolyn."

"Marie, it's good to see you," Carolyn said. "How's Russ?"

"Oh, all right, I guess."

Carolyn turned to Phyllis and asked, "Do you know Marie Tyler?"

"I don't believe so," Phyllis said.

Carolyn performed the introductions, adding, "And that's Amber and Aaron. Marie and her husband, Russ, go to the same church I do."

"It's nice to meet you, Marie," Phyllis said.

"You, too." Marie turned back to Carolyn and went on, "You know I'm on the PTO board at the school."

"No, I didn't know that, but I'm not surprised."

"Yeah, I'm the fund-raising chairperson. You know what that means at this time of year."

"The carnival," Phyllis and Carolyn and Eve all said at the same time.

Marie nodded. "That's right."

Sam leaned back in his chair, propped a foot on the other leg's somewhat knobby knee, and said with a smile, "Coachin' at the high school, I never had much to do with the elementary carnivals, except one year when they decided to put on a donkey basketball game in conjunction with it." He shook his head. "Before that was over, I sure wished I'd never agreed to let those donkeys in my gym."

"Well, we're not going to have any donkey basketball games," Marie said, "although we may have a pony ride. But it'll be outside on the playground."

Phyllis had taught junior high history, but she had been involved in several elementary school carnivals when her son, Mike, was that age. She had been a member of what was then called the PTA—the Parent-Teacher Association—at the school he'd attended. These days it was called the Parent-Teacher Organization, but pretty much only the name had changed. The group was still composed mostly of parents and run by a board of half a dozen or so volunteers, almost always women. It was very rare to find a man willing to be on a PTO board. Finding enough volunteer moms to take care of everything was a big enough chore.

The PTO spent most of the year raising funds. The money was spent on things the school needed that weren't included in the budget, such as copy machines, extra books for the library, and playground equipment. One of the major fund-raisers was the school carnival, usually held sometime during October. In the old days, they had often been tied in with Halloween, but of course such things were forbidden now. They had to be called fall carnivals or harvest festivals or something noncontroversial like that.

The classic school carnival was set up on the playground, with open booths around the edges, which were formed by bales of hay or sketchy wooden frameworks. Each homeroom in the school was responsible for one of the booths, where games designed to appeal to young children were played, such as ring toss, throwing a baseball at stacks of milk bottles, and "fishing" in wading pools filled with sand and little prizes. Other games that required more room were conducted out in the middle of the playground. There were also face-painting and temporary tattoo booths and sometimes dunking booths, pony rides, miniature trains, "bounce houses," and anything else the PTO board could scrounge up to make a little money. There was no charge to attend the carnival, but to take part in any of the games required a fifty-cent ticket at each booth. Kids raced from booth to booth, clutching strings of tickets and the prizes they had already won. Inside the school, in the gymnasium and the cafeteria, other activities would take place, such as entertainment by local musicians and dancers, and there was a snack bar selling cold drinks, hot dogs, nachos, and candy.

And there was usually a bake sale, too, Phyllis suddenly remembered, which was why it came as no surprise to her when Marie Tyler said, "I could really use some help, Carolyn, and from the looks of this, you and your friends have a lot of experience with bake sales."

"Oh, I don't know . . . ," Carolyn said, as Phyllis was silently pleading, *Don't get us involved in this. Please, Carolyn.*

Marie leaned closer to the table and lowered her voice to a conspiratorial volume. "It would mean a lot to me if I could find somebody willing to take over the bake sale. There's just so much involved in putting on one of these carnivals, and to tell you the truth, Shannon's really been on my ass lately about getting it all done."

Phyllis tried not to let her lips tighten in disapproval at Marie's crude language. She didn't like to be judgmental, and she knew perfectly well that this was a different day and age from the one in which she had grown up. But it still bothered her to hear a lady talk like that, especially in front of little ones.

Carolyn looked over at her and asked, "What do you think, Phyllis?"

I think you're trying to pass the buck to me and make me be the bad guy, Phyllis thought. But she said, "We pretty much have our plates full with the Retired Teachers Association—"

Before she could actually say no, another woman walked up to the table. She was older and heavyset, and the brightly colored dress she wore made her look even bigger. Her hair was dyed a startling shade of black. She said in a booming voice, "Hello, ladies. And you, too, of course, Sam."

"Howdy, Dolly," he said with a nod. "Good to see you again."

"Marie, how are you?" Dolly Williamson said as she put her arms around Marie and gave her a hug. Phyllis wasn't surprised that Dolly knew who Marie was. The former superintendent was still so plugged in to the school district that she probably knew all the PTO board members from every campus.

"I'm fine, Mrs. Williamson," Marie said. "I was just trying to recruit Carolyn and her friends to run the bake sale for the carnival at Loving."

"Why, I think that's a wonderful idea!" Dolly beamed at the four people behind the table. "I know you'll all do a fine job."

"Wait a minute," Phyllis began, but she had a sinking feeling that it was already too late. Once Dolly got an idea in her head, she was the original unstoppable force.

"After all," Dolly went on as if she hadn't heard Phyllis, "you're doing so well here."

"Haven't sold much," Sam said.

"You will, you will. Everything looks so good." Dolly

turned back to Marie. "This was lucky for you, my dear. Now you can concentrate on the rest of your job."

"I know," Marie said. She gave Phyllis and the others a smile and added, "Thank you guys so much."

Phyllis felt like pointing out that she wasn't a "guy," and neither were Carolyn and Eve. But there was no point in worrying about such things now, she told herself. What mattered was that she had been roped into helping with the carnival bake sale, along with her friends. They might have been able to withstand the pressure from Marie, but once Dolly had walked up and found out what was going on, they were lost.

Dolly gave Marie another hug and waved a pudgy hand at the others, then went into the store. Marie said, "I'll give you a call, Carolyn, and let you know all the details you'll need to know. Thanks again."

Carolyn nodded and smiled weakly. "You're welcome."

"This'll help keep Shannon from giving me so much shi—I mean, trouble." Marie waved and added, "Bye, guys," as she led her kids into the parking lot and headed for the family SUV.

Carolyn turned to the others and said, "I'm sorry. I don't know what happened."

"Dolly happened," Sam said. He chuckled. "Sort of like a force of nature, isn't she? Doesn't have to stay around very long, but when she rolls through, she brings changes."

"Well, maybe it'll be fun," Carolyn said. "It might be, you never know. And we *do* have experience at putting on bake sales."

Eve said, "Perhaps you do, dear. I was never really the domestic type." She smiled over at Sam, with whom she had been flirting ever since he had rented a room from Phyllis and moved into the big old house on the tree-shaded street a few blocks from the courthouse square. "Which isn't to say that I couldn't still learn if I needed to. If the right man came along and asked the right question . . ."

Sam called to a family going into the store, "You folks want to buy some cookies?"

Phyllis leaned over to Carolyn and asked, "Who's this Shannon that Marie was talking about?"

"Shannon Dunston," Carolyn replied. "She's the president of the PTO board at Loving. And from what I hear, she runs things with an iron fist, as the old saying goes."

"That's odd. Usually you try to get people to do things by being nice to them, especially when you're relying on volunteers."

"That's not the way Shannon looks at it. Although I shouldn't say that, since I don't really know her. I'm just going by what I've heard."

"Well, maybe with our help, she'll get off Marie's, uh, posterior." Phyllis looked at the other three. "Right . . . guys?"

Chapter 2

"I have an idea," Carolyn said as she came into the kitchen.

From under the sink, where she was struggling to fit a pipe wrench around a balky pipe, Phyllis said, "That's nice."

She could have hired a plumber to fix the leaking pipe. She could have even asked Sam to have a go at it. He had all sorts of tools and spent a lot of time building and repairing furniture on Kenny's workbench in the big garage, and more than once he had told Phyllis he would be glad to help out with any handyman work that needed to be done around the house.

But she was stubborn enough to feel that *she* ought to at least try to do it. This was her house, after all, and when Kenny was alive he had taken care of it. She owed it to his memory to continue the tradition.

On the other hand, even when she got the wrench on the pipe, she couldn't budge it. Years of teaching in the public schools had taught her to choose her battles wisely and be selective about which brick walls she picked to bang her head against.

Dressed in jeans and a comfortable shirt, she scooted out from under the sink and placed the big wrench on the floor.

"What on earth are you doing?" Carolyn asked.

"Leaky pipe." Phyllis pushed back several strands of graying brown hair that had fallen over her eyes, then reached up to grab hold of the kitchen counter and steady herself as she climbed to her feet.

"You should let Sam do that."

Phyllis didn't let on that she had come to the same conclusion. Instead she said, "You were saying something about having an idea."

"Oh, yes. About the bake sale at the carnival."

Several days had passed since their encounter with Marie Tyler at Wal-Mart. During that time Carolyn had called some of their friends in the Retired Teachers Association, trying to line up people who could be counted on to supply goods for the bake sale. Of course, parents of the students at Loving Elementary would be asked to donate cakes and pies, too, but young people were so busy these days you couldn't rely on them to provide enough help. Another lesson teachers quickly learned was that if something absolutely had to be done, you'd better be prepared to do it yourself.

"Everyone does a regular bake sale," Carolyn went on. "The RTA just did the one at Wal-Mart."

Phyllis didn't need to be reminded. It had been a long afternoon without many results. They had raised less than a hundred dollars.

"People are tired of them. I think we need to do something different."

"All right," Phyllis said. "What can you do different with a bake sale, though? The whole thing's pretty cut-and-dried."

Carolyn held up both index fingers. "We keep the auction where we get people to donate the fanciest, most elaborately decorated, most unusual cakes they can come up with and then auction them off to the people who attend the carnival."

An idea occurred to Phyllis. "You know, I saw something in a magazine—"

Her mouth clamped shut. She had almost made a mistake.

She had almost spilled a possible plan to an archrival.

Phyllis and Carolyn were friends, of course. They had known each other for many years and shared this house for several. But that didn't mean they didn't also have a healthy sense of competition with each other. Both women had entered numerous baking and cooking contests, including the one at the Peach Festival held in Weatherford every summer, and at times the competition between them had become rather intense. Carolyn had emerged triumphant more often than not, and Phyllis tried to tell herself not to let that bother her, but it was difficult not to, sometimes.

The previous summer, all that had taken a backseat to the tragedy at the Peach Festival and the other murders that had occurred, but those troubles were behind them now and Phyllis's thoughts were turning to other matters. Even though the auction wasn't exactly a contest, Phyllis had a feeling that her friend would try to come up with the cake that sold for the largest amount of money. That was in Carolyn's nature.

And in her own, too, Phyllis was forced to admit as she realized why she was being secretive about what she had seen in the magazine. She didn't want Carolyn stealing her idea.

"What were you saying?" Carolyn asked.

"Never mind," Phyllis said with a wave of her hand. Carolyn was still holding up both index fingers. "So, what was your idea that would make it different?"

"We can have a contest, too."

Here we go, Phyllis thought. "A contest?" Carolyn had gotten around to that even more quickly than Phyllis had expected.

"Yes, but not with the fancy cakes. Those will just be for show, and for the auction."

"Okay," Phyllis said, not sure now where Carolyn was going with this.

"The contest will be to see who can come up with the best-tasting healthy snack."

Phyllis frowned. "Healthy snack? Isn't that an oxymoron?"

"It doesn't have to be." Carolyn waved her hands with enthusiasm. "Think about it, Phyllis. When we were teaching, didn't you absolutely hate seeing what those poor children put in their mouths all the time? Twinkies and potato chips and candy bars and on and on, everything either packed with sugar or salt, nothing but empty calories and fat. It was awful. And most of the time it was the parents who put those things in their kids' lunches."

Phyllis knew that Carolyn was right, at least to a certain extent. Kids had never eaten healthy, not back in the sixties and seventies when her own son, Mike, was a little boy and not now. But Phyllis had tended to worry more about her students who came to school with *nothing* to eat, rather than the ones consuming junk food. Then there were the students who were abused or sick . . . When it came to children, there were definitely enough worries to go around.

"So you think we should have a contest for healthy snacks?"

"That's right. Everyone who wants to enter would pay a small entry fee . . . a donation to the school, really, is what it amounts to . . . and the people who come to the carnival would have to pay to be the judges. A couple of tickets would entitle them to sample all the entries, and then they could vote on which one was the best. At the end of the carnival, when we auction off the cakes, we'll also announce the big winner of the contest." Carolyn beamed. "Everyone likes snacks. And everyone likes a contest, too."

Maybe she was right, Phyllis thought. It wouldn't cost anything to try, and again, it was a variation from the run-of-the-mill bake sale. She wasn't sure how well the idea of healthy snacks would go over with the kids, though. The little Twinkie-munchers *liked* their goodies crammed full of sugar and sodium and fat.

"So you'll enter, Phyllis?"

"I don't know. I have a lot to do around here."

Carolyn waved a hand at the sink. The cabinet doors were still open underneath it. "What, fixing leaky pipes? You should leave that to someone who knows what he's doing."

Phyllis caught that reference to *he*. "You think a woman can't fix a pipe? You think we're just suited for baking and things like that?" She knew she sounded irritated. She couldn't help it.

"I never said that. I just assumed you'd want another chance to try to beat me at something."

"Oh, you're entering the contest, are you?"

"I certainly am."

"Even though you're in charge? Doesn't that strike you as being a conflict of interest?"

"Not at all," Carolyn said. "All the entries will be assigned a number, and they'll be judged anonymously. We won't know who came up with the winning snack until it's all over."

Phyllis was tempted; she truly was. Although she got tired of losing to Carolyn, she enjoyed their competition. This time, though, she was going to remain above the fray, as the old saying went.

Anyway, she had a much better idea for a fancy decorated cake than she did for a healthy snack that kids probably wouldn't like, anyway.

She shook her head and said, "I'll donate a cake for the auction, but I just don't have time to come up with something for the contest. I'm sorry, Carolyn. Right now I have to get back to this job." She knelt, picked up the wrench, and crawled under the sink again.

"You're sure?"

"I'm sure." Phyllis's reply sounded hollow inside the

cabinet. She lifted the heavy wrench and again fit it around the pipe.

"Well, all right." Carolyn's footsteps retreated from the kitchen. Phyllis decided to wait a few minutes to be sure she was really gone before scooting out from under the sink.

Before she could do that, more footsteps entered the kitchen, heavier ones this time, and Sam Fletcher's deep voice asked, "What are you doin' under there, Phyllis?"

She knew that she probably looked utterly undignified. Not only that, but she could tell that her shirt had hiked up a little as she moved around, revealing a few inches of bare belly. She tugged it down and said, "One of the pipes is leaking."

"Want me to take a look at it?" He hunkered down so that he could peer into the cabinet under the sink.

Something about lying there like that with Sam so close by made her uncomfortable. She slid out, but that pushed her shirt up again and she had to grab it and pull it down. "Please," she said as she sat up. "I don't know whether to tighten it or loosen it or what to do."

He took the wrench from her and lay down on his back, putting his head and shoulders into the cabinet. Phyllis remained where she was, sitting on the kitchen floor beside him.

"Carolyn looked a little disappointed when she came out of here," Sam commented as he worked with the wrench.

"She wanted me to enter a cooking contest she's going to put on at that school carnival."

"Another contest, eh? You going to enter?"

"No, I don't think so. She's doing a cake auction, too, and I think I'd rather do that."

"Well, I'm sure you'll come up with something mighty fine."

"Oh, it doesn't really matter. It's just to raise money for the PTO."

"And braggin' rights, I expect."

Rather than respond to that comment, Phyllis leaned over and looked under the sink. "Do you know what's wrong with it?"

"Might need a new washer. . . ." Sam tugged on the wrench. Something cracked, and suddenly water spurted out, splattering over his face. "Oh, shoot! Phyllis, cut the water off! Wait—never mind—I got it!" He twisted something on one of the pipes, and the water slowed to a trickle, then stopped entirely.

"What a mess," Phyllis said as Sam scooted out from inside the wet cabinet.

"Sorry." He raked dripping hair out of his eyes. "I'll get a towel and mop it all up. I'm afraid plumbing's just not my strong suit."

"Don't worry about it. I should have called somebody to take care of it to start with."

"I'll pay for a plumber. I'm the one who cracked that pipe."

"Oh, no, you were just trying to help. It's my responsibility."

"I insist—"

Eve walked into the kitchen at that moment and stood there for a couple of seconds looking at them as they sat side by side on the floor, both splattered with water, Sam's head soaked.

"My," Eve said coolly, "what have you two been doing?"

Without waiting for an answer, she turned and walked out of the kitchen.

The level of awkwardness in the room immediately rose. It shouldn't have, Phyllis told herself. It wasn't as if Eve had walked in and found them rolling around on the floor in each other's arms or anything like that. Phyllis liked Sam and enjoyed his company, and she knew the feeling was mutual, but that was all there was to it. Both of them were too . . . mature . . . to be thinking about anything else.

"I'll get that towel," Sam said as he climbed to his feet. He paused to extend a hand to Phyllis. "Let me help you up."

"I'm fine, thanks." She grabbed the cabinet and pulled herself up as she had before. She didn't meet Sam's eyes, and she noticed that he wasn't making an effort to look at her, either. She wasn't sure whether she ought to feel relieved or disappointed about that.

Relieved, she decided. Definitely relieved.

Chapter 3

As soon as she got a chance to do so in private, Phyllis found the magazine where she had seen the idea for a fancy decorated jack-o'-lantern cake. It started with two Bundt cakes—white, chocolate, or even pumpkin spice—with the flat sides layered together. Then it was covered with orange frosting to make the cake resemble a pumpkin. Chocolate frosting was then used to form the mouth, nose, and eyes of the jack-o'-lantern. The illustration in the magazine showed an ice-cream cone in the middle for the stem, but Phyllis thought it might be cute to frost a cupcake green for the stem. It didn't appear to be a project that would be terribly difficult to do, and yet the finished product had a striking appearance. Even though school carnivals weren't allowed to be called Halloween carnivals anymore, the one at Loving Elementary was going to take place only a few days before that spooky holiday. The jack-o'-lantern cake would tie in perfectly. Surely someone would be having a Halloween party and would think a pumpkin cake was perfect for it. That would increase the chances of bids. The more Phyllis thought about it, the more she was convinced that was what she wanted to make. She told herself she would go to the store the next day and get the ingredients. She would have to practice. Like most things in life, any baking project was a process of trial and error, something that beginning cooks sometimes didn't understand. You couldn't expect everything to turn out right the first time.

But she couldn't cook much until the water was back on in the kitchen, so instead the next day was spent dealing with a plumber who replaced the cracked pipe and the worn-out washer that had caused the problem in the first place.

Eve was still acting rather cool toward her and Sam. During the months Sam had lived here, Eve had flirted with him every chance she got, and while Sam had certainly been polite and friendly toward her, he hadn't responded in any other way—at least not as far as Phyllis knew. Maybe Eve was getting tired of having her advances go unreturned. Maybe she had read more into the situation in the kitchen than had really been there. Phyllis didn't know about that, but she sensed that saying anything about it to Eve might do more harm than good. It would be better to leave the situation alone and let it blow over in its own good time.

Or as her father probably would have put it, *Don't poke that bear with a stick.*

That evening the phone rang, and when Phyllis answered it, Marie Tyler was on the other end. She asked to speak to Carolyn, who talked to her for several minutes before hanging up. Carolyn turned to Phyllis and said, "That was Marie. They're having a planning meeting for the carnival at the school tomorrow, and she wants us to come."

Phyllis frowned. "Us?"

"Actually, she just asked me to attend, but I wish you'd come, too, Phyllis. When we were teaching, you were always better at dealing with parents than I was."

Phyllis made an effort to keep her eyebrows from going up in surprise. It wasn't like Carolyn to admit that anybody was better than her at anything. Something had to be bothering her. Phyllis thought about asking her what it was, but she knew Carolyn would tell without asking if she wanted Phyllis to know what was bothering her. Instead, Phyllis said, "I suppose I could go along."

"Thank you." Carolyn hesitated. "To tell you the truth, after all the stories I've heard about Shannon Dunston . . ." Her voice trailed off and she shook her head. "I just thought it might be a good idea to have some moral support there."

Phyllis remembered the comments Marie had made about Shannon when they were talking at Wal-Mart. "How did someone people don't seem to like very much wind up getting elected president of the PTO?"

"No one else wanted the job, I imagine. You know how hard it is now just getting people to serve on the board, let alone as officers."

Phyllis nodded. She was sure Carolyn was right. More families had both parents working than they did a few years earlier. She imagined it would be hard to take off work for the things the PTO did at the schools all through the year. Bosses probably wouldn't understand losing their employees to Santa's Workshop or the Spring Book Fair.

The next morning they took Phyllis's car and drove out to Loving Elementary. Weatherford had grown so much, with housing developments sprawling all around the previously undeveloped outer edges of the city, that several new elementary schools had been built in recent years to relieve the overcrowded classrooms in the old ones. The new schools were located a short distance out of town, close to where the students actually lived. This was a fairly new way of doing things. When Phyllis had first started teaching, more than forty years earlier, schools had always been built in a central location, and students who lived in outlying areas were forced to come to them, rather than the other way around.

Oliver Loving Elementary School was on a farm-to-market road off the old Fort Worth highway. It was built in the shape of a large T. The hallways where the classrooms were located ran to the right and left from the lobby at the front entrance. Straight ahead was another hallway with the gym on one side and the office, the library, and the cafeteria on the other. In front of the school was a small parking lot, with a larger lot off to one side where the bus lane was located.

There were a few spaces in the small lot when Phyllis and Carolyn arrived. As they got out of the Lincoln, Phyllis couldn't help but hear loud voices coming from a man and woman who stood next to one of the other cars.

The woman, a pretty brunette around forty, was saying, "Think again. I know you have the money, Joel."

"Of course I do, but the office renovation cost more than I expected and it would really help me out if you would—"

"And why exactly would I be interested in helping you out?" Scorn dripped from the woman's voice as she interrupted the man. "I don't owe you any favors."

"You could cut me a little slack, for old times' sake, if nothing else."

"Old times? Old times? You mean like when we were *married*? You mean when I thought we had a happy family? Is that what you mean?"

Phyllis and Carolyn exchanged a glance and walked briskly toward the school entrance, being careful not to look at the arguing couple. Another thing that had changed during the decades Phyllis taught was the exploding divorce rate. In her first classes there had been only a few students whose parents were divorced. By the time of her retirement, the situation had turned around. The students who lived with both birth parents were the uncommon ones. So many of the kids had stepparents, stepsiblings, half siblings, parents who had been married three or four or even five times . . . Phyllis knew that sometimes marriages broke up and it just couldn't be helped. But she hated to see the dissolution of families become such an epidemic.

The voices behind them had grown louder and more angry by the time Phyllis and Carolyn reached the entrance. Phyllis felt a sense of relief as they went inside. Violence at a school had once been unheard of. Now angry ex-spouses had been known to cause trouble and even get into fights at school. It was a dangerous world out there and becoming more so all the time.

They stopped in the office to ask where the carnival planning meeting was being held. Phyllis had been to Loving Elementary before but didn't know any of the staff. A secretary directed them to a conference room down the hallway to the right.

It was just before ten o'clock in the morning, which meant that the kids had been in class for almost two hours. As Phyllis and Carolyn walked down the hall, Phyllis heard the voices of the teachers inside the classrooms, mixed with an occasional burst of laughter or the voice of a child asking a question. She had never taught elementary school; her subject had been eighth-grade history. But all schools, even these new ones, had similar smells and sounds and an indefinable something in the air that told you immediately where you were. Most of the time Phyllis was glad that she had retired and didn't miss teaching at all, but there were moments, especially when she was inside a school, when something inside gave a little twinge and tried to pull her into the classroom. She wanted to be up there in front of that roomful of students again, looking out at their faces—some eager, some bored, some openly hostile—and seeing the promise in all of them, even in the ones who had no idea it was there.

But then the feeling passed, thank goodness. She had done her time. The torch had passed to other educators.

They came to the conference room. The door there was open, too. It was a fairly small room, with most of the space taken up by a long, narrow table. Half a dozen women were seated at the table, talking among themselves. They looked up as Phyllis and Carolyn entered the room. Some of them smiled, Phyllis noticed, but a few just looked curiously at them.

"Oh, hey, there you guys are," Marie Tyler said as she got

to her feet. She turned to the others and went on, "This is Carolyn Wilbarger and, uh, Phyllis, right?"

"Phyllis Newsom," Phyllis said. Some of the women at the table looked vaguely familiar to her. They were old enough that they might have had kids in some of her last classes. That was another thing she had noticed about modern women. Some of them had kids, waited ten or fifteen years, and then had more. Even though very few families had seven or eight children spanning more than a dozen years in age, as had once been common, it wasn't unusual to find one where the oldest children were in high school, even college, and the youngest still in elementary school. Carolyn had told her about one case where mother and daughter had been pregnant at the same time and had even delivered during the same week, resulting in the older woman becoming a new mom and a first-time grandmother in the space of a few days.

"Carolyn and Phyllis are going to help us out with the bake sale," Marie continued. "Both of them are retired teachers, and they can't wait to pitch in with the carnival."

That was stretching things a little, Phyllis thought, but she was willing to forgive Marie's enthusiasm.

"I remember you," one of the women said to Phyllis. "You taught at the junior high, didn't you?"

"Eighth-grade history," Phyllis confirmed. She hoped she hadn't given this woman's child a bad grade. Of course, if she had, the kid should have worked harder.

The woman smiled. "You were one of my daughter's favorite teachers. I'm Abby Granger." She had short blond hair and freckles and looked like a woman who spent a lot of time outdoors. Phyllis would have been willing to bet that the family had horses.

She returned Abby's smile and said, "It's good to see you again, Mrs. Granger. How's Kayla doing?" Phyllis wasn't sure how she had plucked that name out of her memory. She hoped it was the right one.

It was. Abby said, "She's doing fine. Starting her junior year at A&M."

Phyllis nodded. "Say hello to her for me."

Marie went around the table making the rest of the introductions. "This is Holly Underwood . . . Kristina Padgett . . . Lindsey Gonzales . . . and Irene Vernon."

Phyllis and Carolyn said their hellos, and Lindsey Gonzales, who despite her name was a tall, blue-eyed blonde, waved them into chairs and said, "We'll get started as soon as Shannon gets here."

"We can't start until then," Marie said. "We wouldn't dare."

The women all exchanged looks, and Phyllis was reminded all over again that the board president, Shannon Dunston, was not one of their favorite people. She wondered if they had all known beforehand that they would have a hard time getting along with Shannon, or if that had become apparent only after she had taken the reins of power.

"So you're going to help us with the bake sale," Holly Underwood said. She was one of the older board members, somewhere between forty and fifty, with quite a bit of gray in her brown hair.

"Actually, I have an idea about that," Carolyn began.

"Save it until Shannon gets here," Marie said. "There's no point in discussing anything until then, because she'll have to approve anything we do."

Phyllis couldn't stop herself from asking, "Don't you vote on things?"

Again the women looked at each other, and then Abby Granger said dryly, "Some votes are more equal than others."

Phyllis wondered if it was too late for her and Carolyn to back out. After all, they weren't members of the board. They weren't even members of the Loving Elementary PTO. They were just here to lend a helping hand to a worthwhile cause.

More people had probably gotten into more trouble that way, Phyllis reflected.

The women chatted among themselves for several more minutes as a feeling of impatience grew in the air. A few of them glanced at their watches. A couple took cell phones from their purses and checked for text messages.

"I don't understand," Irene Vernon finally said. "The meeting *was* scheduled for today, wasn't it?"

Marie nodded. "Yes, and Shannon is usually very prompt. We're the ones who usually get in trouble for being a few minutes late."

A moment later they all looked around as the sound of footsteps came from the hall, moving swiftly and purposefully toward the conference room. A woman appeared in the doorway. She came into the room and put a large purse down on the table with a little more force than was absolutely necessary.

"Good," she said, her voice as sharp as her movements. "You're all here."

Phyllis wasn't a bit surprised to see that the newcomer was the angry brunette from the parking lot.

Chapter 4

The woman switched her gaze to Phyllis and Carolyn. "Who are you," she demanded, "and what are you doing here? This is a special meeting of the Loving Elementary PTO board."

Marie said, "Shannon, this is Carolyn Wilbarger and Phyllis Newsom. I told you they'd be here, remember?"

Actually, thought Phyllis, Marie had only been expecting Carolyn, but clearly she didn't mind that Phyllis had tagged along. Shannon Dunston minded, though. She was glaring at both of them like they were interlopers.

"We're supposed to help with the bake sale at the carnival," Carolyn said.

Shannon took a deep breath and blew it out through her nose. "All right. Let's get this meeting started. We've already wasted enough time." She sat down in the chair at the head of the table. "Let's hear your reports."

One by one, the women began explaining the preparations they had undertaken to get ready for the carnival. Phyllis had never given the matter much thought, but she was surprised just how much went into putting on one of these things. There were all sorts of supplies to be gathered; construction work to carry out; arrangements to be made for the rental of a bounce house, a dunking booth, and a little train that was pulled by a tractor; paperwork to be filled out for the school district, which would be charging the PTO a fee for the use of the property; even a liability insurance policy that had to be bought just for the day of the carnival. With all these expenses, Phyllis felt like asking how the PTO or any other organization that put on a fund-raiser ever made any money.

Each of the board members had a different task assigned to her, with Marie in overall charge of the preparations because she was the fund-raising chairperson. In addition, she had volunteered to personally oversee the bake sale, Phyllis gathered, before realizing that taking on that chore was too much on top of her other duties. So she had turned to Carolyn for help, and Carolyn, in turn, had called on Phyllis.

Eventually, Marie turned to them and said, "Ladies, what about the bake sale? I'd suggest printing up fliers about needing donations of baked goods. You can give them to the room mothers to distribute to all the parents—"

"Room parents," Shannon broke in. "You can't say room mothers. It's sexist."

"Well, yes, of course. I didn't mean anything by it. It's just that when all of us were kids it was always the moms who served as room parents. The dads didn't—"

"They still don't. We all know nothing would ever get done if it was up to the fathers to do it."

No one made any reply to Shannon's coldly voiced comment. After a moment of awkward silence, Carolyn glanced at Phyllis, who smiled and nodded in a show of that moral support for which Carolyn had asked.

"Actually, I have an idea about the bake sale," Carolyn said. "I'm not sure we should do a traditional one."

"There's always a bake sale at the carnival," Shannon said.

"Yes, but they don't make much money these days. A lot of the baked goods are usually left over and have to be thrown away or taken home by the volunteers." Carolyn ventured a smile. "You ladies are all young enough so that you can afford to have some pies and cakes and cookies around the house without threatening your figures, but I'm not."

Some of the women smiled, but Shannon said, "Get to your point. If we don't even have a bake sale, why are you here?"

"I think you should have the cake auction that you've had in the past," Carolyn said. "And at the same time, you can have a contest for the healthiest snack."

Several of the women looked at Marie. Phyllis knew what they were thinking: Marie was the one who had brought Carolyn into this, and now she was coming up with odd ideas.

"That's . . . interesting," Marie finally said. "Why don't you tell us more, Carolyn?"

"It's just that children eat so much junk food these days. I thought people might enjoy having something that's not only good, but good *for* them, too."

Phyllis tried not to wince at that. She knew Carolyn was struggling.

Shannon said, "Well, that's just the most—"

"I have a recipe," Phyllis said. She ignored the angry glare Shannon sent her way for interrupting and forged ahead. "I have a recipe for peanut-butter-and-banana cookies that are made with oatmeal and applesauce. I make them for my grandson sometimes, and he loves them. They have very little sugar, and all the ingredients are nutritious."

"That sounds good," Abby said, showing some interest.

"And we could come up with other things like that," Carolyn said. "I'm sure some of you have recipes that you like to fix for your children, rather than just letting them stuff their faces with junk food all the time."

Lindsey Gonzales said, "My son would eat a case of potato chips in a week's time if I'd let him." Several of the other women nodded. Phyllis could see a little enthusiasm for Carolyn's idea growing on their faces.

Carolyn went on to explain how the contest would be set up. "The entry fees would be small," she concluded, "and so would be the fee to sample the snacks and vote for the best one. I think if you combined the money you'd take in there with what you'd get for the cakes that will be auctioned off, you'll make just as much or more than you would with a traditional bake sale. I know the interest in it will be higher among the parents."

Another idea occurred to Phyllis. "You could also collect all the recipes beforehand and make a little cookbook that you could sell. It would probably be small, so you could just copy the recipes on regular paper and fold and staple them. The cost would be low."

"You've won me over," Marie said. "I think we should do it."

"I think it's a mistake to get too far away from the traditional," Shannon said. "People don't like change. People *hate* change."

Marie suggested, "Maybe we should vote on it."

For several seconds, the two women looked at each other, and Phyllis could practically see the sparks of dislike crackling between them. Shannon was clearly a woman accustomed to getting her own way in everything, and she didn't like it when anyone opposed her. And just as clearly, that attitude chafed at Marie.

Finally, Shannon said, "Fine. This board is a democracy, after all. We'll vote on it. All in favor of the bake sale ideas from Mrs. . . . Wilbarger, was it?"

"That's right," Carolyn said. "Carolyn Wilbarger."

"All in favor," Shannon said again.

Marie, Holly, Abby, Kristina, and Irene all raised their hands. Lindsey hesitated, glancing nervously at Shannon a time or two before she finally lifted her hand, too. It didn't really matter. The vote had already passed.

"All right," Shannon said, not bothering to ask if anyone was opposed. "Just don't blame me if the PTO doesn't make as much money as it would have the other way." She reached for her purse. "Does anyone have anything else to discuss?"

Shrugs and head shakes around the table answered the question.

"Then we're done here." Shannon picked up her purse and stood. "We'll get together again on Friday. I expect a lot of progress on the preparations by then."

She stalked out of the conference room, leaving the other women still sitting around the table.

Several seconds of uncomfortable silence passed. No one seemed to be in a hurry to get up and leave. Phyllis knew she shouldn't say anything, but the question inside her was bursting to get out.

"I hope you'll all pardon me for asking, but . . . what exactly is Shannon doing to help get ready for this carnival?"

"Making life hell for the rest of us," Marie said. She looked over at Lindsey. "And don't you go running to her to tell her I said that, either, okay?"

The blonde looked offended. "Hey, I don't like Shannon any more than the rest of you do."

"Yeah, but you're the most scared of her."

Lindsey tried to look defiant, but the expression dissolved into a worried grimace. "It's just that she can be so *mean*. I don't like mean people."

Marie turned to Carolyn and Phyllis. "I'm sorry about the way Shannon treated you. We're kind of used to her, or at least we ought to be. Usually she's not quite that snippy to outsiders. She can actually be very charming when she wants to be."

"Which is not that often," Abby put in.

Phyllis said, "She was probably just upset because she was arguing with a man out in the parking lot before she came in. We saw them when we got here."

"A man?" Marie asked as she sat forward. "What man?"

"I don't know. He was a little taller than her, dark brown hair, nice-looking. He wore glasses."

Marie leaned back in her chair. "Ah. Joel. Her ex-husband."

Phyllis put the names together. "Joel Dunston. He's a doctor, isn't he?" She thought she had seen the name on the directory at the medical building where her own doctor had his office.

"That's right. He's an *otolaryngologist*." Marie put a sarcastic edge on the word.

"Ear, nose, and throat man," Abby said. "You didn't dare call him that around Shannon, though, when she was still married to him. She insisted on calling his specialty by its proper name."

"Since the divorce she mainly just calls him a cheap bastard," Marie said.

That brought smiles from some of the other women and a chuckle from one or two of them. Lindsey didn't smile, though. She said, "We shouldn't sit around and gossip."

"You're right, we shouldn't," Marie agreed with a nod. "But Carolyn and Phyllis deserve to know what they're getting into, don't they?"

Lindsey just grimaced and shrugged.

"This is the second year on the board for all of us," Marie went on. "Shannon was on it last year with us, but she wasn't divorced yet the first part of the year. She wasn't president, either. Molly Rutherford was. Her son went on to middle school this year, so she's part of the PTO there. Anyway, Shannon had never been on a PTO board before, and she was as gung ho as she could be. She was up here at the school *all* the time, so much that a few of the teachers complained to the principal about her interfering with their classes. You never saw anybody so full of ideas and energy."

"It sounds like she would have been an asset to the school and the PTO," Carolyn said.

"You'd think so, wouldn't you? Unfortunately, she's also got a bossy streak a mile wide, and you never met a bigger perfectionist, not only for herself but where everybody else is concerned, too. And since she was a doctor's wife and had plenty of time and money, she thought everybody else should be as devoted to the school as she was. All those great ideas she had? She nagged other people into doing the actual work required to carry them out."

"A master delegator, that's Shannon," Kristina said.

Marie nodded. "Molly tried to rein her in, but it was impossible. Shannon worked everybody on the board like dogs. Then finally, last spring, her husband got tired of her being here at the school all the time and neglecting him."

Lindsey said, "It was so sad."

"He had an affair?" Carolyn guessed.

Marie shook her head. "Joel gave her an ultimatum. Either she cut back on all of her school activities, or he was leaving."

Phyllis said, "I take it she didn't cut back?"

"She tossed all his stuff on the lawn and told him to get the hell out, and good riddance. Joel wouldn't back down, and neither would Shannon. They were both too proud for that. They got a divorce, and they've hated each other ever since."

Lindsey said, "You can't blame Shannon for being upset. She was married before, you know. She has an older son from another marriage. And now she's had another one fail."

"Oh, come on," Marie said. "She drove Joel to it. We all know that. What else was he supposed to do? She didn't have any more time for him while they were still married than she does now that they're divorced."

"They have time enough to fight," Abby said.

Again, Phyllis couldn't stop herself from asking a question. "If you knew she was like that, why did you make her president?"

"Hey, none of us wanted the job." Marie laughed ruefully. "Anyway, at the end of the school year, after they broke up, we all felt sorry for Shannon. And for a while she seemed to settle down a little, like the breakup had humbled her. When we were trying to come up with officers for this school year and she said she'd be willing to take on the job of president, we thought it might be good for her. We didn't know she was going to spend the whole summer stewing in her anger so that when school started again she'd come back as a royal bitch."

Marie looked quickly at Lindsey, who held up her hands and said, "I know, I know, don't go running to Shannon. I swear, you guys must think I'm the worst tattletale in the world."

Marie didn't deny that. She just turned her attention back to Phyllis and Carolyn and said, "Now that you know what you're getting into, are you still sure you want to be involved with the carnival?"

They looked at each other. Phyllis shrugged and said, "It's up to you."

Carolyn nodded. "I said I'd do it, and I don't like to break my word. Of course we'll continue."

"Good luck, then." Marie looked around the table. "Good luck to us all."

She didn't have to add, *We'll need it.*

Chapter 5

In the car on the way back to the house, Carolyn said, "I don't remember you ever making peanut-butter-and-banana cookies for Bobby."

Phyllis had been afraid she would catch that. At the time, she had wanted to help Carolyn, who obviously had been struggling to convince the PTO ladies that her idea for a healthy snack contest was worthwhile. So she had thrown out the first thing she could come up with.

"Well, I haven't actually ever *made* it," she said, "but I've thought about it. I'm sure Bobby would like it." In fact she had no doubt of that. Her grandson, who was almost a year old, would probably love all the ingredients she had mentioned.

"I think I read somewhere that you're not supposed to give peanuts to children under two or three." Carolyn paused, then said with a tone of accusation in her voice, "You changed your mind, didn't you? You're going to enter the contest."

"What? No. I was just talking, trying to help you drum up some interest in the idea. I'm not going to enter the contest. I'm just going to make a cake for the auction and maybe help with the cookbook."

"Well, good."

Phyllis took her eyes off the road long enough to look over at Carolyn in surprise. "You don't want me to enter?"

"I was sort of hoping that we could work together on this without competing against each other. I might try to come up with a recipe for the contest, but I don't plan to bake a cake for the auction."

"Really?"

"My lands, Phyllis, have you ever known me to go in for a lot of fancy cake decorating? The proof is in the eating, not how something looks."

Phyllis said slowly, "All right." She wasn't sure if she believed Carolyn or not. In many of the baking contests they had both entered in the past, presentation had been a vital part of the competition.

But come to think of it, she didn't recall Carolyn ever baking any cakes that called for elaborate decorating. And in everyday life, whenever someone needed a cake with a name or HAPPY BIRTHDAY or some other sentiment on it, Phyllis had always been the one who took care of that.

She went on, "I guess you'll be in the contest, then, and I'll be in the auction. I have to admit, it'll be nice not competing for a change."

"Not losing, you mean," Carolyn said.

"Ho, ho! You just couldn't resist, could you?" Phyllis smiled to take any sting out of the words.

Carolyn changed the subject by saying, "That Shannon is really a witch, isn't she?"

"I have a feeling Marie would spell the word one letter differently. I always feel sorry for someone like that who's so full of anger and resentment. They must have a lot of unhappiness in their lives."

"You're too kindhearted, Phyllis. Someone like that ought to be slapped a few times. Then maybe she'd start treating people decently."

"That usually doesn't work. People just slap back."

"I suppose you're right. Well, maybe we won't have to deal too much with Shannon as long as Marie's there to act as a buffer."

"I'm a little surprised the two of you are friends from church."

"Because of the age difference, you mean? Marie's mother and I were in the same Sunday school class. You might remember her. Pamela Hoffman?"

Phyllis shook her head.

"They moved here while Marie was in high school, so neither of us ever had her in class," Carolyn went on. "Pamela and I were friends for a long time, until she passed away. I got to know Marie because I saw her so much at the rest home, you know, while I was visiting Pamela there."

"She seems nice. A little harried and plainspoken, maybe, but most young people are these days."

"Yes, she has a lovely family. Russ is some sort of engineer, or works with computers, or something. I never can keep things like that straight."

Neither could Phyllis, so she knew exactly what Carolyn meant.

They got back to the house a few minutes later. As Phyllis pulled into the driveway and pushed the button on the remote control unit to raise the right-hand door on the two-car garage, Carolyn said, "I'll get started on a handout for the parents. We'll need to let all of them know about the contest and the auction as soon as possible. You'll print them for me, won't you, Phyllis?"

Even though Phyllis was far from being any sort of expert with the computer, she was better at such things than Carolyn. And that was one area where Carolyn didn't mind acknowledging Phyllis's superiority.

"Sure, I'll be glad to."

"I can pay you for the paper and ink. . . ."

"Don't worry about that. It's for a good cause."

Sam was at the workbench in the rear of the garage. Phyllis brought the Lincoln smoothly to a halt several feet short of where he was standing. He was cutting a piece of wood with the table saw and finished what he was doing as the two women got out of the car. Then he turned, pushed his safety goggles up onto his forehead, and said, "Hello, ladies. How was your meeting?"

"It went fine," Phyllis said. She lingered there, unsure why at first.

"I'll get started on that handout," Carolyn said again as she opened the door that led from the garage into the kitchen. She went into the house and pulled the door closed behind her.

"That's a nice thing you're doin', helpin' out Carolyn that way," Sam said. "Not to mention helping the kids at that school with the funds the carnival will raise. Anything I can do to help?"

Phyllis smiled. "How are you at cake decorating?"

"Well, I can use a caulk gun. Sort of the same principle, isn't it?"

"I suppose so," Phyllis said with a laugh. "What about healthy snacks?"

"I can eat 'em. As long as they're not *too* healthy, like broccoli or cauliflower or things like that."

"I was thinking more of peanut-butter-and-banana oatmeal cookies made with applesauce."

Sam smacked his lips. "Sounds good."

"Maybe I'll come up with a recipe some time. Not for the contest, though."

"Why not?"

"I'm not entering the contest," Phyllis explained, "and Carolyn's not going to make a cake for the auction."

"Again, why not?"

"Because we're not going to compete against each other." Phyllis added, "And before you can ask, that's the way Carolyn wants it. She's not good at decorating cakes, and she knows it."

Sam nodded and drawled, "A man's got to know his limitations. And I reckon Carolyn does, too."

"That's from a movie, isn't it? That line about knowing your limitations? I've heard you say it before."

"Yeah, Clint Eastwood says it in one of those Dirty Harry movies. I can't remember for sure which one. Might've been the second one, *Magnum Force*. The famous line from the first one is 'Do you feel lucky, punk?' And 'Go ahead, make my day,' comes from the fourth one, *Sudden Impact*. So, yeah, it was probably from *Magnum Force*."

"What about the third one?"

"*The Enforcer*? Nobody remembers much of anything from it or the fifth one, *The Dead Pool*."

She patted him lightly on the arm. "You maybe watch a little too much TV, Sam."

"More than likely." As Phyllis started toward the kitchen door, he went on, "I really would like to help out with the carnival, though. Maybe I could build some of the booths. I'm pretty good with my hands."

"Now there's an idea. I'll get Marie's number from Carolyn, and you can call her. I'm sure she could tell you who to talk to about that."

"I'd appreciate it. Like I said there at Wal-Mart, I never got to be around the carnivals much. Sounds like fun."

Phyllis went on into the house and found Carolyn and Eve in the kitchen, discussing the meeting at Loving Elementary. Eve turned to Phyllis and asked with a smile, "What were you and Sam talking about out there, dear?"

Phyllis wondered if Eve had an ulterior motive for asking that question. For goodness' sake, it wasn't like she and Sam had been out in the garage smooching or anything like that! Eve had no reason to feel jealous.

"Sam wants to help out with the carnival, too," Phyllis said. "He's talking about maybe helping build some of the booths."

"I'm sure he'd be good at it. He's always building things. He's very good with his hands, you know."

Again Phyllis wondered what Eve meant by that. On the

surface, at least, it was just an innocent remark. Sam himself
had said almost exactly the same thing. Phyllis told herself
that she was being too suspicious and trying to read too
much into everything. Eve seemed friendly again this morning, as if she had gotten over being miffed at finding Phyllis
and Sam sitting together on the kitchen floor. *Be grateful for
that,* Phyllis told herself, *and move on.*

"I told him you could give him Marie's number," she said
to Carolyn.

"Certainly." Carolyn and Sam hadn't gotten along all that
well when Sam first rented the empty bedroom upstairs, but
over the months she had become friendly with him, even
though she was still a little reserved around him at times.
The reserve had all been on Carolyn's part. Sam was the sort
of man who was friendly with everybody right from the
start.

That quality might be tested, Phyllis thought, if Sam ever
had to spend much time around Shannon Dunston.

After lunch, Phyllis finally got around to going to the
store for the ingredients she would need for her first trial run
at the jack-o'-lantern cake. She planned to use a mix for the
cake part just to simplify things, although when the time
came to bake the one that would actually be in the auction,
she would start from scratch. After all, someone would be
buying it to eat, not just because it was pretty, and she
wanted it to taste as good as possible. And no cake from a
mix could ever be as good as one from scratch, at least to
Phyllis's way of thinking.

While she was pushing her cart along the aisles in the
food section at Wal-Mart, she heard a voice behind her say,
"Mrs. Newsom, isn't it?"

Phyllis turned and to her surprise saw Shannon Dunston
standing there, also with a cart. She shouldn't have been surprised, she told herself. Everyone had to shop, even unpleas-
ant people.

The really unexpected part was that Shannon was smiling

now and seemed quite friendly. She had obviously gotten over her bad mood from that morning.

Or maybe she was manic-depressive, Phyllis thought. That would explain it, too. Then she mentally chided herself for not giving Shannon the benefit of the doubt. Marie had said that Shannon could be pleasant when she wanted to.

"Hello, Mrs. Dunston."

"Please, call me Shannon," the younger woman said as she brought her cart alongside Phyllis's. "I hope you didn't get the wrong impression from the meeting this morning. I know I can be a little impatient at times. There's always just *so* much to do, and it seems like I'm running and running and running all the time, and it's so hard to get people to actually help—" She stopped, shook her head, and smiled again. "But I don't have to tell you that. You were a teacher. You know. And I know you saw me arguing with my ex-husband, too. You couldn't have missed it."

"I didn't really pay any attention. . . ," Phyllis began.

"Oh, you don't have to apologize. Joel is so obnoxious he practically shouts it from the rooftops. Can you believe he wanted to skip some of his child support payments just because he spent too much money remodeling his office? He promised he would catch up later, but that doesn't do Becca any good now, does it?"

"Becca is your daughter?" Phyllis asked, hoping that would get Shannon off the subject of her hostility toward her ex-husband.

"That's right. She's in the fourth grade at Loving." Shannon glanced in Phyllis's cart. "I see you have bananas. Are you going to use them in the snack you plan to make for the contest?"

Phyllis gave a guilty little start. She had hesitated when she passed the bananas, but after a moment she had finally given in to temptation and put them in her cart. She already had peanut butter, oatmeal, and applesauce at home. The recipe idea still lingered in the back of her mind, intriguing her with its possibilities. But she wasn't going to enter it in the contest. She had told Carolyn that she wouldn't.

She said, "Actually, I don't think I'll be competing—"

"What? But you have to! It was your recipe that won everyone over to Mrs. Wilbarger's idea. It really has to be in the contest." Shannon got a determined look on her face. "I insist."

Phyllis didn't know what to say. She didn't like being browbeaten, and she had given her word to Carolyn, but Shannon was forceful and clearly accustomed to having people go along with what she wanted.

And the recipe would make a fine healthy snack, too. Good, and good *for* you, as Carolyn had said.

Before Phyllis could decide what to do, she was distracted by a young man who had come up behind Shannon. He wore a T-shirt with the sleeves cut off to reveal several colorful tattoos, and he not only had rings through both earlobes, but his nose was pierced, too, with a silver stud on the left nostril. His head was shaved. Just the sight of him made Phyllis nervous.

And then a surge of outright fear went through her as the young man's hand reached out, straight toward the purse hanging from Shannon's shoulder.

Chapter 6

Phyllis opened her mouth to call out a warning to Shannon that the man was about to grab her purse, but before she could say anything, the young man said, "Hey, Mom, can I have a couple bucks? I want to go back to Mickey D's and get something to eat."

Shannon turned her head to look at him, and the sharpness and impatience she had demonstrated during the meeting that morning were back again as she said, "You can have something to eat when we get home. Where did you wander off to, anyway?"

The young man shrugged. "Went to look at the CDs."

"You didn't take any of them, did you? I don't want the alarm going off again when we leave the store."

"No," he said sullenly. "I didn't do anything. I just looked at them."

"Good." Shannon glanced at Phyllis. Clearly, she didn't want to introduce the young man to her, but she felt compelled to do so. "Mrs. Newsom, this is my son, Kirk."

Phyllis nodded. "Hello."

The young man returned a curt nod and said, "'Sup."

Phyllis had watched enough TV to think about saying, *Word, dawg,* just to see what his reaction would be, but she thought better of it.

Anyway, Kirk had already turned his attention back to his mother. "I just want to get some fries—"

Shannon didn't let him finish. "I already said no."

"Fine, whatever." Kirk stuck his hands in the pockets of his tattered jeans and wandered on down the aisle.

"I'm sorry about that," Shannon said to Phyllis. "Obviously, I didn't discipline Kirk enough when he was a child."

Phyllis remembered what Lindsey Gonzales had said that morning about Shannon having an older son from her first marriage. She hadn't thought about the son being that old.

"You don't look old enough to have a grown child."

"I had Kirk when I was eighteen. Young and foolish, you know. I'd gotten married right out of high school to my childhood sweetheart. I should have known better. Those things never work out."

Phyllis wouldn't have gone so far as to say that. But early marriages *did* take an awful lot of work to make them successful, and often people just weren't willing to put the effort into it.

"Anyway," Shannon went on, "what about the contest? You're going to enter, aren't you? Of course you are. It'll be a lot of fun, and it's all for such a good cause."

"It *is* for a good cause," Phyllis had to admit.

"It's settled, then. I'll look forward to trying those healthy cookies."

"All right." The words were out of Phyllis's mouth before she could stop them. She would just have to make Carolyn understand what had happened. Shannon had trapped her into agreeing.

"I'll see you at the meeting Friday." Shannon smiled and pushed her cart on down the aisle, catching up with her son, who had taken something off one of the shelves to look at it.

"Put that down," Phyllis heard her say. "My God, I can't leave you alone for a minute."

Phyllis turned her cart around and went the other way, blowing out her breath in a sigh as she did so. Even though Shannon had been making an effort to be nicer than usual, the encounter was still troubling to Phyllis. Not only had she gotten roped into agreeing to compete in the healthy snacks contest, but she'd had to witness the way Shannon treated her son. Even though Phyllis didn't care for that whole pierced, tattooed, shaven-headed lifestyle, she couldn't help but feel a little sorry for the young man. There he was, over eighteen years old, and his mother was still treating him like he was seven or eight.

Phyllis had long since learned, though, that she couldn't change the way people treated their children, and except in extreme cases such as abuse, she didn't even have the right to try. Teachers did what they could to help youngsters who had less than ideal home situations, but in the end, most of the time they had to just butt out and learn to live with it. To do otherwise was to risk driving themselves to distraction with worry.

By the time she got back to the house, she thought she had come up with a solution to her problem. She put away the groceries, then found Carolyn in the living room, sitting on the sofa and writing something on a legal pad.

"I'm still working on the handout for the parents," Carolyn said. "Would you like to read what I have so far?"

"Sure." Phyllis took the pad and sat down in an armchair to read what Carolyn had written. When she had finished, she handed it back and said, "It sounds fine. You even have the information about turning in the recipes for the cookbook. I think you've got it covered."

"I hope so. Are you sure you don't mind typing it up and designing it?"

"No, not at all." Phyllis took a breath. "You know, I ran into Shannon Dunston at Wal-Mart."

"Really? So you had to deal with her twice in one day. Better you than me."

"Here's the strange part," Phyllis went on. "She was a lot nicer than she was this morning, and she absolutely insisted that I make that cookie recipe for the contest."

Carolyn looked up sharply. "What? You said you weren't going to enter the contest."

"I know, but Shannon was so determined—"

"That you gave in and said you'd do it." Carolyn's voice had hardened considerably.

"Well, yes, I said I'd make the cookies, but I was thinking that I wouldn't actually enter them in the contest. It would just be . . . an example of a healthy snack, I guess you could say. People could sample it, but they couldn't vote for it. That way it could go into the cookbook."

Carolyn looked at her for a moment, and enough time ticked by for Phyllis to start feeling uncomfortable. Then Carolyn said flatly, "No."

"No what?" Was she forbidding her to enter the contest? That wasn't right, no matter what they had said earlier about not competing.

"No, if you're going to use the recipe, you should enter it in the contest. There's no point in going to that much trouble otherwise."

"Really, it wouldn't be any trouble—"

"I insist," Carolyn said. "If Shannon insists, so can I. Obviously, you *want* to make the cookies, and so you should enter them. There's nothing else to be said." She sniffed coldly. "It's a free country, after all."

This was turning out all wrong, just as Phyllis had been afraid that it would. "I don't have to do it if it's going to bother you."

"Why should it bother me? I'm certainly not afraid of a little competition, if that's what you mean! After all, we both know I've managed to beat you plenty of times before."

Phyllis could understand why Carolyn might be a little upset, but she didn't have to be rude about it. "As Shannon pointed out, it's all for a good cause—"

"Of course."

"Anyway, even though she was acting a lot nicer, she was still determined to get her own way."

"Like someone else," Carolyn said.

That did it, Phyllis thought. Now *she* was getting mad.

"You know, this is fine," Carolyn went on before Phyllis could say anything, "because I was just thinking about coming up with a cake for the auction after all."

"I thought you said you didn't like to decorate cakes."

"Well, we all say things we don't exactly mean sometimes, don't we?"

This had gone on long enough. Phyllis was going to put a stop to it before it got out of hand, and she was going to do that by changing the subject. She stood up and reached toward Carolyn. "Give me what you've written and I'll get to work on it."

"Oh, I don't think that's necessary anymore. I can do it."

"You don't like using the computer—"

"I'm perfectly capable of taking care of it myself."

"I'm sure you are," Phyllis said, "but I don't mind—"

"No thanks." Carolyn got to her feet and started toward the stairs.

"All right," Phyllis said after her. She thought but didn't say, *Be that way.*

But as Carolyn went upstairs and Phyllis sank back into the armchair to brood, Phyllis wondered how much of what she felt was really annoyance with Carolyn—and how much was the guilt she felt over breaking her word to her friend.

Thank God for Sam Fletcher, thought Phyllis. First Eve had been irritated with her, and now Carolyn. But good old dependable Sam was still her friend.

For the next few days Phyllis threw herself into her preparations. She baked the jack-o'-lantern cake first but didn't let anyone see it except Sam. She didn't fully trust Eve not to tell Carolyn about it, and of course since Carolyn had declared that she was going to make a cake for the auction, too, the old spirit of competitiveness that had existed between them for so long was back in the forefront.

Phyllis moved some pans around in the cabinet hunting for her Bundt pan. She had two, but they were slightly different. This time she'd just bake two cakes one after the other using the same pan. Since one of the pans was a new silicone type, she decided to use that. It would be easiest to find another pan like it before the day of the carnival.

Since she was using a white cake mix, she thought about adding food coloring to the cake to make it orange, too. She decided against that, however. The icing was going to have enough food coloring, and she didn't want to run out. She probably would use a little in the cake for the auction to make it a lighter orange than the frosting.

She lightly sprayed the Bundt pan with oil and set it on a cookie sheet. The silicone pan was too flexible to use without something under it. Even with having to use an extra pan under it, she liked the silicone pan because it was so easy to get the cake out after it had baked.

Following the recipe on the box, she quickly blended the cake mix with eggs, water, and oil. She poured the mixture into the Bundt pan and put it into the hot oven. She set a timer and went ahead and cleaned up the dishes that she'd need again in a little while.

After the cake had baked to a golden color and cooled enough to be removed from the pan, Phyllis repeated the process.

Since she still had the kitchen to herself, she went ahead and whipped up a double batch of buttercream icing. She was a little surprised at how much food coloring it took to finally make the icing a perfect pumpkin orange. Keeping in mind that this was just a practice cake, Phyllis didn't worry too much about getting the face exactly right. She used a green ice-cream cone for the stem, as in the magazine, but she wasn't really satisfied with the way it looked. An upside-down cupcake might work better for the carnival cake, she thought. That way she could make the icing on it look more like a stem.

Phyllis put the cake in the cabinet, away from prying eyes.

Later, after Carolyn and Eve were both out of the house, she took the cake from the cabinet where she had hidden it. Sam was upstairs in his room watching a movie on his DVD player, but he was willing to stop it to come down and see what Phyllis wanted.

"There it is," she told him as she waved a hand at her creation sitting on the kitchen counter. "What do you think?"

"Looks like a jack-o'-lantern, all right. Pretty scary, eh, kids?"

Phyllis had a feeling he was making some reference to movies or TV, but she didn't get it. "Is that all you have to say?"

"Well, I haven't tasted it yet, so looks are all I've got to go by," he pointed out. "But I'm sure it's good. Everything you bake is." He paused. "You gonna cut it?"

"I might as well. It was just for practice, after all." She picked up a knife. "You want a big piece, I suppose?" She knew he had quite a sweet tooth.

"Yeah. Maybe not a piece with an eye on it, though. That'd be a mite creepy."

After Sam had eaten his slice of cake and proclaimed it delicious, Phyllis wrapped up the rest of it and drove over to the north side of town to share it with her grandson, Bobby, after calling first to make sure her daughter-in-law, Sarah, was going to be home. When she got there, Bobby toddled down the walk to meet her, followed closely by his pretty blond mother. Phyllis scooped the boy up into her arms and kissed his cheek as Bobby hugged her tightly around the neck with his chubby arms. "G'anma!" he said happily.

Phyllis didn't particularly like being called *Grandma*, but she would put up with it from this little boy.

"Bring me anyt'ing?" he asked.

"Bobby," Sarah scolded mildly. "Is that any way to say hello to your grandmother?"

"It's all right," Phyllis said. "As a matter of fact, I did bring you something, Bobby. I brought some jack-o'-lantern cake."

"Cake!" he said clapping his small, chubby hands together.

Sarah had started to frown a little, so Phyllis told her, "Don't worry, we'll just give him a small piece." She handed Bobby to Sarah and turned back to the car to get the covered plate she had used to carry the cake.

"That certainly looks good," Sarah commented as the three of them went into the neatly kept brick house. The place didn't have the personality that the big two-story frame house where Mike had grown up did, but unless you wanted to buy an old house, you couldn't get anything except these brick cookie-cutters anymore. And people had a right to live where and how they wanted to, Phyllis reminded herself, although as a parent it was sometimes difficult for her not to speak up and offer an opinion. Anyway, Mike and Sarah and Bobby all seemed very happy.

Sarah got out saucers and a knife to cut the cake, then hesitated. "Do I try him with the fork?" she asked. "Or should I just let him use his fingers?"

Bobby waved his hands in the air, wiggling his fingers as if answering her. Sarah laughed and cut several wedges of cake.

"Why a pumpkin? It's not Halloween yet," she asked as she broke off a small piece from one slice and handed it to Bobby, who stuffed it in his mouth.

"It's a trial cake for an auction at a PTO carnival," Phyllis explained. She hadn't talked to Mike or Sarah for several days, and they didn't know yet about her involvement with the carnival at Loving Elementary.

Sarah took a bite and frowned.

"It's doesn't taste good?" Phyllis asked anxiously. "I haven't really tried it yet myself."

"No, it's not that. The cake tastes just fine. Really good,

in fact." Sarah handed another piece to Bobby, who had finished the first bite she'd given him. "I was just thinking about the fact that you're entering a baking contest again. This will be the first one since the Peach Festival, won't it?"

"Yes, but nothing's going to happen," Phyllis said, feeling a little uneasy in spite of herself. The memory of everything that had happened that day—the dead man, the paramedics, then the police and the revelation that the death had been a case of cold-blooded murder—was still all too vivid in Phyllis's mind.

But this was a PTO carnival at an elementary school. Nobody was going to get murdered at something like that. Phyllis forced the very thought out of her head as an utter impossibility. She took a bite of the cake instead.

Sarah and Bobby were right. It was good, even if it was from a mix.

Chapter 7

Phyllis left the rest of the cake there so that Mike could have some when he got home from his shift as a Parker County deputy sheriff.

As she turned into the driveway at her house, Sam pulled his pickup to a stop at the curb in front, where he usually parked it. Phyllis put the Lincoln in the garage, but instead of entering the house through the kitchen she left the garage door open and walked out into the front yard to meet Sam. She knew he had been going over to the elementary school to talk to the custodians about helping with the construction of the carnival booths. That was what Marie had told him to do when he called her about volunteering. The school custodians were traditionally in charge of any construction that needed to be done.

"How did it go?" Phyllis asked.

"Just fine," Sam replied with a nod. "I even knew one of the fellas. He used to be a custodian up at Poolville when I was still there."

They climbed the steps to the porch together. As they reached the top step, Eve emerged from the house and said, "Why, hello there, you two. I was just about to sit out here for a while and enjoy the weather. It's such a beautiful day. Why don't you join me?"

Eve was right about it being a pretty day. The sky was a deep blue, dotted here and there with white fluffy clouds, and the air had the sort of crispness to it, without actually being chilly, that was only found in autumn. Eve sat down in the big porch swing and patted the empty space beside her as she smiled at Sam.

He sat down on the porch steps instead, and stretched his legs out in front of him as he leaned back and rested his elbows on the porch. He looked supremely comfortable. Phyllis sat down on the swing next to Eve and said, "Sam's going to help the custodians at the school put together the booths for the carnival."

"I've been wanting to do something to help out with that, too," Eve said. "As you know, I'm not a cook, but maybe they'd like to have a kissing booth. I'm sure I could run one of those just fine. Don't you think so, Sam?"

"Yes, ma'am, I expect you could," he said.

Phyllis wondered what he meant by *that*. Did he really think Eve was kissable? Of course, it was no business of hers what Sam thought about such matters. . . .

"I'm not sure that would be a good idea," Phyllis said. "Remember that other carnival kissing booth you volunteered at, Eve?"

"You mean at which I volunteered?" Eve said, still and always an English teacher even though she was retired. "That commotion wasn't my fault. You'd think all those women would have realized it was for a good cause and didn't really mean anything when I kissed their husbands."

"You'd think," Phyllis said.

From his lounging position on the steps, Sam said, "I remember some of the carnivals at our elementary school had a dunkin' booth set up. Kids really got a kick out of dunkin' their teachers in a big tub of water."

Eve laughed. "If you're hinting that you'd like to see me in a wet T-shirt, dear, all you have to do is ask!"

Sam immediately turned a deep shade of red. Phyllis didn't know whether to laugh at him or be annoyed with Eve for making such a suggestive comment. She didn't do either, because Sam quickly changed the subject by saying, "You know, there's been some trouble there at the elementary school lately. The custodian I know told me about it. Seems somebody got into the school and stole some computers and stuff."

"Broke in, you mean?" Phyllis asked.

"Well, that's the funny part. The sheriff's department came out and investigated, of course, and the deputies didn't find any sign of forced entry. Best they can figure, somebody found a way in—a door that accidentally got left unlocked or something like that. Or else they got their hands on a key somehow. The custodians say they're careful about making sure everything's locked up tight. So at this point nobody really knows what happened."

"That's such a shame," Eve said. "Imagine, someone stealing from a school."

"Some people will steal from anybody," Phyllis said, "even schools and churches and places like that."

Sam nodded. "It's a mean ol' world sometimes."

The discussion sobered all three of them, so despite the beautiful day they went inside before much longer. Anyway, Phyllis told herself, she had to start thinking about supper.

And she wished she could get rid of the image in her head that involved Eve, Sam, and a kissing booth. . . .

When Phyllis and Carolyn arrived for the Friday morning meeting at Loving Elementary, they didn't have to ask for directions this time, although they did stop in the office to let the secretary know they would be in the school. The days when people could wander in and out of a school with nobody paying any attention to them were long gone.

As they walked down the hall toward the conference room, they heard voices—loud, angry voices. Actually, Phyllis realized as they came closer, there was only one voice, and it belonged to Shannon Dunston.

". . . been doing, then, since you obviously haven't been

doing what you were told to?" Shannon was saying. Someone answered her, but Phyllis couldn't make out the words. She and Carolyn traded frowns of concern. There was still a little tension between the two due to Phyllis entering the snack contest, but that was momentarily forgotten in the face of this new trouble.

When they reached the open door of the conference room, they saw several of the members of the PTO board sitting at the table. Shannon stood at the head of the table, a fierce glare directed toward Lindsey Gonzales. Kristina Padgett and Irene Vernon sat across the table from Lindsey, who was alone on her side. Marie, Holly Underwood, and Abby Granger weren't there yet.

"I'm sorry, Shannon," Lindsey said. She looked and sounded like she was fighting back tears. "I've just been really busy this week."

"Those posters should already be collected and put up in the businesses all over town," Shannon snapped. "People aren't going to come to the carnival if they don't even know about it."

"Ladies," Phyllis said, "you might not be aware of it, but we could hear you down the hall."

"You mean people might hear that Lindsey can't even do a simple job?"

"I'll do it!" Lindsey burst out. "I'll do it this afternoon! I swear I will, Shannon."

"Never mind," Shannon said, scorn dripping from her voice. "I'll take care of it. That's the president's job, isn't it, doing everything that doesn't get done?" She swept her withering gaze around to the other two board members in the room.

Phyllis waited to see if Lindsey, Kristina, and Irene were going to get up and walk out. Phyllis would have, if Shannon had attacked her like that. Clearly, Shannon didn't understand—or didn't care—that the board members were volunteers. They didn't have to be here. If they wanted to, the entire board could just quit and dump all the responsibility for the carnival in her lap.

But no one stood up. The three women just sat there, pointedly looking at the table and not meeting Shannon's gaze. After a moment of awkward silence, Shannon said, "Where are the others? Can't anybody be on time?"

As Phyllis and Carolyn pulled out folding chairs to sit down at the table, the chair legs scraping on the tile floor, Phyllis heard footsteps in the hall. A few seconds later, Marie appeared in the doorway, a smile on her face. That smile vanished quickly as she must have sensed the hostile atmosphere in the room. "Uh-oh," she said. "What happened?"

"Lindsey hasn't collected the posters that the children made for the carnival," Shannon said. "She was supposed to have taken them around town and put them up in all the businesses by now."

"Oh, honey," Marie said as she looked at Lindsey, "you should have let me know you were having trouble. I would have helped you."

"I kept thinking I'd get around to it," Lindsey said miserably. "I meant to."

Shannon said, "You know what they say about good intentions and the road to hell." She looked at Marie. "Do you know if the others are coming?"

"Yeah, I saw Holly and Abby pull into the parking lot behind me. They ought to be here any minute." More footsteps sounded from the hall. Marie looked around and went on, "Here they come now."

The other board members entered the conference room a moment later. Everyone sat down. The meeting could get under way now, even though it was obvious it had been going on unofficially even before Phyllis and Carolyn arrived.

Phyllis knew the sort of posters Shannon had been talking about. Although it wasn't mandatory, the children designed and illustrated them—often with varying degrees of help from their parents, Phyllis suspected—and then they were taped up in the windows of the businesses around town to publicize the carnival. Each poster had to include the date and time and how much fun it would be. Most of the kids drew simple pictures of the activities that would be going on at the carnival, but others—likely the ones with the most parental involvement—were more creative and downright fancy. But it was all in good fun, and since the goal was to get as many people to attend and spend money as possible, whatever worked was just fine.

Nothing else was said about the posters and Lindsey's failure to collect them from the classrooms and post them around town. During the meeting, Shannon called on each of the board members in turn, asking for reports on what they had accomplished since the last meeting. As far as Phyllis could tell, preparations for the carnival were proceeding satisfactorily, but Shannon found some nit to pick with everyone's reports, some more so than others.

Since they weren't members of the board, Shannon turned to Carolyn and Phyllis last. "What about you ladies?" she asked, softening her tone slightly. "Are we ready for the auction and the snack contest? The carnival is a week from tomorrow, you know."

"Yes, I know," Carolyn said. She had brought along a large tote bag this morning, and as she opened it up, Phyllis saw why. Carolyn took out a thick sheaf of papers. "I'd like to put these notices in the teachers' boxes for them to pass out, so the kids can take them home."

"A lot of them will never get there, you know," Shannon said. "The kids will throw them away or lose them."

"Yes, I know, but I'm not sure how else we can get the word out to the parents. Some of them will get to where they need to go."

Shannon nodded. "I suppose so. I can get you a list of most of the parents' e-mail addresses, too, so you can e-mail them directly. The school office has that information."

Carolyn looked a little leery of the idea of doing a mass e-mailing like that. Phyllis knew that Carolyn still wasn't completely comfortable with the computer and at times had trouble retrieving her own e-mail, let alone sending out a few hundred of them at the same time. So she said, "That would be great, Shannon. If you'll get the addresses for us, we'll take care of that." Phyllis thought she could handle the task, and she knew that if she had any trouble, Sam could help her. He was probably the most computer-literate of the four of them who shared the big old house.

"All right," Shannon said. "Give me your address, and I'll have the school secretary save the e-mail list on my jump drive so I can send it to you later."

Carolyn just looked more confused. So she pressed on, picking up one of the handouts she had made. "All the information about entering the contest and donating cakes or other baked goods for the auction is on here." She handed it to Shannon and then passed copies to the rest of the board members, as well as handing one to Phyllis. This was the first time Phyllis had seen what Carolyn came up with. It was strictly functional, done probably in a word-processing rather than a graphics program, but all the necessary information was there, as Carolyn had said. Phyllis could have made it look a little flashier, but this would do the job. She smiled and nodded approvingly as she handed the sheet of paper back to Carolyn.

The others were satisfied with it, too. Shannon looked around the table and said, "All right, does anybody have anything else to bring up?"

No one said anything. Lindsey still didn't look up from the table. She hadn't said much during the meeting.

"I'll be checking with all of you during the next week," Shannon went on when it became obvious no one was going to speak up. She picked up her purse. "Now I'll go get those posters and get started on that, I suppose." She walked out of the conference room.

"Would it have killed her to say keep up the good work, or something like that?" Marie said when Shannon's brisk footsteps had faded away down the hall. She turned to Lindsey. "I'm sorry that happened, sweetie. Shannon was out of line."

"No, she wasn't," Lindsey said, and Phyllis saw a couple of streaks on the blonde's face where tears had rolled down her cheeks. "I fell down on the job. It's all my fault."

The others tried to make her feel better, reminding her that in the past they had all been the target of Shannon's wrath, too. After a minute, Lindsey managed a weak smile. They all got up and left the conference room together, trailed by Phyllis and Carolyn.

Quietly, Carolyn said, "Thanks for stepping in when Shannon started talking about all that computer stuff. I get lost so easily when it comes to that."

"It's not a problem," Phyllis assured her. "I'm glad to do whatever I can to help."

As they reached the parking lot, Carolyn said, "You know, I was probably too hard on you about entering the contest, Phyllis. I can understand how somebody would agree to something just to get that woman off their back."

"I appreciate that," Phyllis said sincerely. "It's been bothering me a lot that I upset you."

Carolyn shook her head. "Don't worry about it. Like I said, I understand." She paused as she opened the passenger-side door of Phyllis's Lincoln. "But don't think for a minute that I'm not going to beat you."

Phyllis returned her friend's smile and said, "We'll see about that."

Chapter 8

Phyllis spent the weekend experimenting with the healthy cookie recipe. Now that Carolyn had made peace with her, she was able to throw herself wholeheartedly into getting ready for the upcoming competition without feeling guilty about it. She tried to make the cookie into a giant pizza using coconut and a thin layer of jam for the topping, but the cookie was too soft for this to work, and the jam was overpowering. Phyllis decided it would work better to just make regular-sized cookies. The taste was the most important thing.

While the last batch of cookies was cooling, Phyllis decided she'd better find out if Carolyn was right about young children and peanut butter. On the Internet, she found out that Carolyn was indeed right: Bobby would have to wait until he was older before he could have anything with peanut butter. It would still make a nice recipe for the carnival. She'd just need to make sure any smaller kids were allowed to eat food with peanuts before letting them sample.

On Monday Phyllis drove over to Fort Worth, twenty miles to the east, for a doctor's appointment. Her regular physician, Dr. Walt Lee, practiced in Weatherford, but she also saw an allergist several times a year for help with her hay fever. This was a particularly bad season for it. The pollen levels wouldn't drop significantly until after the first freeze, and Phyllis's eyes had begun watering and itching too much for her to wait that long for relief.

After getting a shot and a prescription for some eyedrops, Phyllis returned to her car and got ready to leave the doctor's office in southwest Fort Worth. Since she was already over there, she decided she would shop a little, since it was a nice area with a multitude of stores. She didn't go there very often because the traffic was bad.

She stopped at the exit of the doctor's office parking lot to wait for traffic to clear on the busy boulevard. While she was sitting there, she spotted a familiar face in a car that slowed down right in front of her to turn into the next parking lot, which happened to belong to an Applebee's.

At first Phyllis wasn't sure she had seen whom she thought she saw. But then the car slid into a parking space in front of the restaurant and stopped. Sure enough, it was Shannon Dunston who got out, and she was accompanied by a tall, dark-haired man who possessively took her arm as they went inside. The man definitely wasn't Shannon's ex-husband, Dr. Joel Dunston. Shannon must have started dating again.

Phyllis couldn't help but feel a twinge of sympathy for the poor guy.

Then she told herself she ought to be ashamed for thinking that. Shannon's social life was none of her business.

And besides, maybe enjoying a little male companionship would mean that Shannon wouldn't be quite so cranky in the future.

Phyllis scolded herself for thinking *that*, too.

By the day before the carnival, Phyllis had received all the recipes that would be in the cookbook. Since most of the recipes came through e-mail, all Phyllis had to do with most of them was copy and paste them into her newsletter program. Once she had all the recipes laid out, she needed a cover. She had a digital camera that she bought when Bobby was born. She thought about just taking a picture of the plate of cookies after she made them, but Carolyn would probably be upset if she used her entry for the cover. She could go to the school and take pictures, but then it occurred to her that there might be a picture of Loving Elementary on the school Web site. Sure enough, after she'd connected to the Internet it was short work to go to the Web site, copy the picture of the school, and paste it onto the cover page. Once she was satisfied, she set it up to collate and print one hundred copies. She had a booklet stapler that she had bought when she was a teacher. The printer was fairly fast, so it was printing the booklets about the same speed that Phyllis could straighten and staple them. It really didn't take as long to get it all done as she had been expecting.

One of the things Phyllis had discovered with the peanut-butter-and-banana recipe was the fact that the cookies tasted even better the next day. She spent Friday morning at Wal-Mart getting all the needed ingredients for both the cookies and the cake, while doing the rest of the grocery shopping for her and the others in the house. She'd bought bananas earlier in the week, so they would be nice and ripe.

After she'd put everything away in the cabinets, it was time to make the batch of cookies for the carnival. She slipped a David Sanborn CD into the under-counter CD player and started working to the soft saxophone melody. She put all the ingredients needed on the counter and pre-heated the oven to 375 degrees.

Phyllis pulled out two baking sheets from the bottom cabinet. She tore sheets of parchment paper to fit the pans. Parchment paper worked well for this cookie and, since she didn't have to oil the pan, it cut the fat just a little more.

In a large mixing bowl, Phyllis measured, mixed, and blended the sugar with the butter and egg with the mixer on medium until it had a nice creamy look. Then, one by one, she measured, added, and mixed the flour, baking powder, baking soda, and salt until all the ingredients were well blended.

She took out a small bowl, peeled a brown-speckled banana, and broke the banana into pieces in the bowl. It was easy to mash the banana with a fork.

She went back to the large mixing bowl, setting the mixer on low. She then proceeded to measure and add the oats, peanut butter, applesauce, and finally the mashed banana. She stopped the mixer just long enough to run a spatula around the sides of the bowl to make sure it was all mixed.

Using two spoons, she scooped and dropped spoonfuls onto the parchment paper–covered pans. When she had the first pan full, she put it into the oven and set the timer for twelve minutes. While the first pan was baking, she started dropping spoonfuls of the dough onto the second pan so it would be ready to go in as soon as the first pan came out.

The room filled with the smell of roasting peanuts. It brought back childhood memories of when her father would roast pans of peanuts. This recipe was definitely a winner as far as she was concerned.

Since she spent Friday afternoon baking the cookies that would serve as her healthy snack entry, she had Saturday morning to make the cake. For a change, she knew beforehand what Carolyn was entering in the contest. She'd seen her muttering and throwing out failed attempts all week. She had been stuck on flavored popcorn for the first part of the week, but finally came up with some nice low-fat pizza rolls. She'd given Phyllis the recipe before most of the other entrants had sent theirs. If Carolyn's entry won . . . well, then, more power to her. Phyllis wasn't going to lose any sleep over it.

She was actually more concerned with seeing what Carolyn was going to donate to the auction. She hoped her friend wouldn't embarrass herself by attempting something beyond her abilities.

The carnival was scheduled to begin at one o'clock

Saturday afternoon. Phyllis was up early Saturday morning, baking the cake that she would decorate to look like a jack-o'-lantern. She wanted it to be as fresh as possible for the auction.

During the week, Sam had spent quite a bit of time at the elementary school, helping the custodians with their preparations. Eve had finally settled on working at the ticket booth. It wouldn't be as much fun as a kissing booth, she said, but at least that way she would get to see just about everyone who attended the carnival.

So for more than a week, the festivities at Oliver Loving Elementary School had dominated the conversation and thoughts of the four retired teachers, and now that the day was finally upon them, Phyllis was eager to experience the excitement of the children and parents who would be there. Most of the kids had been looking forward to this since the beginning of the school year.

Phyllis had doubled her old reliable yellow cake recipe, added a little food coloring to make it a light orange, and had baked it in two Bundt pans and two foil cupcake baking cups. Of course, the cupcakes took a lot less time to bake and cool. One cupcake was for the jack-o'-lantern's stem, and the other was for a taste test. It never hurt to make sure she hadn't forgotten to put something in the recipe. Even Carolyn made a mistake on one of her flavored popcorn attempts. Phyllis had heard mutterings about vegetable oil when the result made its way into the trash.

The cupcake was just right. To tell the truth, Phyllis preferred her cake without icing. A really good cake didn't need icing, but a fancy decorated cake required a lot of it.

In a large bowl, Phyllis beat powdered sugar with butter and shortening at a low speed until it was blended. She added milk and vanilla and beat that on medium speed until the mixture was smooth. She had to add a few more drops of milk to make it the right spreading consistency. She removed about one third of a cup of the buttercream frosting and set it aside in a small bowl for decorating the stem. Adding red and yellow food coloring to the remaining frosting and blending it made the orange frosting that Phyllis wanted to cover the cake.

She had bought a nice decorative Halloween plate at the dollar store and she used this to assemble her cake on. The first Bundt cake went down with the flat side up. On the flat side, Phyllis added a small layer of orange frosting. Lining up the indentions, she carefully put the second Bundt cake flat side down on top of the first one. It was easy to then cover the cake with a thin layer of the orange icing. She didn't want it too thick, since she wanted the shape of the cake to show through well.

Phyllis took the reserve icing, added green food coloring to the frosting, and blended it into a nice leaf green. She peeled the foil baking cup off the cupcake and quickly frosted the bottom and sides. The frosted cupcake was carefully placed on the hole on top of the cake to make the stem. The frosting on the cake and cupcake would hold it in place.

Now it was time for the face. She decided to just make a traditional jack-o'-lantern face using chocolate icing. Phyllis put water in a coffee cup and set it in the microwave to heat to boiling. She broke off one square of unsweetened chocolate and chopped it up. This went into a saucepan with a teaspoon of butter, and she heated it over a low heat until it melted. Removing the pan from the burner, Phyllis added powdered sugar and a little of the boiling water from the coffee cup. She beat this by hand with a whisk until the frosting was smooth. She added a little more of the boiling water to the icing mixture and beat it until it was the perfect spreading consistency. The chocolate icing went into a decorating bag with a medium writing tip.

On a piece of scrap paper, Phyllis sketched out how she wanted the face to look. Using a toothpick she marked off the corners of the triangular eyes and nose, and the ends of the mouth. It was easier to fill in the small holes left by the toothpick than it was to remove unwanted icing.

Once she had the marks where she wanted them, she piped the chocolate icing, making the triangles and filling them in. She was quite pleased with the end results.

Carolyn came into the kitchen as Phyllis was putting the finishing touches on the jack-o'-lantern cake. At late as it was now, there was no longer any point in worrying about secrecy. Phyllis stepped back from the table where the cake was sitting and said, "What do you think?"

"It's very impressive," Carolyn admitted. "You've outdone yourself, Phyllis. This is going to make my effort look pretty weak."

Phyllis glanced over at her. "What sort of cake did you make?" She knew that Carolyn had been working late in the kitchen the night before, and she had gone over to her daughter Sandra's house that morning to finish up whatever she was working on and to make her low-fat pizza rolls.

"Oh, you'll see when we get there," Carolyn said with an offhand wave. "And speaking of that, we probably need to get there about noon to start setting everything up."

Phyllis nodded. "I'll be ready." She tried not to let on that Carolyn's reticence about what she was doing for the auction had her intrigued.

She put the jack-o'-lantern cake in a box that she'd bought earlier in the week just for the cake, since she knew she didn't have anything around the house to carry it in. She had two other boxes ready, one with the peanut-butter-and-banana cookies and another with the cookbooks. All she had left to do was rinse the dishes, add them to the breakfast dishes in the dishwasher, and get it running.

Carolyn took her own car, since she had to go by Sandra's house to pick up whatever it was she had left there that morning. Phyllis offered Eve a ride, but Eve said, "No, that's all right, dear, I'll be coming with Sam later. His work is al-

ready all done, so he doesn't have to get there early and neither do I."

Phyllis couldn't very well argue with that, so she wound
up driving alone to the school once she had put the boxes
into her car. When she got there, she parked in the front lot
because she planned to go in through the main entrance.
From the road she had seen a few cars parked in the side lot,
toward the rear where the playground was located. There
were probably some people back there already setting up
booths and such.

As Phyllis was taking the cake out of the car, another vehicle pulled into an empty space nearby and Shannon Dunston got out. "Hello, Phyllis," Shannon said. She seemed to
be in a pretty good mood. She even smiled a little. "Are you
ready for the big day?"

"I hope so."

"Here, let me give you a hand," Shannon offered, taking
Phyllis a little by surprise. She reached past Phyllis into the
car and picked up the boxes with the cookies and the cookbooks. "I love these carnivals," Shannon went on as Phyllis
locked her car and the two women started toward the front
door of the school. "The money they raise goes to help the
kids, and they have such a good time, too. And they're really
the reason we're doing all this, aren't they?"

"That's right," Phyllis said, somewhat warily. It almost
seemed as if Shannon were a completely different person
today.

Maybe the man Phyllis had seen with her earlier in the
week really *had* had a positive effect on her.

"I really want to get it right this time," Shannon said.
"You met my son, so you know what I'm talking about."

Phyllis began, "I'm sure he's a fine young man—"

"Kirk has been a trial to me for years now," Shannon
broke in. "I'd like to blame his father . . . but I have to take
some responsibility for the way he turned out, too. I was determined, though, that my daughter, Becca, was going to

have every chance to do better. That's why I've worked so hard for the PTO. Nothing is more important to me than her."

Phyllis found herself feeling a little sorry for the other woman. Shannon had thrown herself into being a mom, and ultimately that might have contributed to the breakup of her second marriage. Maybe it would have been better for the little girl, Phyllis thought, if Shannon had spent a little less time at school and a little more with her husband. Then the girl would still have both parents together. Of course, other people's personal lives were none of her business, Phyllis reminded herself.

When they got to the entrance, Shannon reached out to grasp the handle on one of the glass doors. The door didn't budge when she pulled on the handle. She tried the other one. "Locked," she said. "The custodians should have unlocked them by now. Oh, well," and she delved into her purse with her free hand, "I have a key." She fished out a ring of keys, found the right one, and unlocked the doors, then held one of them open while Phyllis carried the jack-o'-lantern cake inside.

They went past the office and down the hall to the cafeteria. No one was there, but all the tables and benches were set up as if it were a regular school day. Normally on Friday afternoons the custodians folded them up and stacked them to one side so the cafeteria floor could be waxed and buffed, and the tables and benches would be set up again on Monday morning. But today there would be a concession stand in here selling nachos, pizza, and soft drinks, so people would need places to sit down and eat. Also, the baked goods donated to the auction and the entries for the contest would be laid out on a couple of the tables.

Several people followed Phyllis and Shannon into the cafeteria. Irene and Holly were in charge of the concession stand, so they had to get ready as well. They had their husbands with them, and quickly introduced the men to Phyllis and Shannon before getting to work. More people began drifting through the cafeteria—custodians, teachers, PTO board members, other parents who had volunteered to help out. And people began arriving with goods for the auction and entries for the contest. Phyllis took charge and managed as best she could, but she was glad when Carolyn showed up a short time later.

Carolyn was carrying a couple of boxes. In one was a chocolate cake that looked just like a giant Hostess cupcake. Phyllis was impressed. Carolyn thought up a cake for the auction that didn't require a lot of decoration, but would appeal to the kids and their parents.

Phyllis glanced into the other box to see how the low-fat pizza rolls turned out. They looked really tasty.

The cafeteria became even more crowded and hectic as one o'clock approached. Through the windows of the cafeteria, Phyllis could see the side parking lot filling up. A big crowd was going to be on hand. Most of the kids who were going to attend the carnival were being kept out of the building, but they were already swarming over the playground equipment farther out from the paved area where the booths were set up. Some children tagged along with their mothers when they came into the cafeteria to drop things off for the auction or the contest, and Phyllis had to shoo a few of them away from the tables where the cakes, pies, and cookies were displayed. She knew they didn't mean any harm, but they might not be able to resist the temptation to help themselves.

As Shannon bustled through to check on things, Phyllis asked her, "Where's your daughter today? Surely she's going to be here."

"Oh, yes, Becca wouldn't miss it. She's with her father. Joel promised to bring her to the carnival." Shannon shook her head. "As if Joel knows anything about keeping his promises. He won't break this one, though. He wouldn't dare."

Shannon hurried on to whatever needed her attention next, and Phyllis refrained from shaking her head as she watched the younger woman stalk out of the cafeteria. For a few minutes there earlier, Shannon had gained some sympathy from her, but the edge in her voice as she spoke about her ex-husband told Phyllis that the bitterness and anger were still strong inside Shannon.

Carolyn came over carrying a knife. "Can you help me cut up the contest entries so people can have samples of them?" she asked.

"Sure," Phyllis agreed. Carolyn handed her the knife. Phyllis got busy cutting the entries into bite-sized samples, starting with her cookies. The cookies were soft, so they cut easily.

By the time she was finished with that, the hands of the big clock on the cafeteria wall showed that the hour was almost one. Phyllis took out a handful of the cookbooks and set them next to a computer-printed sign stating the reasonable price of the books. The Oliver Loving Elementary School Fall Carnival would be officially under way any minute now.

Carolyn moved over beside Phyllis and asked quietly, "Are you ready for this?"

"Are you?"

"Of course."

"Good," Phyllis said as the sound of voices suddenly swelled from the hallway outside the cafeteria. "Because here they come."

Adults and children began pouring into the big, high-ceilinged room. Since the carnival began at one o'clock, some families had opted to have their lunch there, and the concession stand did a booming business right from the start, as people lined up for pizza and nachos. A veritable tide of youngsters washed over the playground as well. From where she was, Phyllis could see part of the paved area through the windows. A line of eager children formed at every booth she could see. A few minutes later, she saw a tractor chugging across the open field on the other side of the playground, pulling a train of about a dozen little cars, each of which held two kids. She couldn't see the bounce house, but she would have been willing to bet that it was full by now. A lot of people were going to have a lot of fun here today.

"Hi, guys," a bright, happy voice said from behind Phyllis and Carolyn. "Everything going all right?"

They turned to see Marie Tyler standing there with a tall, dark-haired man. She went on, "Those cakes look great! Oh, there's one that looks just like a jack-o'-lantern! How adorable!"

"That's Phyllis's," Carolyn said, with maybe only a hint of jealousy in her voice. She looked over at the man with Marie, nodded, smiled, and said, "Hello, Russ."

"Hi, Mrs. Wilbarger," he said. "Thanks for helping out with all of this. I think Marie would have been pulling her hair out if you hadn't agreed to give her a hand."

"It was my pleasure," Carolyn said graciously. "I don't think you've met my friend Phyllis Newsom, have you?"

"Oh, that's right," Marie said. "Phyllis, this is my husband, Russ. Honey, this is Carolyn's friend Phyllis."

Phyllis hadn't said a word since Marie and her husband had come up. She had been trying not to stare too hard at Russ Tyler. Now she forced herself to acknowledge the introduction. "I'm pleased to meet you," she lied.

It was a lie because she wasn't glad to meet Russ Tyler at all.

Unless she was very badly mistaken, Marie's husband was the man she had seen in Fort Worth a few days earlier, holding Shannon Dunston's arm like a lover as he walked with her into that restaurant.

Chapter 9

She had to be wrong about what she had seen, Phyllis told herself. She'd been having allergy trouble and her eyes had been watering a lot. That must have blurred her vision. So there was a chance she hadn't really seen Russ Tyler with Shannon.

But even as she tried to convince herself, she knew she hadn't been mistaken. She had gotten a good look at the couple as they entered the restaurant.

Maybe there was a reasonable explanation. Maybe Shannon and Russ were just friends. Maybe they had been meeting Marie there for lunch. Maybe they worked together. . . . No, wait, Shannon didn't have a job. That was why she was able to devote so much time to the PTO.

And Marie and Shannon wouldn't have been getting together for lunch, either. Phyllis knew that in her bones.

Oh, hell, she thought with uncharacteristic vehemence. *Oh, hell.*

But she kept a smile plastered on her face as Marie said, "I'd better go see how Irene and Holly are doing with the concession stand. Come on, honey."

Russ lifted a hand in farewell and said, "See you later, ladies. Nice to meet you, Phyllis."

She managed to nod pleasantly enough. But at the same time she was thinking about how Marie obviously loved him, and about how they had two children together, and she asked herself what in the world he was thinking by jeopardizing all that by having an affair with Shannon Dunston.

Phyllis took a deep breath. Maybe they weren't having an affair. Maybe it was just a casual thing, getting together occasionally for lunch. Marie might even know all about it.

But Phyllis doubted that very seriously.

"Are you all right?" Carolyn asked quietly. "Something's bothering you, isn't it?"

Phyllis shook her head as she watched Marie talk to Holly and Irene for a moment and then leave the cafeteria with Russ. "I'm fine," she said. And she was. Luckily, none of this was even remotely any of her business. She could try to just put it all out of her head. A part of her wanted to warn Marie that there might be some hanky-panky going on between her husband and Shannon, but at the same time, her years as a teacher had taught her to butt out of people's personal lives. What happened at school was all that had really concerned her, although as a human being she felt sympathy for other people's problems. Everyone involved in this one would just have to work it out for themselves.

As the carnival went on, Phyllis found herself too busy to worry about anything except keeping up with the constant flow of people in front of the tables as they admired the auction items and handed over tickets so they could sample the healthy snacks. Each entry had been assigned a number, and at the end of the table was an empty jar and a stack of pieces of paper cut into small squares, along with some pencils. When people had tried all the snacks, they could write down the number of the one they liked best and drop the piece of paper in the jar. Half an hour or so before the auction was scheduled to begin, the voting would be ended and Phyllis and Carolyn would take the jar to the school principal, who had agreed to do an impartial count of the votes.

There were plenty of entries to select from. As Phyllis looked along the table, she saw baked pita triangles with seasonings, banana bread, berry muffins, roll-ups with whole wheat tortillas, apple breakfast bars, a low-fat carrot cake, walnut-raisin cookies that Phyllis remembered from the recipe had cottage cheese in them. She was really curious what they tasted like. People had embraced the idea of coming up with healthy snacks better than she had at first thought they would.

The cake auction was going to be spectacular, too. Phyllis was amazed at the variety of cakes people had come up with. There was a sandcastle that sparkled with sugar, a rose garden, and a cute carousel with animal crackers. She saw some cakes she wouldn't have minded bidding on herself, but she knew she probably wouldn't. She had to watch how much sugar she took in, and her own baking ideas usually provided more than enough.

Marie came through the cafeteria several times, sometimes with Russ and sometimes alone. She carried a zippered money bag. Since the concession stand operated on a cash basis, rather than using tickets like the booths and other attractions, the money taken in there had to be collected every so often to keep it from building up too much. Phyllis assumed that Marie was taking the cash back to some place in the school where it could be locked up safely, probably in the principal's office.

Around the middle of the afternoon, Shannon and her ex-husband came into the cafeteria, along with a pretty little brown-haired girl Phyllis assumed was their daughter, Becca. Joel Dunston gave the girl some money to go to the concession stand; then he and Shannon sat down at the far end of one of the tables. They didn't sit side by side, Phyllis noticed, but rather across from each other. Both of them leaned forward over the table so that they could talk quietly. Judging by the expressions on their faces, the conversation they were having wasn't a pleasant one. They both looked like they were barely keeping their anger in check.

They sat back and smiled as Becca returned to the table carrying a bowl of nachos and a soft drink. Phyllis hoped the little girl wasn't paying too much attention to her parents, or else she would see that the smiles on their faces were patently phony. People ought to be able to put aside their differences for the sake of their children, at least for a little while, Phyllis thought, but sometimes they were unable or unwilling to do so.

When Becca finished her food, she came over to gaze in amazement at the fancy decorated cakes, then moved on to the table with the snacks. "Can I try them?" she asked Phyllis.

"If you have two tickets, you can sample and judge the snacks. If you want a cookbook, it's four tickets."

Becca dug in the pocket of her jeans and came up with a crumpled wad of tickets. She tore off two and handed them across the table.

"You can have one sample of each, and you should pay attention to the numbers on them, because down there at the end of the table you can vote for which one you like the best." Phyllis pointed to the jar, which was now about a third full of the little pieces of paper.

"Okay." Becca picked up one of the samples.

"Have you been enjoying the carnival?" Phyllis asked.

"Oh, we just got here. My dad was running late, as usual, and my mom's mad at him about it, as usual." The little girl sounded bored by her parents' squabbling. "My mom told him he was going to be late for his own funeral. He said he'd be right on time for hers. He said he might even get there early, so he could enjoy it longer."

Phyllis caught her breath. Even though Becca didn't seem particularly upset and had reported her parents' hurtful comments in matter-of-fact fashion, Phyllis knew the little girl had to be bothered by hearing such things. No child would enjoy her parents' clawing at each other like that.

"What do you think of the snacks, dear?" Phyllis asked in an attempt to change the subject.

"They're all really yummy," Becca said around a

mouthful of carrot cake. "Are they really supposed to be good for you?"

"Yes, indeed."

"They sure don't taste like it. They're too good for that."

Phyllis didn't argue with her, knowing the commonly held belief among children—and most adults—that if something tasted good, it couldn't possibly be good for you.

With a self-possession beyond her years, a quality that children from dysfunctional families often seemed to possess, Becca sampled the rest of the entries and finally picked up a pencil and square of paper to record her vote. She folded the paper and dropped it into the jar, then turned and waved at Phyllis before heading back to the table where her parents were still sitting and talking with tautly angry expressions on their faces. They forced smiles again as Becca rejoined them. Joel stood up and took the little girl's hand. She practically tugged him out of the cafeteria, clearly anxious to see what else the carnival had to offer.

Phyllis kept an eye on Shannon, hoping the woman wouldn't get up and come over here to indulge in more bitter sniping about her ex-husband. She didn't; Shannon left the cafeteria instead, turning the opposite way in the hall from the direction Joel and Becca had gone.

A while later, Russ Tyler wandered by. He nodded to Phyllis and Carolyn, saying, "Hello, ladies." Marie wasn't with him, and neither were Amber and Aaron, the Tyler children. He walked on through the cafeteria and left by the same exit that the Dunstons had a short time earlier. Phyllis couldn't help but notice that Russ turned in the same direction Shannon had gone.

At the *school carnival*? Phyllis thought. Surely they hadn't set up an illicit rendezvous *here*!

A part of her wanted to hurry after Russ and confront him with her suspicions, maybe even catch him and Shannon together. Phyllis knew she couldn't do that, though. She had to stay here in the cafeteria and help Carolyn tend to the tables, and anyway, she reminded herself for what had to be the dozenth time, it wasn't any of her business what Shannon and Russ did or didn't do. She didn't *want* to catch them in the act.

Carolyn came up beside her and said, "You look like something's bothering you again."

"No, I'm just . . . ready for this carnival to be over. I guess I'm a little tired. I'm not as young as I once was."

"None of us are," Carolyn said.

Phyllis was able to force her mind back onto the business at hand, at least for a while. Then Joel Dunston came into the cafeteria alone, crossed the big room to the tables where Phyllis and Carolyn stood, and asked, "Have either of you ladies seen my wife? Shannon Dunston? She's the president of the PTO."

Even though Phyllis knew who Joel was, she realized that he had no idea who she was. They had never been introduced. Phyllis noticed that he referred to Shannon as his wife, not his ex-wife. Maybe despite the anger that existed between them, he was having trouble adjusting to the divorce. Maybe he still had feelings for her. If that was the case, then the last thing he needed was to find her in the arms of Russ Tyler.

"Yes, we know Shannon," Carolyn said. "I haven't seen her since earlier in the afternoon, though. What about you, Phyllis?"

Phyllis shook her head and said, "Sorry." She wasn't going to tell Joel which direction Shannon had gone. Anyway, that had been a while earlier. Shannon could be anywhere in the school by now.

Several children came running up to the table. "Slow down, slow down," Carolyn told them, years of being a teacher coming out in the stern tone of her voice. "What do you children want?"

"A piece of cake!" one of them cried as he pointed at Phyllis's jack-o'-lantern cake.

"We can't cut that one," Carolyn explained. "It's for the auction."

"You mean it's just for show?" a little girl asked. "It's not for eating?"

"Whoever buys it at the auction can eat it," Phyllis explained.

"How about that one?" the little boy who had wanted a piece of the jack-o'-lantern cake asked. He was pointing at the sandcastle cake. Carolyn told him that one was off-limits for the time being, too.

"If you want one of the things on this table, you can ask your mother or father to bid on it," she said. "But if you have two tickets, you can sample all the snacks on the other table."

The little boy wrinkled his nose in distaste. "Somebody told me they're good for you. I don't want any of that stuff."

Several of the other kids weren't so picky, and dug out tickets to sample the snacks. Phyllis and Carolyn had to keep an eye on them to make sure none of them got more than one piece of anything, and by the time the kids moved on, Joel Dunston was gone. The area around the tables had been busy enough so that Phyllis hadn't noticed when he left.

She wondered if this time he had gone the same direction as Shannon and Russ. She hoped that if those two *had* gotten together, they'd had the sense to do it behind a locked door.

Phyllis was distracted by a little girl, probably a kindergartner, who ran up to the tables, tugging her father along with her. Sporting pigtails and a T-shirt with Elmo from *Sesame Street* on it, she was utterly adorable. She pointed to the jack-o'-lantern cake and said, "Punkin!"

"Yeah, that's right," the man told her. He flashed a grin at Phyllis. In his twenties, he wore a black Harley-Davidson T-shirt and had close-cropped blond hair. "Are those cakes for sale?"

"No, we're going to be auctioning them off in a little while," Phyllis explained.

"I want the punkin cake, Daddy!" the little girl said.

He smiled down at her and said, "We'll see," in a tone of voice that Phyllis knew meant he had no intention of bidding on any of the cakes. "Let's get some of these snacks instead," he went on as he handed over four tickets and then started picking out samples for them.

Frances Hickson, the principal of Loving Elementary, showed up a short time later and said, "I guess it's about time for me to count those votes, isn't it, ladies?"

Phyllis glanced at the clock and was surprised to see that it was four. The carnival had been going on for three hours. They had been busy enough that it didn't seem that long.

Carolyn raised her voice and called out to the people in the cafeteria, "Last call for the snack contest! Anyone who wants to sample the snacks and vote on them, now's the time!"

A few people hurried up to the table and handed over tickets for both the snacks and the cookbooks. When they were done and had cast their votes, Carolyn put the lid on the jar and handed it to Principal Hickson. The school administrator, a nice-looking, fortyish woman with short dark hair, smiled and said, "The auction starts at four thirty, right? I'll have the results back to you by then. I'll just take the jar into the music room to count the votes."

"Thank you," Carolyn said. As the principal walked away with the jar, heading for the music room behind the stage, Carolyn turned to Phyllis and went on, "I guess we can continue selling samples and cookbooks; people just can't vote on the snacks anymore."

Phyllis nodded. "Yes, we want to get rid of as much of this stuff as we can."

For the next thirty minutes, they continued collecting tickets from anyone who still wanted to sample the snacks, including some kids who were coming back for seconds or

even thirds on them. Then Principal Hickson returned with
the jar of ballots under one arm and a piece of paper in the
other. "We have a winner," she said with a smile.

"You're going to be in charge of the auction, right?" Carolyn said. "You can announce the contest results, if you
don't mind."

"Sure," the principal agreed. She set the paper with the
results on the table and placed the jar on top of it, then went
back into the kitchen and returned a moment later with a
portable public address system. She set it on the end of the
table, turned it on, and picked up the handheld microphone.

"If I could have your attention, please," she said, her
voice booming out from the speakers. The portable PA system was tied in with the school-wide system, so Principal
Hickson's voice could be heard all over the campus. She
went on, "We're about to have the cake auction in the cafeteria, and before that gets under way I'll be announcing the
results of the snack competition. So anyone who's interested
in these things, y'all come on in and we'll have some fun
auctioning off these goodies!"

Sam and Eve were among the people coming into the
cafeteria following the principal's announcement. Sam had
come through earlier in the afternoon, said hello to Phyllis
and Carolyn, and sampled all the snacks and voted for his favorite. Phyllis hadn't seen Eve since she got there, though.
She thought that someone Eve's age shouldn't look so good
in a pair of tight jeans, but Eve undoubtedly did. Phyllis
wondered if Sam had noticed, then decided that of course he
had. He was a man, after all.

The cafeteria began to fill up. Some people weren't interested in what was going on inside and so would stay outside
on the playground, but after a long afternoon a lot of the parents were ready to sit down for a while. The noise level
grew. Several of the PTO board members drifted in. Phyllis
saw Marie and Russ and their two children. Joel Dunston

and Becca walked into the cafeteria a few minutes later. Phyllis didn't see Shannon anywhere in the room, though.

"Welcome, everyone," Principal Hickson said into the microphone. "I hope y'all have had a good time here at Oliver Loving Elementary School this afternoon!"

A wave of applause came from the crowded tables.

"I know a lot of you have sampled the snacks up here on this table today and voted for your favorite," the principal went on. "What some of you may not know is that all these snacks are nutritious. That's right, they're good for you!"

Mock groans came from some of the kids, followed by laughter.

"We've counted the votes, and we're ready to announce which of these snacks you folks liked the best."

"What does it win?" someone called from the audience.

"Well, now . . ." Principal Hickson looked around at Carolyn and Phyllis, who shook their heads and shrugged. "The prize is knowing that they pleased a lot of folks," the principal said as she turned back to the crowd. "And maybe we'll see if we can hunt up a blue ribbon or something, how about that?"

More applause.

"Anyway, here we go." Hickson reached over and took the paper from under the jar. "The winner of the snack competition is . . . Phyllis Newsom!"

Phyllis caught her breath in surprise. She had hoped to win . . . she had thought that her peanut-butter-and-banana cookies might deserve to win . . . but she hadn't believed it would actually happen. She glanced over at Carolyn, who looked pained for an instant but then put a smile on her face as she said, "Congratulations." Unlike the smiles worn by Shannon and Joel Dunston earlier in the afternoon, Carolyn's expression was genuine. She was being more than gracious about being defeated; Phyllis had to give her that. She seemed to be honestly glad that Phyllis had won.

"Thank you," Phyllis said. She looked out at the

applauding audience and saw the big grin on Sam's face. That made the effort worthwhile, too.

Principal Hickson turned and smiled at her and said, "We'll look for that blue ribbon later, okay?"

"Okay," Phyllis said.

"Now it's time to get on with the auction." Since the microphone was a cordless one, Principal Hickson was able to move over behind the other table as she continued, "My goodness, I don't think I've ever seen a prettier assortment of cakes. I know a lot of you will want to bid on these. We'll start with this giant Hostess cupcake. Do I have a bid for this beautiful chocolate delight?"

Before anyone could call out a bid, a shocked silence fell over the cafeteria. It lasted for several seconds, and during that time, the sound of someone screaming came down the hall and into the big room, loud and clear.

Chapter 10

Pandemonium erupted.

A lot of the parents had their kids with them and knew they were safe, but some didn't. As they heard that shrill indication of bad trouble, those adults reacted instinctively and lunged to their feet. They had to check on their children and make sure they were all right. Every parent in the room who couldn't be sure otherwise had the terrifying feeling that something bad might have happened to their child.

It was a stampede through the doors, the thunder of feet and the startled shouts drowning out the continued screams. Principal Hickson called, "Wait! Everyone stay calm!" but despite the amplification of the PA system, everybody ignored her. She dropped the microphone and joined the rush out of the cafeteria.

Phyllis and Carolyn traded shocked glances, unsure what they should do. Sam and Eve hurried up to the tables. "You have any idea what all the commotion's about?" Sam asked.

Phyllis shook her head.

"I'll go find out," Sam said. "You ladies stay here."

"I'm going with you," Phyllis declared, and Carolyn and Eve nodded in agreement. They had all been teachers too long for their instincts to allow them to stand back whenever there was trouble in a school.

The four of them left the cafeteria and followed the sound of the uproar down the left-hand wing, toward the conference room where Phyllis and Carolyn had met with the members of the PTO board. The crowd was converging on the far end of the corridor. Phyllis and the others hurried in that direction, too. Phyllis wasn't sure what was down there; she hadn't been that far along this hall during her previous visits to the school.

People began turning back when they reached the end of the hall. Some of them looked sick. Others just seemed horrified and scared. Parents picked up their kids and hurried to get them away from whatever it was. But other people were still trying to get past, and that created a logjam. It took several minutes for Phyllis, Sam, Carolyn, and Eve to work their way along the side of the corridor, next to the wall, before they finally reached the end of the hall. Sam's broad shoulders led the way.

A short cross hall ran from the front to the back of the wing. A couple of classrooms, empty now, were across it, at the very end of the building. At the back of this short hall was a single door that led outside. At the front, the hall ended in a blank brick wall. There was a closed metal door to the right. None of this was any cause for alarm.

What had caused the screaming—and what had prompted Principal Hickson to say raggedly into her cell phone, "We need an ambulance and the police *right now!*"—was the body lying on the gray-carpeted floor of the short hallway, around the corner so that it wasn't visible from the main hall. Phyllis leaned against the wall. She was stunned by the sight of Shannon Dunston sprawled on her side, eyes wide and lifeless. The pale blue blouse she wore had a dark red stain on the front of it, and Phyllis knew it had to be blood.

"Good Lord," Sam muttered. Phyllis wouldn't have been able to hear him over the commotion if he hadn't been right beside her. One of his big hands gripped her shoulder. "Are you okay?"

Phyllis managed a shaky nod. "Yes, I'm all right." Although she was afraid that she already knew the answer, she asked, "Is . . . is she dead?"

"Looks like it to me," Sam replied, his rugged face grim.

"How terrible!" Eve said. "Who is she? She looks familiar to me, but I can't place her."

Carolyn said, "That's Shannon Dunston, the president of the PTO. I don't know that you ever met her."

"I'm sure I did, but I don't recall where."

Phyllis didn't see that it mattered now whether Eve had ever met Shannon or not. No one would ever meet Shannon again. For all of her faults, there had been a moment or two when Phyllis had caught a glimpse of a troubled, hurting human being inside that shell of bitterness and impatience. Phyllis couldn't help but feel a little sorry for Shannon now that she was dead.

Now that she had been murdered.

Phyllis's breath hissed between her teeth as that thought occurred to her. Sam looked over at her and asked, "What's wrong?"

"What happened to her?" Phyllis asked as she nodded toward the body.

"I don't know. With that much blood, there must be a wound of some sort. . . ."

"She was murdered."

Principal Hickson overheard Phyllis's comment and turned sharply toward her. "What was that? What did you say, Mrs. Newsom?"

Phyllis stiffened her spine. "I said Shannon was murdered. Somebody killed her."

"I thought it must have been some sort of terrible accident. It . . . it never occurred to me that . . . oh, Lord! Someone was murdered! In my school!"

"Who found her?" Phyllis asked. "Who was doing all that screaming?"

"I . . . I'm not sure. When I got here, Mrs. Gonzales was

leaning against the wall. She was crying and she had her hands over her mouth. I suppose it could have been her."

"Lindsey Gonzales?"

"Yes. But she could have come up after someone else screamed. There were already quite a few people here."

Phyllis looked around but didn't see any sign of Lindsey. The blonde must have been one of those making their way down the hall, away from the scene of the murder. Someone would have to question her and find out exactly what she had seen.

But that wasn't her job, Phyllis reminded herself. True, she had figured out who had committed that murder at the Peach Festival, but she was no detective. The only reason she had started poking around in that crime, and the others that had plagued Weatherford during that tense summer, was because a friend of hers had been under suspicion.

Still, some things were just common sense, and someone needed to speak up now. "This is a crime scene," she said. "Everyone needs to stand back and not disturb things any more than they already have."

"That's right," Sam said. He raised his voice and went on, "Everybody move back now! You don't want the cops to find you trompin' all over the scene and disturbin' evidence!" During his years as a basketball coach he had shouted out hundreds of defensive alignments to his teams, so his deep voice was powerful and carried authority. The crowd in the corridor began to move back.

Someone came pushing forward urgently, though, calling, "Let me through! Let me through, damn it! Somebody said my wife was hurt!"

Joel Dunston broke through the crowd. His eyes were wide and panicky. As he started to lunge around the corner, Phyllis said, "Sam, stop him!"

Sam got in Joel's way and grabbed him, but not before Joel had caught a glimpse of the bloody figure lying on the floor. He let out an inarticulate shout of pain and grief, like the cry of a wounded animal.

"Hang on to him, Sam," Phyllis said as she saw Becca Dunston slip through a gap on the crowd. She stepped quickly toward the little girl. It was bad enough that Joel had seen his ex-wife's murdered body. Phyllis wasn't going to allow Becca to witness that terrible sight. She caught hold of the girl's shoulders and said, "Wait right here, honey."

Becca looked up at her with tear-filled eyes and asked, "Is . . . is my mom all right? Somebody said she was hurt."

"Why don't we go back up to the library and wait?" Phyllis suggested without answering Becca's question. "I'm sure your father will want to talk to you later."

As she steered Becca back up the hall toward the front of the school where the library was located, the crowd suddenly parted to let several uniformed men through. They were Parker County sheriff's deputies, Phyllis realized, and the one in the lead was her own son, Mike. He stopped short when he saw her.

"Mom?"

Phyllis kept her hands on Becca's shoulders and nodded her head toward the far end of the hall. "Down there," she said quietly. Mike looked like he wanted to ask questions, but instead he returned her nod and led the other deputies toward the scene of the crime.

Of course, it might *not* be the scene of the crime, Phyllis reminded herself. Just because Shannon's body had been found down there in that little blind hallway didn't mean that she had been killed there, although it certainly seemed likely.

And there she went, thinking like a detective again when she had no business doing so. "Come on, dear," she said as she guided Becca toward the library.

Phyllis wasn't surprised that the sheriff's department had responded to Principal Hickson's 911 call. While the school was fairly close to town, it was outside of the Weatherford city limits, meaning that the sheriff had jurisdiction here. His men would handle the investigation into Shannon's death.

Phyllis and Becca went to the library, but the doors were locked. That left the cafeteria. Phyllis would have preferred the quiet of the library, but she had no choice in the matter. She wanted to keep Becca occupied for a while. She took the girl into the cafeteria and asked, "Would you like something to eat?"

Becca shook her head. "No. My stomach doesn't feel too good. I . . . I'm worried about my mom."

"So am I, dear. But we'll just have to wait until someone comes to talk to us." Phyllis tried to wrestle the subject away from Shannon. "Did you go to all the carnival booths and ride all the rides?" She had already noticed a flower painted on the little girl's cheek, so she knew Becca had been to the face-painting booth.

Becca managed to nod. "Yeah, I did just about everything there was to do. My dad bought me a bunch of tickets."

"Did he stay with you all afternoon?" Phyllis told herself that she wasn't checking on Joel Dunston's alibi. She was just trying to keep Becca talking. But she already knew that Joel *hadn't* been with Becca all afternoon. She had seen him come through the cafeteria by himself a little earlier.

Becca shook her head. "No, he doesn't like to do all that little kid stuff. He can stand it for a while, but not all day. He told me to go on and have fun, so I did."

"What about your mom? When was the last time you saw her?"

"I don't know. She and my dad had that fight in here, right after my dad and I got here. Then I saw her again out on the playground after that. She asked if I was having a good time." Becca sniffled. "I told her I was."

"Where did she go then?" Phyllis wanted to bite her lip. She hadn't brought the little girl in here to interrogate her, but that seemed to be the way it was turning out.

"I don't know. She went back into the school. She said she had to go see about some money."

Phyllis frowned. "What money?"

Becca shook her head and said, "I don't know. Just some money. That's all she said."

Marie Tyler had been collecting the cash from the concession stand and putting it somewhere safe. Phyllis supposed she had done the same with the money taken in by Eve and the other volunteers who were selling tickets. But as the PTO president, Shannon could have been doing the same thing. Phyllis found herself wondering just how much cash was generated by an event like this. The carnival was a fund-raiser, after all. The goal was to raise as much money as possible. She supposed the total could be well up in the thousands of dollars.

Stop thinking about possible motives, she told herself. It wasn't up to her to solve Shannon's murder. That would be the responsibility of Mike and the other members of the sheriff's department.

Marie Tyler came into the cafeteria with her kids in tow. She looked around, spotted Phyllis, and started toward her.

"Have you seen Russ?" she asked as she came up to the table. Her face was pale and drawn, and Phyllis was pretty sure she had heard by now what had happened to Shannon. She might have even seen the body, although Phyllis hadn't noticed her among the crowd at the far end of the hallway.

Phyllis shook her head and said, "I'm sorry. I haven't." *Not since I saw him following Shannon,* she added silently.

"I have to find him," Marie said. She looked around a little wide-eyed, then returned her gaze to Phyllis and said, "Would you mind keeping an eye on my kids for a minute? Thanks."

Then, without waiting for an answer, as usual, she hurried off, leaving Amber and Aaron standing there beside the table, looking a little confused and scared.

"Sit down, you two," Phyllis said, since there was really

nothing else she could do. "Would you like something to eat?"

"I'm hungry," Amber said, and her little brother nodded.

Phyllis looked at Becca and said, "Are you sure you don't want something?"

The little girl shrugged. "I guess I could eat something."

"Fine. All of you stay right here. I'll be right back."

Phyllis stood up and went toward the tables at the front of the room where the auction goods and the snack competition had been set up. With all the commotion going on, everybody had forgotten about the auction. Some of the items were gone, though. Either the people who had donated them had come by to reclaim them, figuring that under the circumstances the auction was off, or else some sticky-fingered youngsters had simply carried them off.

That was certainly the case on the snack table, which was practically empty by now. With Phyllis and Carolyn gone and all the confusion filling the school, kids had simply helped themselves to the goodies. Phyllis felt a flare of anger at such behavior, but she told herself to forget about it. There were much more important things going on.

Her jack-o'-lantern cake was still on the auction table. It would have been difficult to carry off without somebody noticing. If anyone had a right to cut it, she did, she decided, so she looked around for the knife she and Carolyn had used earlier and spotted it lying on the table. She planned to cut three small pieces off the cake, one each for Becca, Amber, and Aaron.

She had just picked up the knife and had it poised over the rounded edge of the jack-o'-lantern cake when Mike hurried into the cafeteria and said, "Mom, no! Don't use that knife!"

Chapter 11

Phyllis froze and stared silently at her son, startled into speechlessness by Mike's words and actions. He came toward her, one hand outstretched, and went on, "Just put the knife down now. Please, Mom."

Phyllis finally got her tongue back. She said, "Michael Newsom, what in the world is wrong with you?"

"I just need you to put the knife down."

She waved it. "This knife?"

Mike winced. "Yes. Please."

"Well, just what do you think I'm going to do with it?" Phyllis demanded. "Do you think I'm about to go berserk or something?"

"Of course not. But that might be the murder weapon."

Phyllis's eyes widened. She tore her gaze away from her son's intent face and turned her head to stare at the knife in her hand. Then she said quietly, "Oh," and her fingers opened involuntarily. The knife clattered to the table.

Mike rushed forward, taking a plastic evidence bag from his pocket. He turned it inside out, used it to pick up the knife, and then pulled the bag right side out again. He blew his breath out in relief as he ran his thumb and forefinger along the bag's opening, sealing it.

"There," he said. "Now the evidence won't be contaminated any more than it already is."

"Mike, what are you talking about?" Phyllis cast a

worried glance toward the table where Becca Dunston and the two Tyler youngsters were sitting. She didn't want them overhearing anything they shouldn't, but she had to know what was going on. "What makes you think that knife is"— she lowered her voice—"the murder weapon?"

"The ambulance and the paramedics got here right after the other deputies and I did," Mike explained. "Calvin noticed something on Mrs.—"

Phyllis lifted a hand to stop him from saying the name.

"On the victim's blouse," Mike went on. "The medical examiner and the crime scene guys aren't here yet, but it's pretty obvious that the cause of death was a knife wound. And on the edge of the hole in the blouse that the knife made, Calvin found something."

Phyllis knew her son was talking about Calvin Holloway, an emergency medical technician who was one of Mike's best friends. She said, "What was it?"

Mike looked down at the bagged knife in his hands. "Calvin said he thought it was cake frosting."

Phyllis stared at the knife, too. She and Carolyn had used it quite a bit during the afternoon to cut samples from the various snacks, including a carrot cake with sugar-free icing. She saw some of that frosting dried on the blade. "Oh, my God," she said softly. "My God. You mean we used it to cut . . . and somebody used . . . Oh, no." She suddenly felt sick to her stomach.

Mike put a hand on her arm. "Take it easy, Mom," he said. "We don't know anything for sure yet. Anyway, there's a good chance that even if this is the murder weapon, the killer lifted it from here not long before he used it, then put it back during the confusion after the body was discovered. I don't imagine it was used for anything after the murder."

"But I was about to—"

"That's why I stopped you. When Calvin said that about the cake frosting, something clicked in my brain, and I realized that this was the most likely place anybody could find a knife with frosting on it. So I came to see if it was still here."

"Thank goodness you got here when you did," Phyllis said fervently. The idea that she could have used the knife to cut a piece of cake for the murdered woman's daughter was grotesque. Just thinking about it made her stomach even more queasy.

"I'll turn this over to the lab and let our forensics experts decide whether or not it's the murder weapon. I've got a hunch it is, though."

So did Phyllis. With all the people going in and out of the cafeteria all afternoon, anyone could have picked up the knife without her noticing and slipped it back onto the table after all the commotion broke out.

She stiffened as she remembered that Joel Dunston had been standing beside the table not long before Shannon was killed. And since she hadn't noticed him leaving the cafeteria, it went without saying that he could have pocketed the knife and carried it off with him.

And he had said that he was looking for Shannon. . . .

Phyllis's eyes went to Becca again. How terrible it would be for the little girl to not only lose her mother to a killer but also to have her father convicted of the murder.

She was getting way ahead of herself, and she knew it. There could be dozens of other explanations. Phyllis was glad it would be up to Mike and the other deputies, instead of her, to figure out what had really happened.

People began coming back into the cafeteria, among them Sam, Carolyn, and Eve. They walked over to Phyllis and Mike, and Sam said, "The medical examiner is here, and he's got that whole wing of the school blocked off now."

Mike nodded. "I'd better take this knife and get back to the investigation."

Eve looked at the knife and said, "Oh, dear. Is that what I think it is?"

"Could be, Mrs. Turner," Mike told her. He nodded

politely to the four retired teachers—Phyllis had raised him too well for him to do otherwise—and hurried out of the cafeteria.

Phyllis asked Sam, "Did you overhear anything while you were down there?"

"The paramedics said it looked like a stab wound to the chest. Probably got the heart. Mrs. Dunston wouldn't have lived long after that."

A little voice piped up, "Mrs. Dunston? You mean Becca's mama?"

Phyllis looked around in horror and saw that Aaron Tyler had come up to the table without any of them noticing. He went on. "You said you were gonna get us somethin' to eat." Then he turned his head and shouted, "Hey, Becca, did you know your mama got stabbed in the heart?"

Phyllis felt like her own heart had plummeted all the way to her feet. It got even worse a second later when Becca covered her face with her hands and began to sob, great racking wails that shook her slender body.

Phyllis hurried over to the table and sat down beside the little girl. She couldn't do anything except put her arm around Becca and say comfortingly, "It's all right, Becca. There, there. It'll all be all right."

That was a lie and Phyllis knew it. For Becca Dunston, it would probably be a long, long time before everything was all right again—if it ever was.

The carnival had been almost over when Shannon's body was found, and after that grisly discovery the festivities were definitely finished. But the deputies issued orders that no one was to leave just yet, which meant that the parking lot was full of cars with angry, impatient people sitting in them or milling around them. Sheriff's department cruisers with their red and blue lights flashing were parked across all the exits, blocking them.

Of course, there was no way of knowing just who and

how many of the people in attendance at the carnival had left before the deputies arrived. The killer could have slipped away in the confusion and been long gone by the time the law got there. But no one else could leave without at least a cursory interview with one of the deputies. Those orders had come directly from Sheriff Royce Haney when he found out that a murder had been committed at an elementary school. School violence was always a powerful magnet for the news media, and the sheriff wanted to get on top of this case as quickly as possible.

Mike couldn't blame him for that. And he knew that Sheriff Haney was more concerned with finding the killer than he was with the impression his department would make in the media. But it never hurt to keep the uproar under control as much as possible.

Haney himself arrived shortly after the ME did, and sought Mike out immediately, since he knew that the young deputy had been one of the first on the scene. Haney took Mike over to a corner of the hallway and said, "What have we got here, Deputy? Boil it down for me."

Mike took a deep breath before he started his report. "The victim is Mrs. Shannon Dunston, age forty-one. Pending the medical examiner's findings, cause of death appears to be a single stab wound to the chest that probably nicked her heart. She was found lying in a short hallway at the end of the main hall that runs through this wing of the school."

"Who found the body?" Haney interrupted.

"We don't know yet," Mike replied with a shake of his head. "We're still interviewing witnesses. All we know is that someone found her and started screaming, and that brought quite a few other people on the run. According to the school principal, Frances Hickson, a woman named Lindsey Gonzales was on the scene and appeared to be very upset. It's possible she was the one who discovered the body."

"Has she been interviewed yet?"

Again, Mike had to shake his head. "We haven't located her. It's possible that any number of people could have left the school before we arrived and locked down the campus, and she must have been one of them."

"They're bound to have her address in the school office," Haney said. "Get it and find her."

"Yes, sir."

"What about the murder weapon? Was it in or near the body?"

"No, sir, but I recovered a knife from the school cafeteria that might have been used to kill Mrs. Dunston."

"What makes you think that?"

Mike hesitated, but there was no way he could get around answering the question. "The cake frosting," he said.

The sheriff stared at him but didn't say anything.

Mike went on, "One of the paramedics found what appeared to be cake frosting on the dead woman's blouse, at the point of entry. I happened to know that there were a lot of baked goods in the cafeteria, including cakes, so I thought the murder weapon might have come from there."

"And how did you happen to know that, Deputy?"

"Because my mother and her friends were here helping out with the carnival bake sale. Well, it wasn't a bake sale exactly. . . ."

"Your mother?" Haney said.

"Yes, sir."

"She's not conducting her own investigation, is she?" Haney asked dryly.

Mike felt a flash of irritation at the sheriff's tone. "No, sir, she's not involved at all," he said. "But if you recall, she has a pretty good record at clearing homicide cases."

Haney frowned and said, "Be sure to tell her that I don't think we'll need her help on this one."

Mike nodded but didn't say anything. He didn't really trust himself to speak at that particular moment.

After a second or two, Haney went on, "So we've got, what, a couple hundred suspects?"

"There are probably more people than that still here, and as I said, we don't know how many left before we arrived. But a lot of them are little kids, sir, and I'm sure that most of the adults wouldn't have had any reason to want Mrs. Dunston dead."

"But there are that many who *could* have taken the knife from the cafeteria and then returned it there after the murder, correct?"

Mike had to nod in agreement. "Correct, sir."

Haney grimaced and said, "Keep interviewing everyone, for as long as it takes."

"People are getting impatient," Mike pointed out.

Haney grunted. "Let 'em. I don't care if some of them are here all night. They're not leaving until we've talked to them."

"Yes, sir."

"Now show me the murder scene."

They had already ducked under several strips of crime scene tape that were crisscrossed across the hallway where it joined the lobby at the front of the school. The two lawmen walked down to the far end of the corridor, where a knot of deputies stood at its junction with the short hallway. They stepped aside to let Haney take a look at the body, which still lay where it had been found. The medical examiner had moved Shannon onto her back, but only after numerous photos had been taken.

"Got a time of death yet?" Haney asked the ME.

"It's still tentative, but I'd say within the past two hours," the man replied. "Cause of death appears to be a stab wound to the chest. I can give you the details after the autopsy, but I'll be mighty surprised if it turns out to be anything else."

Haney looked at the closed metal door to the right of the hallway. "What's in there?"

"According to the principal, that's the book room, where

they store all the textbooks when they're not being used,"
Mike said. "It's supposed to be locked up, but we haven't
tried the knob yet. We're waiting until it can be dusted for
prints."

"Get busy on that, and on the rest of the crime scene, as
soon as you can." Haney looked down at Shannon's corpse
and shook his head. "And find out who'd want this woman
dead badly enough to stick a knife in her. That's the big
question we have to answer, gentlemen."

Chapter 12

Phyllis sat with Becca in the cafeteria until the little girl's father appeared, his face pale and haggard. Even though Joel Dunston had been divorced from Shannon, seeing her dead body appeared to have aged him considerably.

"Becca," he said hoarsely, and she practically flew into his arms, throwing her arms around his neck and hugging him tightly as she sobbed. He patted her awkwardly on the back and muttered, "We'll get through this somehow. I promise you we will. At least . . . at least we still have each other."

While Joel was attempting to comfort his daughter, Marie Tyler came into the cafeteria through another door and hurried over to the table where Phyllis and the others sat. "I can't find Russ anywhere," she said, her voice tight with tension and worry. "Have any of you seen him?"

Carolyn said, "Not since before . . . Well, not lately."

"I don't understand it. Where could he have gone?" Marie took her children's hands and walked off through the cafeteria, looking despondent and more than a little lost.

A horrible thought flashed through Phyllis's mind. If Joel had caught Shannon and Russ together, he might have killed both of them.

But then Russ's body would have been found there, too, wouldn't it?

Unless Joel had killed Shannon and Russ had fled. Joel could have gone after him and killed him elsewhere. . . .

But in that case, then how had the knife gotten back to the cafeteria? It really didn't seem likely that Joel would have stabbed Shannon, chased down Russ, killed him, and then returned to the carnival to put the murder weapon back where he had gotten it. It could have happened that way, but Phyllis didn't believe it.

That still left Russ Tyler's whereabouts a mystery. Maybe he was hiding somewhere, afraid that Joel would get him, too.

Phyllis wasn't sure she could accept that scenario, either. The school was swarming with deputies now. If Russ had witnessed Shannon's murder, all he had to do was come forward and tell what he had seen.

Unless *he* was the one who had stuck that knife in Shannon's chest. Then, in a panic of fear and guilt, he wouldn't want to talk to the authorities.

Or maybe the killer wasn't either Joel *or* Russ. Marie could have found her husband with Shannon and lost her head, in which case Russ was hiding out because he didn't want to be forced to reveal that his wife had killed the woman he was having an affair with . . . if he was really having an affair with her, which Phyllis certainly didn't know for sure . . . and didn't the fact that the knife had been taken from the cafeteria mean that the murder hadn't really been a spur-of-the-moment thing but instead had been planned . . . ?

The theories and questions whirled around inside Phyllis's head until she was dizzy. She was glad when Sam said, "Let's all get out of here and go home." Phyllis nodded gratefully. She wanted to lie down for a while.

Carolyn looked at the remains of the auction and snack contest and said, "I guess we'd better pack up everything that's left and take it with us."

Mike came up behind her in time to hear her say that. He

shook his head and said, "I'm sorry, Mrs. Wilbarger, but you can't do that."

Carolyn turned around to face him. "Why not?"

Mike waved a hand at the tables. "All these cakes and such might be evidence. Maybe we can match the frosting that was found on Mrs. Dunston's blouse to one of them."

"So you're impounding all of them?" Phyllis asked.

"That's right." Mike shrugged. "Sorry."

Phyllis looked at the jack-o'-lantern cake and shook her head. "I don't suppose it really matters. I don't think any of us are in the mood for snacks or sweets right now, anyway."

Sam asked Mike, "You boys come up with anything yet on the killin'?"

"I can't really talk about that." He looked around at the four of them. "You weren't fixing to leave, were you?"

Sam nodded. "We thought we would. These ladies have had a hard day."

Mike shook his head and said, "I'm sorry, but you can't go. Not until you've been interviewed."

"Interrogated, you mean?" Carolyn asked with a touch of resentment in her voice. She hadn't forgotten about how both she and her daughter Sandra had been considered suspects in another murder before being cleared, largely through Phyllis's efforts.

"Just some routine questions," Mike said. He took a notebook and pen out of the pocket of his uniform shirt. "I can go ahead and get that out of the way, so you folks won't be stuck here."

Phyllis sighed and sat down at one of the tables. "All right," she said. "Whatever it takes to get us out of here."

The other retired teachers sat down, too, and Mike perched a hip on the table as he asked, "Did all of you know the murdered woman?"

"Carolyn and I did," Phyllis said. "I'm not sure if Sam and Eve ever met her."

"I didn't," Sam said.

Eve said, "I'm not sure if we were ever introduced, but I *know* I saw her somewhere before."

"She was the president of the PTO, right?"

Phyllis nodded and quickly sketched in the details of how she and Carolyn had gotten involved in putting on this school carnival. Mike wrote quickly as she gave him the names of the PTO board members.

"There's a chance this Mrs. Gonzales was the one who discovered the body," he commented, "but it appears she left the school before we got here."

"I saw her down there at the end of the hall," Phyllis confirmed. "She looked awfully upset, as she had every right to be. Shannon lying there like that was a terrible sight."

"Yep, I imagine so. How familiar are you with the school? How long could the body have been there before somebody found it?"

The four of them looked at each other. Still taking the lead, since Mike was her son, Phyllis said, "None of us ever taught here. Carolyn and I attended a few meetings to discuss preparations for the carnival, but those were the only times I ever set foot in the place until today."

Sam said, "I was out here a few times, too, helpin' the custodians build those booths out on the playground. Never poked around the school much, though. But I don't reckon there would have been much reason for anybody to go all the way down to the end of that hall this afternoon. Nothin' to do with the carnival was down there."

"So Mrs. Dunston's body could have been lying there for fifteen minutes or even half an hour without anybody coming along to find it?"

Phyllis said, "That seems reasonable to me."

Mike looked up from his notebook and frowned. "What do you reckon she was doing down there in the first place, if there was nothing connected with the carnival going on in that part of the school?"

Because it was an out-of-the-way corner where she could

get together with Russ Tyler. Phyllis couldn't stop that thought from going through her head. But she didn't say anything. She had nothing to go on but a brief glimpse of Shannon and Russ going into a restaurant in Fort Worth. She wasn't sure she wanted to build a damning theory on such fragile evidence, especially when it might put several people at risk of being considered murder suspects.

On the other hand, she didn't want Shannon's killer to get away with it. Despite her flaws, Shannon hadn't deserved to be wantonly murdered like that.

She needed to think about it some more, Phyllis decided. She knew that what she was doing could be considered with-holding evidence . . . but she just needed to think.

Nobody had an answer for Mike's question about Shan-non's reasons for being down at the end of the hall, so he moved on and asked one that made Phyllis even more un-comfortable. "Can any of you think of any reason why someone would want Mrs. Dunston dead?"

Carolyn said, "You mean besides the fact that she treated all the volunteers who worked with her like dirt?"

Mike's eyebrows rose. "Hard to get along with, was she?"

Phyllis sighed and nodded. "We didn't know her all that well, you understand, but it was obvious that she was a per-fectionist and browbeat everyone else on the board. She piled work on them and didn't like it when it wasn't done just to suit her."

"She didn't mind telling you when she wasn't pleased with something, either," Carolyn put in.

"So the rest of the board hated her?"

Phyllis said, "I'm not sure I'd go so far as to say that."

"Some of them did," Carolyn declared, outspoken as al-ways. "And the rest of them were afraid of her."

"I'm sure they'll all be interviewed," Mike said. "I under-stand she was divorced?"

"Twice," Phyllis said. "Most recently from Dr. Joel

Dunston." There was no point in keeping quiet about that. The Dunstons' divorce was a matter of public record, and the authorities would have no trouble finding out about it, no matter what Phyllis said.

"The ear, nose, and throat guy," Mike said. "I've heard of him."

Phyllis nodded. "Yes. He and Shannon had a daughter together. The girl's name is Becca. She goes to school here. I don't know what grade she's in. Third or fourth, I'd guess."

Mike wrote in his notebook again, then asked, "How did they get along?"

"Shannon and her daughter?"

"No, I meant the ex-husband. How did Mrs. Dunston get along with him?"

Phyllis hesitated, then said, "Not well. Joel Dunston brought Becca to the carnival today. They were late getting here, and Shannon wasn't happy about it. They had an argument here in the cafeteria, right after Dr. Dunston and Becca arrived."

"A violent argument?"

Phyllis shook her head. "No, not violent. Intense, I'd say. You could tell they were both angry, but they didn't raise their voices, and they tried to put on a good front while the little girl was around. Not that they fooled her. Children are usually sharp enough to see right through that."

"But maybe the argument continued and got violent later," Mike suggested. "Did any of you see Dr. Dunston later in the afternoon?"

Carolyn said, "He came back into the cafeteria not long before the cake auction got started."

"Which was . . . ?"

"About four thirty," Phyllis supplied.

"Was he still here when the auction started?"

She had to shake her head. "No, he left sometime before that. I didn't really notice when. We were busy."

"I didn't see him go, either," Carolyn said.

Phyllis could tell that Mike was excited. She supposed that in any murder, the spouse or ex-spouse was the most logical suspect. In this case, there were the added factors of the open hostility that existed between Shannon and Joel Dunston, and the proximity between the two of them this afternoon. When the classic questions of means, motive, and opportunity were asked, Joel was a possible answer for all of them.

"We'll definitely want to talk to him," Mike said. "He's still around, isn't he?"

"He was here with his daughter just a little while ago. I didn't see him leave; I'm sure he's still somewhere on school property, unless one of the other deputies talked to him and let him go."

Mike shook his head. "Not likely." He looked at some of the notes he had written farther up the page and went on. "You said Mrs. Dunston was divorced twice. Do you know anything about her first husband?"

"Just that she had a son with him," Phyllis said. "And that they were childhood sweethearts and got married right out of high school."

"You wouldn't happen to have a name for that first husband, would you?"

Phyllis shook her head. "No. But her son's name is Kirk. I suppose he has his father's last name, but I have no idea what it is."

Carolyn frowned at her in puzzlement and asked, "How do you know all this?"

"Well, I told you I ran into Shannon in Wal-Mart that day—you know, when she talked me into entering the healthy snack contest."

"I know," Carolyn said.

"Her son was with her that day, and when Shannon and I were talking, she mentioned those things about her first marriage."

"Does this kid still live with her?" Mike asked. "How old is he?"

"I don't know where he lives. But she said he was born when she was eightteen."

"That would make him twenty-one or twenty-two, depending on when his birthday is, so he's not really a kid. If he's that old, he's a grown man."

"She didn't treat him like one," Phyllis said. "It seemed like she was as rough on him as she was on everyone else."

That caught Mike's interest, too. "Really? I don't suppose he was here this afternoon, was he?"

"I didn't see him. Of course, there were a lot of people around, and he might not have come inside the cafeteria. Even if he did, I might not have noticed him . . . although he'd be a little hard to miss."

"Why's that?"

"Oh, he's one of these young men . . . you know . . . with all sorts of tattoos and . . . piercings . . . and he has his head shaved—"

"That's him!" Eve said.

The others all turned their heads to look at her. "What do you mean, 'That's him,' Mrs. Turner?"

"That's the young man I saw arguing with Mrs. Dunston earlier this afternoon," Eve said. "I knew when I saw the body that she looked familiar. They were outside on the playground, near the ticket booth, and they were so angry with each other, I swear I thought he was going to hit her!"

Chapter 13

With sudden interest, Mike straightened from his casual pose and took a quick step toward Eve. "You're sure about that?" he asked her.

Eve nodded emphatically. "I was afraid for a minute that I might have to find someone to separate them if they started fighting. Of course, it didn't work out that way. They just argued for a while and then left."

"Which way did they go?" Mike asked.

"On into the school. But I don't have any idea where they went after they were inside." Eve looked at Phyllis. "You say that boy was her son?"

Phyllis nodded. "It must have been him. I can't see Shannon associating with anyone else who looks like that."

"And you think that he . . . that they kept on arguing when they came inside . . . and then he . . ." Eve looked horrified. "That's almost too horrible to even think about!"

"Nobody's accusing anybody of anything just yet," Mike pointed out. "If this kid—Kirk, you said his name is, Mom?"

Phyllis nodded.

Mike went on, "If this kid was responsible for what happened, he had to get his hands on that knife somehow. None of you saw him in here in the cafeteria during the afternoon?"

Phyllis looked at Carolyn, and they both shook their heads. "We were really busy a lot of the time, though,"

Carolyn said. "I like to think that I'm pretty observant, but I suppose it's possible that he could have come through here without me noticing him."

"That's true for me as well," Phyllis admitted. "I think I would have seen him if he was here, but I can't be sure."

"For that matter, we haven't positively established that the knife you were using is the murder weapon," Mike said. "I guess that's the next step, other than interviewing everybody to find out if anyone saw anything that might help us."

Sam said, "You're liable not to get much out of questionin' folks. Big crowds don't make for good witnesses, from what I've seen in the movies and on TV."

Mike sighed. "Unfortunately, that's one of the things that they get right. Eyewitness accounts are usually pretty unreliable. You never can tell, though. We just have to take the investigation one step at a time." He closed his notebook. "I'll let the sheriff know about this son of Mrs. Dunston's. There's the first husband to look into as well. Maybe he's been nursing a grudge against her ever since their divorce, and he could have been here this afternoon, too."

Sam said, "There's no shortage of suspects, I'll grant you that."

"Does this mean we can leave now, since you've questioned us?" Phyllis asked.

Mike nodded. "I don't see why not. It's not like I don't know where to find you if any more questions come up."

Carolyn gestured toward the tables and said, "But you still want us to leave everything here like it is?"

"Yeah, I think so. I'll suggest to the sheriff that he send somebody down here to keep an eye on it until the crime scene unit can get to it. He's liable to give the job to me." Mike didn't sound too happy about the prospect of being stuck guarding potential evidence, rather than being an active part of the investigation.

They left the cafeteria, Mike walking out with his mother and the other retired teachers so he could let the deputies guarding the exits know that it was all right for them to leave. When he had gotten them through the doors, he turned, waved, and went back into the school.

Before they reached their cars, one of the people still in the parking lot came hurrying over. He was a balding, sandy-haired, mild-looking man about forty years old, wearing jeans and a khaki work shirt.

"Sam," he greeted the former basketball coach, "do you know what's going on in there? I've heard all sorts of crazy talk about somebody being killed."

"I'm sorry to say it isn't crazy talk," Sam responded. "A woman was murdered a while ago."

"Murdered! Good Lord. Do you know who she was?"

"Name was Shannon Dunston."

The man's eyes widened even further in shock. "Mrs. Dunston? The PTO president?"

Sam nodded. "One and the same."

The man shook his head. "That's terrible, just terrible. Do the deputies know yet who did it?"

"Nope. I reckon you knew Mrs. Dunston pretty well, since she was around the school all the time, from what I've heard about her."

"Of course I knew her. Maybe not all that well, but she was always asking the custodial staff to do things."

Sam looked at Phyllis, Carolyn, and Eve. "You ladies don't know Gary, I imagine," he said. "He's one of the custodians here at the school—the one I mentioned who used to work up at Poolville."

The man nodded to the three of them and supplied his name. "I'm Gary Oakley. Pleased to meet you, ladies, although I wish it was under better circumstances."

"So do we, Mr. Oakley," Phyllis said. "I'm Phyllis Newsom, and this is Carolyn Wilbarger and Eve Turner."

"Y'all are retired teachers, like Sam?"

"That's right."

Gary Oakley summoned up a smile. "I saw you in the

cafeteria selling cakes and such. I thought about coming over to see what you had, but I didn't get around to it. Too late now, I suppose."

"Yeah, all the leftover goodies were impounded by the law as evidence," Sam said.

Gary looked surprised again. "Evidence in the murder?"

"The investigators never know what's going to be important," Phyllis said.

"No, I guess not. Still, I don't see what a cake could have to do with a murder." The custodian sighed. "When I heard that somebody had died in the school, I sure figured it must have been an accident or a heart attack or something like that. Never even crossed my mind that it might've been murder. Where was she found?"

"All the way down at the far end of the main hall," Sam said, "by the book room."

Gary nodded. "In that little alcove where the cross-hall dead-ends? That's a pretty out-of-the-way spot, all right. And the deputies don't have any idea who did it?"

"Not so far."

"Terrible, just terrible," Gary said again. "Do you know when they're gonna let people leave?"

"The sheriff said everybody had to be questioned before they could go. The ladies and I have already talked to one of the deputies, so we're leaving now."

"You're some of the lucky ones, then." Gary looked around the crowded parking lot. "Who knows when they'll get around to the rest of us? Say, you don't think I could maybe catch a ride out with you, do you? Since you're free to go, they might think I was, too."

Before Sam could reply, Phyllis said, "None of us could do that, Mr. Oakley. My son is a deputy, and I'm sure the sheriff would be upset if he knew that possible witnesses were trying to leave without being interviewed first."

"Oh, I wouldn't want to cause any trouble for anybody," Gary said quickly. "I just need to, uh, get home to feed my dogs. They don't like it when their supper's late." He shrugged. "But I don't guess they'll starve to death before I get there."

"I'm sure they'll be fine," Sam said. "See you later, Gary."

"Yeah, see you around, Coach."

They went on to their cars as Gary Oakley walked off toward the school. Phyllis frowned slightly as she watched him go. He had seemed awfully anxious to leave before the deputies got around to talking to him, and she wasn't sure she believed his story about wanting to get home and feed his dogs. That sounded like something he had come up with on the spur of the moment.

Which made her wonder about the real reason why Gary Oakley was nervous about talking to the deputies.

As Mike had suspected, Sheriff Haney thought it would be a good idea to have somebody watching over the remnants of the auction and the snack contest, but to Mike's relief the sheriff detailed one of the other deputies to do that. Haney said, "Come along with me. I want to talk to the principal."

They found Frances Hickson in the school office, talking on the phone. A deputy was with her. "I assure you your son is safe, Mrs. Kellaway," she was saying. "In fact, there are deputies all over the school. This is probably one of the safest places in Parker County right now. . . . No, ma'am, I promise you, I'm not trying to be funny. . . . I don't know, but the sheriff is right here. I'll ask him." She covered the receiver's mouthpiece. "Sheriff, some parents brought their children to the carnival and dropped them off, intending to pick them up later. When can they get their kids?"

Haney thought about it for a second and then said, "Parents can pick up their kids anytime. We'll set up a place where we can ask the youngsters a question or two as they leave."

The principal nodded and relayed the information to the distraught parent on the phone, then hung up. She sighed and said, "That phone's been ringing constantly for half an hour now. It didn't take very long at all for word to get around town about the murder, and people are worried about their kids."

"Bad news travels fast," Haney said. "And a lot of folks got away from here before we arrived. Unfortunately, chances are the killer was one of them."

"You think so?"

"If you'd stuck a knife in a woman's chest, would you want to hang around?" Haney asked.

Mike thought that if the knife he had recovered in the cafeteria really was the murder weapon, the killer had hung around long enough—and had been coolheaded enough—to return it to where he had gotten it. Mike decided it was entirely possible that the killer was still somewhere on the school grounds, trying to keep a low profile. But of course it was just as likely, and probably more so, that the murderer had fled immediately.

The phone rang again, and again Principal Hickson had to go through the same routine, reassuring a worried parent and passing along the information that children left at the carnival could be picked up. Haney sent the deputy who had been guarding the school office to issue his orders and set up a station where children could be released to their parents. That left Haney and Mike alone in the office with the principal.

"Why would people leave their kids alone at a carnival, even a school carnival?" Haney commented when the principal was off the phone again.

"It's a well-supervised activity," Frances said. "And I like to think we have a safe campus—" Her expression changed abruptly as she realized what she had just said. "Oh, dear. Nobody's going to think it's safe anymore, are they?"

"Murder is always an aberration, ma'am," Mike said.

"It's not like Loving Elementary is a hotbed of crime or anything like that."

"No, but this isn't the first time we've been out here on an emergency call," Haney said. "There was that burglary a week or so ago. Whoever got in here made off with quite a bit of stuff."

Frances frowned. "But that couldn't have anything to do with what happened to Mrs. Dunston."

Before either of the lawmen could respond to that, the phone rang again. Haney motioned to one of the deputies just outside the office in the lobby and called him in. "Answer the phone," the sheriff instructed, "and if it's people wanting to pick up their kids, tell them to come on as soon as they can." To Principal Hickson he said, "Can we talk in your office?"

She stood. "Of course. Come on back."

She led the way into her private office, which had a window that looked out at the parking lot in front of the school. A couple of chairs were positioned in front of the desk. Haney and Mike sat down there while Principal Hickson sank wearily into the chair behind the desk.

"The day of the carnival is always a stressful one," she said, "but it's never been like this before, thank God."

Haney said, "I'll ask you the same question everybody else is being asked, Mrs. Hickson, so don't think I'm singling you out. Do you know of any reason why someone would want to kill Shannon Dunston?"

"Of course not. To be honest, she wasn't well liked by the staff or the faculty, or probably by the other parents, despite the fact that she worked hard to help the school. But just because someone gets on your nerves is no reason to kill them."

"Not usually," the sheriff said. "What was it about her that got her on everybody's bad side?"

"Well, it was more a matter of her attitude than anything else, I suppose. She could be very sharp with people. They disappointed her easily, and she wasn't shy about letting them know. And when she wanted something, she would harp on you about it until you gave in, just to get her off your back."

"Sounds like you're speaking from personal experience."

"We had our share of run-ins. When Shannon got an idea in her head—" Frances stopped short and leaned forward in her chair. "Wait a minute. Are you asking me if *I* killed her?" The principal's face flushed with anger.

"Not at all," Haney assured her. "But if she was irritating enough to get under the skin of somebody like you, who's used to dealing with unhappy people all the time, I can imagine she might have pushed somebody else right over the edge." He paused for a second to let Frances's resentment fade, then went on, "You were in the cafeteria when the body was discovered, right?"

"Yes, we were about to get the cake auction under way when everybody heard the screams. Does that count as an alibi?" Before the sheriff could answer, she went on, "I don't guess it does, does it? You need to know where I was before that."

Haney shrugged. "Just as a matter of routine."

Frances frowned in thought for a moment, then said, "I was outside part of the time, and I was in the gym part of the time. Some activities were set up in there, you know. I'm sure a lot of people saw me, but I couldn't tell you who. About four o'clock I was in here with Marie Tyler."

"Here in your office, you mean?"

"Well, in the outer office, to be exact. Marie had collected some more money from the ticket booth and the concession stand, and she wanted to lock it up in Katherine's desk."

"Katherine?"

"Katherine Felton, the school secretary. There's a big drawer in her desk. Marie put the PTO cash box in it and locked it up, so it would be safe. You can't be too careful when there are a lot of people milling around." Frances laughed. It had a hollow sound. "I guess that's been proven this afternoon, hasn't it?"

"Is the money still there?" Mike asked curiously.

"It should be."

"How much are we talking about?" Haney asked.

"Goodness, I don't know. Around ten thousand dollars, maybe more."

The sheriff rubbed his chin for a second and then said, "How about if we take a look, just to be sure."

"All right." Frances stood up and took a ring of keys from the pocket of her jeans. She and the two lawmen went back into the outer office, where a deputy was still answering the phone and assuring worried parents that their children were all right.

The bottom drawer on the right-hand side of the desk was larger than the others. Frances leaned over to unlock it and pull it open. Then she stared down into the drawer and frowned as she said, "That's odd. Where . . . ?"

Haney and Mike moved quickly to her side. "What is it?" the sheriff asked.

Mike had a feeling he already knew the answer.

Frances Hickson lifted worried eyes to meet their intent gazes. "It's gone," she said, gesturing toward the drawer that held only some manila files and a box of CD-Rs. "The PTO cash box is gone."

Chapter 14

Phyllis, Carolyn, and Sam all got back to the house within a minute of each other. Eve had ridden in Sam's pickup. Normally the thought that Eve was alone with Sam like that might have bothered Phyllis a little, whether she wanted it to or not, but today Phyllis's mind was too full of other things to worry about something like Eve's tendency to flirt. Anyway, Sam was a grown man. He could fend her off, or choose not to, depending on what he wanted to do.

Phyllis drove into the double garage first, followed a moment later by Carolyn, and Sam pulled his pickup to a stop at the curb in front of the house. Not much was said as they all went inside. They were still too shocked by what had happened at the school.

Although maybe they shouldn't have been shocked, Phyllis thought. Sudden, unexpected death was an all-too-common thing in life. The events not only of today but also those in recent months had proven that. Phyllis had never really believed that people should live each day as if it were their last . . . but it didn't hurt anything to keep the possibility in mind.

She didn't feel like preparing a big meal for supper, so she made sandwiches instead, and everyone took their plates and glasses of iced tea out onto the porch to eat as the light of day faded. Carolyn and Eve took the swing, while Phyllis and Sam sat in two of the three metal chairs that had been on the porch for decades. Sam had repainted them during the summer, and they looked practically as good as new.

"We might as well talk about it," Carolyn said after they had eaten in relative silence for a few minutes. "We're all thinking about it, anyway. Who do you think killed Shannon?"

"Don't reckon I'd have any idea," Sam said. "I didn't know the lady."

"Neither did I," Eve said, "but from what little I saw of her today, I sort of feel sorry for her. She didn't look happy when she was arguing with her son."

Phyllis said, "She wasn't happy. No one who's that angry all the time could be." She hesitated, pondering whether she ought to say anything about seeing Shannon and Russ Tyler in Fort Worth. Finally she decided that she shouldn't. It was bad enough that she hadn't told Mike about what she had seen. She didn't want to put her friends in a position where they might have to withhold evidence, too.

She needed to talk to Russ, she thought, and find out exactly what was going on between him and Shannon. If it was really more innocent than it appeared, then there would be no reason the authorities had to know about it.

But if their relationship *hadn't* been innocent . . . if Russ had somehow been involved in Shannon's death . . . then to approach him might put her in danger, Phyllis realized. She would have to be careful—very careful—and doing so might involve letting one other person in on what she knew.

Her gaze turned toward Sam. He had helped her look into those other murders. She trusted him, and knew she could count on him. Talking to him about this would have to wait until they were alone, though.

As those thoughts were going through Phyllis's head, Carolyn was saying, "It wouldn't surprise me if it turned out to be one of those PTO ladies who killed her, the way she treated all of them."

Phyllis forced her mind back to the conversation and said, "None of them really struck me as murderers."

"You never can tell about people," Carolyn insisted. "You don't know what's going on inside their heads. That's why when someone finally snaps and commits some act of violence, everyone around them is usually surprised. I think anyone is capable of almost anything if they're pushed far enough. At least that way when something bad happens, *I'm* not surprised. Take Lindsey Gonzales. Shannon was terrible to her. I'm sure there have been plenty of times when Lindsey would have liked to pick up a knife and stab her."

That same thought had occurred to Phyllis, and the fact that Lindsey had been right there when Shannon's body was discovered had to be considered, too. But Lindsey didn't really seem coolheaded enough to have carried the murder weapon away with her and then surreptitiously returned it to the cafeteria. Not to mention that she would have had to be planning Shannon's murder ahead of time in order to have taken the knife in the first place. Phyllis might have believed that Lindsey could lash out at someone in the heat of the moment, but was she capable of carrying out a cold-blooded, calculated murder? Phyllis really didn't think so.

"And what about Irene Vernon?" Carolyn went on.

"I don't think I've ever heard her say more than a dozen words," Phyllis said.

"Exactly. You know what they say about the quiet ones."

Phyllis's first instinct was to think that was ridiculous, but she realized she couldn't rule anything out. Truly, she didn't know any of the PTO board members well enough to say that they could or couldn't commit murder.

A few minutes later a sheriff's department cruiser pulled up at the curb behind Sam's pickup. Mike got out, came around the front of the car, and up the walk to the porch. He took off his Stetson, nodded politely, and said, "I thought I'd come by and let you know what's going on with the investigation."

"Are you allowed to do that?" Phyllis asked. "I wouldn't want you to get in trouble with Sheriff Haney."

"Well, he did make a point of telling me that we wouldn't need your help with this one, Mom," Mike said with a smile, "but I don't figure he'd mind me talking about it. Anyway, I have some more questions, so I guess you could consider this a follow-up interview."

"Well, then, sit down and go ahead."

Mike took a seat on the empty metal chair. He said, "First of all, we're pretty sure now that the knife from the cafeteria is the murder weapon. Our lab found traces of blood on it, and the frosting on Mrs. Dunston's blouse seems to match the frosting from that carrot cake."

"It was definitely frosting that was found on her blouse, then?"

Mike nodded. "Yep."

Sam asked, "What about DNA from the blood?"

"We sent samples over to the medical examiner's office in Fort Worth. They'll have to run the DNA test; we don't have the facilities for that. And it'll be a couple of weeks, maybe longer, before we get any results. But that brings me to one of the questions I need to ask you. Did anybody happen to cut their finger or anything like that this afternoon?"

"While we were using that knife, you mean?" Phyllis shook her head. "I didn't."

"Neither did I," Carolyn said. "And neither did anyone else. I'm sure we would have known about it if one of the children had picked it up and nicked themselves. For one thing, the parents would have been screaming about filing a lawsuit."

"More than likely," Mike said with a nod.

"But you have to remember, that knife was used in the school cafeteria," Phyllis reminded him. "One of the ladies who works there could have cut herself yesterday or something like that. That could explain how the blood got on it."

"Was the knife clean when you got it out of the kitchen today?"

Phyllis looked at Carolyn, who said, "I'm the one who took it out of a drawer in there, and yes, it appeared to be clean. A utensil like that should have been washed yesterday afternoon after lunch was finished for the day. I would think that the dishwasher in the kitchen would have sterilized it and gotten any blood off of it. Health department rules cover school kitchens, too, just like restaurants."

Mike nodded. "That's what I thought. We'll question the ladies who work in the cafeteria, just to be sure, but I'm confident that the blood got on the knife today, and the only reasonable place it could have come from was Mrs. Dunston."

"Whoever killed her must have wiped the blade clean," Phyllis speculated. "I certainly never *saw* any blood on it."

"Yes, there were only traces on the blade, down by the handle. Chances are you wouldn't have noticed them. It took our lab guys to find them."

"So the killer had to have been in the cafeteria before the murder to get the knife," Sam mused, "as well as later to put it back."

"That's the way it looks," Mike agreed. "Unfortunately, we're estimating now that close to a thousand people were at the carnival at one time or another today. It's going to be almost impossible to track down all of them. Principal Hickson says she can't even turn over the master list of students who attend the school without us getting a court order first. She doesn't want to violate any privacy laws."

"You can get a court order, though, can't you?" Phyllis asked.

"We should be able to. But even when we've got the list and can question all the parents, if some of them deny being there we might not be able to prove otherwise."

Phyllis leaned forward in her chair. "This wasn't a random killing," she said. "Whoever murdered Shannon had what they thought was a good reason for doing it. They must have planned it out at least a little ahead of time, and they ran the risk of taking that knife from the cafeteria and then putting it back later. After Shannon was dead, the killer had to wipe the knife clean and then conceal it somehow while he took it back to the cafeteria. He couldn't have walked around the school holding a knife in his hand. Someone would have noticed."

"You said *he*," Mike pointed out. "Any particular reason for that, Mom?"

Phyllis shook her head. "No, I was just thinking out loud and speaking in general. A wound like that could have been inflicted by either a man or a woman, couldn't it?"

Mike nodded. "That was the ME's preliminary opinion. Not only that, but the blade went just about straight in and out in a level blow. The angle of the wound doesn't tell us much about the killer's height or whether the person was left-handed or right-handed."

Eve shuddered and said, "I hope the poor woman didn't suffer too much."

Before today, Phyllis probably wouldn't have thought of Shannon as "the poor woman," despite the flashes of sympathy she'd felt for her. It was a different story now. No one deserved what Shannon had gotten.

"The ME thought it probably took her a minute or so to die," Mike said. "I guess she didn't suffer for long . . . but she *did* suffer before it was over, I'll bet."

A somber silence descended over the group on the porch. Phyllis hadn't quite finished her sandwich, but she didn't have any appetite now. She set the plate aside and drank some of her iced tea.

After a couple of minutes, Mike said, "Here's something you don't know about yet. The cash collected by the PTO this afternoon is missing."

"What!" Phyllis exclaimed. "Someone stole it?"

"It sure looks that way," Mike said with a nod. "The sheriff and I were talking to Mrs. Hickson, the principal, and she

mentioned that the cash box was locked up in the school secretary's desk. We took a look, just to make sure it was still
there, not really expecting that it would be gone. But sure
enough, it was. There were several thousand dollars in it."

"Did you check with Marie Tyler?" Carolyn asked.
"She's the fund-raising chairman for the PTO board, so she
could have taken it to deposit it in the bank."

"Mrs. Hickson suggested the same thing, so she and
Sheriff Haney and I went looking for her. When we found
her, she was just as shocked as we were that the money had
disappeared. Maybe more so. She seemed to take it personal. Broke down and cried, right there in the school, because all the work everybody had done was for nothing."

"You believed her?" Sam asked.

Mike nodded. "I did. Of course, I guess she could have
been lying, but when you work in law enforcement for a
while you get sort of an instinct for that."

Carolyn said, "Like being a teacher. After you've been in
a classroom, you *know* when your students are lying to you."

Phyllis agreed, and she trusted Mike's instincts. Her own
feelings told her that she would sooner suspect Marie of
Shannon's murder than she would of stealing that money.
Marie might kill for love, but not profit.

"Was Marie's husband with her?" she asked.

"Tall guy, dark hair? Yeah, he was with her. I figured he
must be her husband, the way he was trying to comfort her
when she got upset."

So Marie had found Russ, Phyllis thought. He had still
been in the school somewhere when Marie was looking for
him.

"Do you think there's any connection between the missing money and Mrs. Dunston's murder?" Sam asked.

Mike shook his head, sighed, and shrugged. "We just
don't know. There could be. Maybe she happened to go into
the school office just as somebody was taking the cash box,
and the thief forced her down the hall and killed her to keep

her from implicating him. People have been murdered before for a lot less."

Phyllis remembered something she had heard that afternoon and leaned forward in her chair. "Mike, Becca Dunston, Shannon's daughter, told me that the last time she saw her mother, Shannon said she was going to check on some money."

Mike looked intrigued and excited by that news. "That would possibly put Mrs. Dunston at the scene of the theft and tie her murder in with it. That's good information to have, Mom."

"But what about the knife?" Phyllis asked as she thought more about what might have happened. "If the person who stole the money is also the killer, why would he have taken the knife from the cafeteria earlier?"

"Yeah, that's the problem," Mike said. "We have to figure that when he took the knife, he intended to use it to kill Mrs. Dunston. That would make the theft and the murder two separate crimes and probably two separate criminals."

"But you can't assume that," Sam pointed out.

"No, we sure can't. At this point we can't assume anything for certain."

Sam shook his head. "I'm mighty glad it's up to you folks to figure out this mess and not me. I'd never make a hand as a detective."

"*Mess* is the right word. Not only do we have the murder and the missing cash to contend with, we haven't made any progress on finding out who burglarized the school a week or so ago. We don't know whether what happened today is connected to that or not. The sheriff seemed to think it might be, though, because the drawer in the secretary's desk where the cash box was kept hadn't been broken into. Somebody had to have unlocked it, just like somebody got into the school earlier without actually breaking in."

"Maybe somebody picked the lock on the desk," Sam suggested. "It can't have been a very complicated one."

"No, but it was locked when Mrs. Hickson went to open it and check on the cash box. That suggests a key was used to open it and then relock it."

"Boy, this stuff just goes 'round and 'round, doesn't it?"

Mike nodded glumly. Phyllis didn't like to see him looking so defeated. The case seemed overwhelming now, but she was sure that as the law continued to sift through all the possibilities and talk to all the people who might have been involved, sooner or later answers to all the questions would emerge.

And once again she felt a pang of guilt about not telling him what she knew about Shannon Dunston and Russ Tyler. But she didn't actually *know* anything, she reminded herself. She liked Marie Tyler, despite the young woman's tendency toward rather colorful language, and she didn't want to ruin Marie's marriage if there was no real reason to do so. That's what would happen if she told Mike that Shannon might have been having an affair with Russ. Even if Russ was cleared of the murder, the damage to his marriage would already be done.

So, even though she was uncomfortable about doing so, she would keep quiet about what she knew for now, until she had a chance to find out exactly what had been going on. Then if she could help Mike, she would.

If that made her a meddling old woman, then so be it.

Sometimes in life it took a little meddling to set things right.

Chapter 15

Mike was off duty on Sunday, the day after the carnival, so he tried to concentrate on his time with Sarah and Bobby and enjoy the chance to be with his family. He had learned early on that when you worked in law enforcement, you had to be able to leave the job behind as much as possible when you weren't on duty. Otherwise it would consume you.

But he couldn't avoid the stories about the murder in both the Weatherford and Fort Worth papers and on the newscasts from the Fort Worth/Dallas TV stations. When he noticed that there was no mention of the missing money in any of the news reports, he knew the sheriff was deliberately holding back that part of the story. That made sense. For one thing, they didn't know for sure that the murder and the theft were connected, and for another, it was always wise to keep something in reserve in case it was needed to trip up a suspect or weed out false confessions.

Monday morning when he reported for his shift, the dispatcher told him that the sheriff wanted to see him. Mike walked down the hall to Haney's office. The door was open, but he rapped lightly on it anyway.

"Come in, Mike," Haney said from behind his desk. His swivel chair was turned so that he was facing a computer and monitor set up on a portable computer table next to the desk. He gestured toward the screen and said, "Take a look at this."

Mike leaned over the desk, resting his hands on its top to balance himself as he studied the monitor. A pair of standard mug shots were displayed on the left-hand side of the screen, complete with the usual identifying numbers across the bottom of them. They showed a balding, sandy-haired man. Information about his arrest record was on the right-hand side of the screen.

"Gary Oakley," Mike read. "Why is that name familiar to me?"

"Because he works as a custodian at Loving Elementary," Haney said.

Mike's eyebrows rose. "What was he arrested for in the past?"

"Burglary," the sheriff said. "He served three years in the penitentiary at Huntsville."

Mike straightened and drew in a deep breath. "They hired a convicted felon to work around little kids?"

Haney leaned back in his chair and said, "That doesn't surprise me. There are stories on the news all the time about convicted sex offenders getting hired to work in schools. They lie about it on their employment applications, and the school district doesn't take the time and trouble to check them out thoroughly enough to catch the lie." The sheriff shrugged. "It's hard to blame the school districts too much. They get hit by funding and personnel cuts, just like we do, and things start to fall through the cracks."

Mike thought about the fact that Bobby would be starting school in a few years and said, "Yeah, but when you're talking about the safety of children, you've got to be more careful than that."

Haney leaned his head toward the computer. "What else do you think about this?"

"Oakley has to be the leading suspect in the earlier burglary of the school and the theft of that cash box. He'd have keys to get into the building and maybe even into the secretary's desk. That would explain why there were no signs of forced entry either time."

"What about the murder?"

"We don't know all those things are connected, do we?" Mike said. "But yeah, I guess if he's a suspect in the other cases, he's got to be a suspect in the murder, too." The wheels of Mike's brain turned over rapidly as he put together a theory. "Say Oakley was taking the cash box out of the drawer when Mrs. Dunston walked into the office. She told her daughter, the last time the little girl saw her, that she was going to check on some money."

"How do you know that?" Haney asked sharply.

"My mother talked to the little girl after Mrs. Dunston's body was found."

The sheriff grunted. "Your mother, eh?"

"It's not what you think, Sheriff," Mike said. "She was just talking to the little girl, trying to keep her calm. She wasn't actually questioning her or anything like that."

Although now that Mike thought about it, he recalled how his mother had started poking around during the investigation of those murders a few months back. . . . She had taken to detective work so well, in fact, that she had solved those crimes.

He put his mind back on the current case and said, "If Oakley took the cash box and was discovered by Mrs. Dunston, he could have forced her down the hall and killed her to keep her from telling anybody what she'd seen."

There was a problem with that, however. Mike remembered what his mother had pointed out as they all sat on the porch of her house on Saturday evening. If Oakley had killed Mrs. Dunston on the spur of the moment to cover up his other crimes, why had he taken the knife from the cafeteria earlier in the day?

Mike was about to say something about that when Sheriff Haney ordered, "Go out to the school and pick him up. I want him brought in for questioning. Better take some backup, too. If he's a killer, he might decide not to come along peacefully."

"Maybe it would be better to pick him up somewhere away from the school," Mike suggested, "or at least wait until after the kids have gone home for the day."

Haney thought about it for a moment, and then shook his head. "I know what you're talking about," he said. "You don't want to put those kids at risk, and neither do I. But if Oakley's our murderer, he's liable to get nervous and decide to run. I think it would be better to get him in custody as soon as possible."

Mike nodded. He knew he couldn't push his questioning of the sheriff's orders any further without running the risk of angering Haney, who was, after all, still his boss.

He thought Haney was wrong, though. If Gary Oakley was cool enough to wipe that knife almost clean and replace it in the cafeteria after using it to kill Shannon Dunston, it wasn't likely he would panic now without even knowing that he was under suspicion. Instead, Oakley would be more likely to proceed with his usual activities and try to appear as normal as possible.

But orders were orders, and Mike would just have to be very careful about carrying them out. He left the sheriff's office and found a couple of deputies, Fitzgerald and Harrison, to accompany him to Loving Elementary. On the way out of the building, he explained that they were going to be taking a suspect into custody and bringing him in for questioning.

Mike took his usual cruiser while the other two men followed in another car. A cold front had blown through the previous night, bringing in clouds and chillier temperatures.

Appropriate considering that today was Halloween, he thought.

Based on what they knew now, Mike had his doubts about Gary Oakley being the killer. It just didn't add up. The fact that the murder weapon came from the cafeteria threw everything out of whack. Oakley had been at the school during the carnival; there was no doubt about that. He had even been questioned briefly before being allowed to leave, like everyone else. And given his record, he certainly had to be considered the prime suspect in both the earlier burglary and the disappearance of the cash box. But that didn't make him a killer.

Of course, there might be facts they didn't know yet, Mike reminded himself. Oakley might break down and confess to everything as soon as they started interrogating him. That possibility was reason enough to bring him in and ask him a few questions.

Mike drove into the front parking lot of the school. Since it was midmorning, there were several empty spaces in the lot. He parked the cruiser in one of them. Fitzgerald and Harrison parked a few spaces away and got out of their car. The wind was blowing hard enough that all three deputies had to hold their hats on as they went into the school.

Gray-haired Katherine Felton, the secretary, looked at them in surprise as they entered the office. She said, "Oh, my goodness. There hasn't been more trouble that I don't know about yet, has there?"

Mike smiled reassuringly at her. "We just need to talk to Mrs. Hickson for a minute," he said. "Is she in?"

"Oh, yes." The secretary pushed a button on the intercom system and said, "Frances, there are deputy sheriffs out here to see you."

A response came immediately from the speaker. "Send them in."

Mrs. Felton turned in her chair to point as she said, "Right back there." Mike didn't bother telling her that he knew where the principal's office was. He had just been there a couple of days earlier.

Frances Hickson was standing behind her desk with a worried look on her face as the three deputies came into her office. "What is it?" she asked. "Has something else happened?"

Harrison and Fitzgerald hung back, letting Mike take the lead. "Do you know if Gary Oakley is here at the school this morning, ma'am?" he asked.

"Gary?" Frances's frown deepened. "I suppose he is. I haven't heard anything about him not showing up for work today. We have two shifts of custodians, you know. A couple of them don't get here until the middle of the afternoon, and then they clean during the evening, after everyone is gone. But Gary is part of the crew that comes in first thing in the morning with the rest of us."

Mike nodded. "Do you have any idea where we could find him right now?"

Frances glanced at the clock on her desk and said, "He's probably in the cafeteria helping to get set up for lunch. The kindergartners and first-graders will be eating soon."

That was all the more reason to grab Gary Oakley now, while they had the chance to do so without putting any kids at risk. Mike nodded and said, "Thank you, ma'am," as he started to turn away.

"Wait a minute," the principal said. "What's this all about? Why do you want to talk to Gary?"

Mike hesitated. He didn't want to tell Mrs. Hickson that Oakley was the leading suspect in three separate crimes at the moment, including murder. He said, "We just need to ask him a few more questions."

He wasn't sure if Frances believed him or not. The woman was smart enough to know it wouldn't take three burly young sheriff's deputies to ask a few simple questions.

"I'll come with you," she said as she started out from behind her desk.

"That really isn't necessary, ma'am," Mike said quickly.

"This is my school, Deputy," Frances said. "Everything that goes on here concerns me."

"I'm afraid I have to insist that you stay here, Mrs. Hickson."

Her eyes widened. "Oh, Lord. I don't believe it. You think Gary killed poor Shannon."

"We just need to ask him some more questions—" Mike began again.

Frances sank wearily into her chair and waved them out of the office. "Go on," she said. "I don't believe it, but do what you have to do."

Mike led Fitzgerald and Harrison out of the office and down the hall toward the cafeteria. The walls seemed strangely bare to Mike, and it took him a moment to realize why that was so. There were no Halloween decorations. When he had gone to elementary school, the walls would have been covered with cardboard jack-o'-lanterns, witches, skeletons, and mummies. Not in these days of political correctness run amok, though, when the absolute worst thing anybody could do was offend someone else's delicate sensibilities. Mike sighed as he reached the cafeteria, wondering if kids today even had any idea of what they were missing.

A pair of doors led into the big room, one of them down at the end of the hall, next to the door that opened out onto the playground. Mike motioned wordlessly for Fitzgerald to cover that one; then he and Harrison went into the cafeteria through the first door.

Gary Oakley and another custodian were carrying one of the tables into its proper position for lunch. The table was turned on its side, the bench seats that formed its legs still folded against the bottom of it. When the custodians had it in place they would unfold the benches and set the whole thing upright. About half the tables were already set up. The others were still folded and leaned against the wall.

Oakley's back was toward the doors as he and the other man carried the table. The other custodian saw the deputies entering the cafeteria and looked surprised, as anyone would have under the circumstances. Oakley must have noticed the man's expression, because he turned his head to look over his shoulder.

"Mr. Oakley," Mike said, "we need to talk to you for a minute."

He was watching Oakley's face closely and saw the sudden leap of fear in the man's eyes. Oakley's gaze darted from Mike and Harrison across the room to Fitzgerald and back.

Uh-oh, Mike thought.

Oakley dropped the table with a crash, spun around, and darted toward the front of the cafeteria. A stage was located there, so that the big room would be converted to an auditorium for PTO meetings, programs, assemblies, and the like. Mike recalled for a second that when he was a kid, it had been common for rooms like this to be referred to by the odd hybrid word "cafetorium."

He didn't know if there was any way out through the stage area. A backstage door might lead into another room, the music room, for example. He just didn't know.

So he broke into a run after Oakley and yelled, "Stop!"

Chapter 16

Oakley didn't even slow down as he slapped a hand on the stage and vaulted onto it. Steps at each side of the stage led up to it, but Mike didn't take the time to veer to either side. He leaped onto the stage right behind Oakley and tackled him just as the custodian started to push his way past the closed curtain. The thick, heavy curtain slowed Oakley down just enough for Mike to be able to catch him.

Both men struggled on the smooth wooden floor of the stage as the curtain swirled around them. Oakley desperately tried to writhe out of Mike's grip, but Mike managed to get a good hold on Oakley's right arm, and twisted it behind the man's back. Oakley yelped in pain. He flailed with his left arm and cracked his fist into Mike's jaw in a backhanded blow. Mike grunted and felt anger surging up inside him. He suppressed it with an effort. A lawman couldn't afford to lose his temper. He tightened his grip on Oakley's wrist and twisted harder. Oakley sobbed and went limp.

Harrison and Fitzgerald reached them just then. Harrison had his handcuffs out. He clicked one of them shut around the wrist that Mike held, then Fitzgerald jerked Oakley's other arm behind his back and Harrison cuffed that wrist, too. Mike let go of Oakley and rolled onto his back to catch his breath as the other two deputies took hold of the custodian and hauled him to his feet.

"You're under arrest," Fitzgerald said.

"I—I didn't do anything!" Oakley said between sobs.

"How about resisting arrest and assaulting an officer?"

"I didn't mean to! I just got scared! I didn't assault anybody!"

Mike climbed to his feet and rubbed his jaw where Oakley had clipped him. "Tell that to my jaw," he said. "If you didn't do anything, why'd you run?" Quickly, he held up a hand before Oakley could say anything. "Don't answer that."

He took a laminated card from his shirt pocket and read Oakley his rights, making sure the man nodded that he understood them before anything else was said. The custodian who had been working with Oakley had come to the front of the cafeteria to watch the ruckus, along with the ladies who worked in the school kitchen. There were plenty of witnesses to the fact that Oakley had been Mirandized properly.

"All right, let's go," Mike said as he tucked the card away. Sheriff Haney would want to handle the interrogation. Mike wanted to ask some questions, but he knew it would be better to wait.

They drew plenty of attention—more than Mike was comfortable with, actually—as they led the sobbing, handcuffed Oakley out of the school. Several teachers and kids saw them and stared in shock. Frances Hickson and Katherine Felton stood in the office doorway watching them, along with the school nurse.

"Gary, I'm sorry," the principal said as they went by, but Oakley didn't seem to hear her. He didn't look up as he stumbled along between Harrison and Fitzgerald. Each of the deputies held one of his arms.

Mike paused just outside the office. "I'm sorry about this, ma'am," he told Frances. "I hope we didn't disrupt things too much."

"Did you hurt him?" she asked accusingly.

Mike touched his sore jaw again and said, "He gave better than he got."

*   *   *

Phyllis read the newspapers and watched the TV news reports with great interest, but by Monday morning the sheriff's department hadn't made any arrests, or really even said much about the case . . . at least on the record. She thought about calling Mike and asking him if there were any new developments, but she didn't want to bother him, or have him think that she was trying to take advantage of the fact that he was a deputy. But she couldn't help being intensely curious. After all, the murder had taken place right there in the school, only a few hundred feet from where she had been at the time.

That thought made her a little nervous, even though obviously she didn't have anything to fear from the killer. Her only connection with Shannon Dunston had been the school carnival, and that was over and done with.

Unless . . . maybe Russ Tyler had seen *her* that day over in Fort Worth, just as she had seen him and Shannon. If he was the killer, he could be worried that Phyllis might link him romantically to Shannon, thereby revealing his motive.

That was reaching too far. "You're just a paranoid old woman," she told herself aloud as she stood in the kitchen, pouring herself a final cup of coffee after breakfast.

"Oh, I don't think you're paranoid, dear," Eve said from behind her. Phyllis jumped a little; she hadn't realized that Eve had come into the kitchen. The retired English teacher went on, "You've always seemed remarkably levelheaded to me."

Phyllis set the empty carafe back on the coffeemaker and turned around. "Thanks . . . I think," she said.

"What makes you think you might be paranoid?"

Phyllis couldn't explain without revealing her suspicions about Russ Tyler, and she couldn't justify those suspicions without telling Eve what she had seen in Fort Worth. So she said, "Oh, nothing. I'm just worried about that murder."

"Yes, I understand. It was a terrible thing. And to think that it happened practically right under our noses!"

"That's exactly what I mean. It makes you realize how fragile life really is."

"And when you get to be our age, I think you appreciate it more," Eve said.

Phyllis nodded. "That's right. I know I don't have that much time left, relatively speaking, but I want to enjoy every bit of it that's still coming to me."

Shannon Dunston hadn't had that chance. True, she had seemed to be an unhappy woman, but surely she'd still had good moments, too. And things might have turned around in her life so that she was even happier; you never could tell about that. The only real constant in life, thought Phyllis, was that nothing ever stayed the same for very long.

And the idea that Shannon would never even have the opportunity for things to get better angered Phyllis. It wasn't right. No one deserved to have their future ripped away like that.

Maybe she *could* help the sheriff's department find out who had killed Shannon. Maybe it was her duty as a human being.

It was time to find out the truth about Russ Tyler.

That could be a tricky matter, though. She sat down at the table to sip her coffee and think about how to proceed.

"What are you going to do today, dear?" Eve asked as she sat down, too.

Figure out how to investigate a murder, Phyllis thought. But she couldn't say that, so she said, "Oh, I don't know. I thought about making a casserole or something and taking it over to Shannon's house. I don't know if her ex-husband has moved back in to take care of the little girl, or if Shannon's son still lives there, or what, but whoever's there, they'll need food."

Carolyn came into the kitchen in time to hear what Phyllis was saying, and she joined in, "That's an excellent idea.

I'll make something, too, and we can take it over there to-gether."

"I can get a sympathy card," Eve said, "and we can all sign it."

Phyllis nodded. "That's what we'll do. Do you know where Shannon lived, Carolyn?"

"No, but I'm sure we can find out from Marie."

Phyllis liked that idea, too. She needed an excuse to talk to Marie, to try to find out more about Russ and the state of their marriage. It would have to be done carefully, though.

Carolyn began working on a green bean casserole. Phyllis knew that was one of the dishes people always brought to bereaved households, but to be honest, she didn't like green bean casseroles. If that was what Carolyn wanted to do, though, it was none of her business. Phyllis decided to cook some sweet potatoes instead, with plenty of marshmallows and brown sugar. That was another widely accepted "grief food," if you wanted to call it that.

When everything was in the oven, Carolyn called Marie to find out where Shannon had lived. While the phone was still ringing, Phyllis said, "Why don't you ask her if she'd like to go over there with us? That might be better, since you and I really didn't know Shannon all that well."

Carolyn nodded her agreement, and a moment later Marie answered. Phyllis could tell from Carolyn's end of the conversation that the younger woman was proving agreeable to the suggestion. Carolyn said, "We'll be by to pick you up about eleven o'clock, then." She said good-bye and hung up.

"Poor Marie," Carolyn went on as she turned to Phyllis. "I could tell she's very shaken up about everything that's happened. I think she really did like Shannon, despite all the friction between them."

Or it could be, thought Phyllis, that Marie was shaken up because she had discovered her husband's affair with Shan-non and killed the other woman. Or that she had discovered Russ was the murderer.

Phyllis warned herself not to jump to conclusions. She had to keep an open mind. She didn't *know* anything yet.

When the food was ready, they covered the dishes with aluminum foil. Eve had run downtown to a card shop to get a sympathy card, rather than going all the way out to Wal-Mart. The three women signed it; then Eve said, "I'll go up and see if Sam would like to sign it. After all, he was at the carnival, too."

And Eve would seize any excuse to be around Sam, Phyllis thought. Still, she had to admit that Eve was right; Sam would probably want to sign the card.

He did so, coming back downstairs with Eve to say, "This is a nice thing you ladies are doin'. I've always admired the way folks rally around a family that's goin' through a time of trouble. Makes me feel like there's a little hope for the human race after all."

"Would you like to come with us?" Phyllis asked.

"No, I reckon I better not. I don't want to be sexist about it, but comfortin' grievin' folks just seems to me like something that ladies are better at. When it comes to death, women bring food and men carry the coffin."

Carolyn said, "That *is* sexist . . . but I think you're right. Too many people have forgotten that there are differences between men and women, and that's the way the Good Lord intended it."

"*I've* never forgotten that," Eve put in, smiling at Sam.

Somehow, that made Phyllis feel better in a way. Eve was nothing if not consistent.

Phyllis and Carolyn left a few minutes later in Phyllis's Lincoln. Carolyn gave her directions. Marie and Shannon had lived in the same neighborhood, an upscale residential area on the south side of town, across the interstate. Traffic was bad part of the way—the huge boom in new business construction along the highway made the traffic almost as thick as in Fort Worth, Phyllis thought—but soon enough they found themselves following a winding street lined with large, expensive brick homes. It was a very nice neighbor-hood, but Phyllis preferred the older, more sedate part of town where she lived, with its massive trees shading the houses and the yards, and its air of history and gentility.

The curb had house numbers painted on it. "This is it," Carolyn said when they reached Marie's address.

Phyllis parked at the curb. Marie must have been watching for them, because she came out the front door of her house before either of the older women could get out of the car. She was dressed in a brown skirt and jacket and looked nice. The cold wind plucked at her skirt as she came down the walk carrying a casserole dish of her own.

She got into the backseat and said, "Hello. This is very thoughtful of you ladies. I wanted to take something over to Shannon's, but I wasn't sure if I ought to or not."

"I just hope somebody's home," Carolyn said, as Phyllis pulled away from the curb.

"There should be. Surely Becca isn't going back to school yet. I know Joel planned to move back into the house for a while. He has his own apartment now, of course, but he wanted Becca to be in the most familiar surroundings for her."

"That's wise," Phyllis said. "Dealing with her mother's death will be hard enough for her without being uprooted from her home at the same time."

"And I guess Kirk is still around, too," Marie added. "He doesn't have anywhere else to go, as far as I know."

"You'll have to tell me how to get there," Phyllis said as she drove between houses where many of the yards had Halloween decorations up. Most people didn't decorate as elaborately for Halloween as they did for Christmas, of course, but she still saw a lot of jack-o'-lanterns. They reminded her sadly of her jack-o'-lantern cake, which as far as she knew was still somewhere in the sheriff department's crime lab.

"Oh, sure," Marie said. "Turn left up here at the next corner. It's not far."

After a moment, Phyllis asked, "How do you know that Shannon's ex-husband was moving back home?"

"That's what Joel told Russ he was going to do. They're still friends."

That was news to Phyllis. She hadn't known that Joel Dunston and Russ Tyler were friends. That made Russ's behavior even more despicable if he had been carrying on an affair with Shannon.

Marie went on, "That's one thing that bothered Shannon. I think she assumed that when she and Joel split up, the people who knew them would take her side and stay friends with her. Instead, even though we all tried to act as neutral as possible around her, I'm pretty sure she knew we all felt a little sorry for Joel. That drove her crazy."

Marie fell silent, and when Phyllis glanced in the rearview mirror she saw that the young woman was biting at her lower lip.

"I shouldn't say things like that," Marie continued after a few seconds. "Nobody should speak ill of the dead."

"You're not speaking ill of Shannon," Carolyn said. "You're just stating facts. Nobody is really neutral when it comes to divorce. They all blame one party or the other."

"Yeah, I suppose you're right." Marie looked out the window. "It's just a shitty situation all around."

Phyllis tried not to sigh at Marie's language. She had more important things to think about.

"You said that Joel Dunston and your husband are friends," she said, trying to sound like she was making idle conversation. "Your husband's not a doctor, too, is he?"

"Russ? A doctor?" Marie laughed. "Lord, no. He gets so sick at the sight of blood that if one of our kids scrapes a knee, I have to put the Band-Aid on it. Russ is a lot more comfortable with things that aren't alive. He's an engineer at Lockheed. He can compute airplane structural stresses and things like that all day, because steel doesn't bleed and doesn't have any feelings."

Neither Phyllis nor Carolyn said anything, and after a second Marie went on, "Geez, I didn't mean to make him sound all cold and heartless. Believe you me, Russ is plenty alive, especially in the bedroom, if you know what I mean."

Phyllis knew what she meant, but she didn't particularly want to think about it. On the other hand, the fact that Russ Tyler evidently had a healthy appetite for the pleasures of the flesh might mean that he would more easily stray from his marriage vows. But then again, Phyllis had read that men who paid plenty of attention to the wife they had at home were less likely to be involved with some other woman.

Feeling uncomfortable with the whole subject, she asked, "Am I still going the right way?"

"Yeah, the house is right up here," Marie said. "There on the left, where that pickup is parked. You can pull in the driveway."

Phyllis did so, glancing as she did at the pickup parked at the curb. It was an old, rather beat-up vehicle, and she guessed that it belonged to Shannon's son, Kirk. It certainly didn't look like the sort of vehicle a doctor would drive.

As they got out of the Lincoln with their casserole dishes and closed the doors, the front door of the house opened and a couple of young men stepped outside. One of them was Kirk. The other, who had close-cropped fair hair and wore a leather jacket over a dark T-shirt, looked vaguely familiar to Phyllis, but she wasn't sure where she had seen him before. He said, "See you later, man," to Kirk, then gave the three women a smile and a friendly nod as he cut across the front yard toward the pickup. He was obviously one of Kirk's friends, Phyllis decided.

Kirk didn't look particularly happy to see them. "Hello," he said warily.

"Hi, Kirk," Marie said. Since she was a friend of the family, at least sort of, she knew him the best. "Is your stepdad here?"

Kirk leaned his shaven head toward the door. "Yeah, he's

inside with the kid." He turned briefly and called through the open door. "Hey, Joel! More people here with food!" Then he muttered, "I gotta go," and stalked toward the double garage.

Marie said after him, "We're sorry about your mother, Kirk."

Without turning around he said curtly, "Yeah, thanks." Then he disappeared inside the garage. That left Phyllis, Carolyn, and Marie standing somewhat awkwardly on the doorstep.

The awkward moment didn't last long, because Joel Dunston appeared in the doorway, summoned up a smile, and said, "Marie. It's good to see you. Why don't you and your friends come inside? The air's cool out here today."

Thinking about the way Kirk had reacted to Marie's expression of sympathy about his mother's death, Phyllis decided that the air wasn't the only thing cool. Kirk's attitude had been downright cold. Hadn't he felt anything for Shannon?

Or was his heart so hardened against her that he could bring himself to murder his own mother?

You're getting way ahead of yourself, Phyllis thought as she went into the house with Carolyn and Marie, all three of them bearing sympathy in casserole dishes.

Chapter 17

Sheriff Haney paused at the door of the interview room and crooked a finger at Mike. "Sit in on this with me, Deputy," he said.

Mike nodded, trying not to appear too eager. He followed the sheriff into the room where Gary Oakley, a dejected figure with his head hung low in despair, sat alone at a scarred wooden table. Oakley didn't even glance up as Haney and Mike sat down in empty chairs across the table from him.

"I'm Sheriff Haney, Mr. Oakley. We want to ask you a few questions."

"I didn't do anything," Oakley mumbled, speaking so quietly that Mike had to lean forward to make out what he was saying.

Haney pressed the RECORD button on a small tape recorder that sat on the table. He gave the date and time, and then said, "Interview with Mr. Gary Oakley. Present are Mr. Oakley, Sheriff Royce Haney, and Deputy Mike Newsom. Mr. Oakley has been apprised of his constitutional rights. Mr. Oakley, do you waive the right to legal counsel?"

"I don't need a lawyer. I didn't do anything."

"On the contrary, between the years 1992 and 1995, you committed at least three burglaries for which you were charged, tried, and convicted. You served time in the Dallas County jail and the Collin County jail for your first two convictions, and at your third trial, you were sentenced to a term of two to seven years in the state penitentiary. You served three years of that sentence and were released on parole in 1998. What have you been up to since then, Gary?"

Oakley finally looked up from the table. "You know what I've been doing," he said in a flat voice. "I worked as a school custodian in Poolville and then at Loving Elementary here in Weatherford."

"You lied on your job applications about being a convicted felon," Haney said. "That's a crime in itself."

"I knew I wouldn't get hired if I told the truth. But I thought it would be all right, because I never intended to break the law again. I still don't."

"You're admitting to lying on your job applications?"

"What's the point in lying about that now? You know who I was. You know what I did."

"What do you mean by saying we know who you were? Aren't you still the same guy?"

With a solemn expression on his face, Oakley shook his head. "No. I'm not the same guy. I've changed."

Haney gave a harsh laugh. "Yeah, every convict claims that he's a changed man . . . right up until the day he deals drugs or molests a kid or murders somebody again."

Oakley leaned back and drew in a sharp breath as if the sheriff had struck him across the face. "I never did any of those things," he said. "I broke into businesses and stole things when I was younger, but I never hurt anybody. I never would!"

"What about Shannon Dunston?"

"I never hurt Mrs. Dunston! I . . . I know somebody killed her, but it wasn't me. I swear it wasn't. I didn't have any reason to."

"What if she caught you stealing something?" Haney didn't mention the PTO cash box in particular. Mike knew the sheriff wanted to keep that card to play later. "Maybe she walked in on you and started to scream, or threatened to tell somebody what you were doing, so you had to kill her to shut her up." Haney dropped his voice a little, skillfully. "You probably didn't really mean to hurt her. Things just got out of hand. . . ."

"No." Oakley whispered the word. He looked across the table at them, and then said it again, stronger this time. "No. I didn't steal anything, and I didn't hurt anybody. The only times I've broken any law since I got out of prison were when I lied on my job applications. I don't even drive over the speed limit!"

"Gary, if you don't cooperate, things aren't going to go well for you—"

"You don't have any evidence," Oakley broke in. "You can't, because I didn't do it. If you've found the murder weapon, it won't have my fingerprints on it."

"How do you know that, Gary?" the sheriff volleyed right back. "Do you know because you wiped it clean?"

"I know because I never touched it," Oakley said stubbornly.

Haney leaned back in his chair. "Let's set the murder aside for a minute," he said. "What about the burglary at the school a week or so ago? That's got your fingerprints all over it, Gary."

Oakley's breath hissed between his teeth. "I heard about that. I prayed nobody would find out about my record, because I knew if they did, you cops would blame me for what happened! But I didn't have anything to do with that, either."

Haney looked over at Mike, bringing him into the interrogation for the first time by asking, "Deputy Newsom, you've read the reports on that case. Tell Mr. Oakley, were there any signs of forced entry at the school?"

Mike shook his head. "None. It looked like somebody must have used a key to get in."

"And as a custodian at Loving Elementary, you'd have the keys to every door in the school, wouldn't you?" Haney asked Oakley.

"There are other custodians," Oakley said, but his

momentary show of strength was beginning to fade. "A lot of people have keys to the school."

"But none of the rest of them are convicted burglars," Haney said heavily. "We checked. You're the only employee with a record."

Oakley put his hands over his face, and for a second Mike thought the man was going to cry. Instead, Oakley just said in a ragged voice muffled by his hands, "You're not going to believe me, no matter what I tell you. You've made up your minds that I'm guilty, so it doesn't matter anymore."

Haney leaned forward intently and clasped his hands together on the table. "That's right. It doesn't matter, so you might as well tell us the truth. What happened Saturday during the carnival? Did Mrs. Dunston come into the office and catch you while you were taking the cash box out of the secretary's desk?"

Oakley lowered his hands. Mike saw what looked like genuine surprise in the custodian's eyes. But before Oakley could say anything, Haney pressed on.

"Did you grab her and take her down that hall at knifepoint? You must know that school inside and out. You knew that if you killed her down there, it would be a while before anyone found her. That's what you did, isn't it? You killed her!" Haney slapped the table, the sound like the crack of a gun in the close confines of the room. "Admit it!"

Mike could see Oakley wavering. Oakley wanted to confess. But at the same time, there was a mixture of stubbornness and bafflement in his gaze as it switched back and forth between Mike and the sheriff. Finally, Oakley said, "I didn't do it. I didn't kill Mrs. Dunston, and I didn't steal anything from the school."

With an ominous glare, Haney shook his head. "You're gonna be sorry about lying to us, Gary. You just blew your chance to get the best result from this."

Oakley dragged in a deep breath. "One of the deputies

said earlier I could call somebody. I know I've got a right to call somebody."

"You said you didn't want to make a call," Haney snapped.

"I've changed my mind. I couldn't think of anybody then. But now . . . I know who I want to call."

Joel Dunston ushered Phyllis, Carolyn, and Marie through a very neatly kept living room and a luxuriously furnished dining room into a gleaming, spotless kitchen, without a speck of dust anywhere. On the refrigerator door were several photographs of Becca playing, lined up perfectly straight and held in place with tiny magnets in the corners. Phyllis wasn't surprised to see that the photos were displayed so neatly. Even in the short time she had known Shannon, she had gotten the idea that Shannon was the sort of woman who wouldn't tolerate any sort of mess.

Except an emotional one.

Phyllis put that thought out of her mind as Joel said, "Just set those dishes on the counter and I'll put them away later. You're all very kind to be thinking of us."

Marie reached for the handle of the refrigerator. "We can just go ahead and put them away for you now, so you won't have to bother with them."

Joel started to make a motion like he was going to tell her not to open the refrigerator, but then he stopped and said, "Okay, thanks."

Marie opened the door, and Phyllis saw that the refrigerator was already mostly full of covered dishes. Joel smiled weakly and said, "People have, uh, been bringing food all weekend. I don't think Becca and Kirk and I will have to worry about going hungry."

Marie found a place for her dish, and then turned to take Carolyn's green bean casserole. Phyllis's sweet potatoes went into the refrigerator last. As Marie closed the door, she said, "I believe all those dishes have the name of who they belong to on them, but I'm sure there's no hurry about getting them back."

"None at all," Phyllis assured Joel.

"I can even come by and pick them up when you're done with them," Marie went on. "How's Becca doing?"

Joel shrugged. "As well as can be expected, I guess. None of us are doing great, of course. That'll take some time."

"She didn't go to school today, did she?"

"No, she's in her room." Joel took a step toward the hall. "I can get her if you want to see her. . . ."

"Oh, no, let her rest," Marie said.

Actually, Phyllis wouldn't have minded asking the little girl a few more questions, but this was hardly the right time or place. But then, was there ever a right time and place for a murder investigation?

Joel stood there awkwardly. Phyllis was afraid that he was going to steer them back to the front door and out of the house, but then he said, "Where are my manners? Would you ladies like some coffee?"

Marie smiled at him. "That would be very nice. Thank you, Joel."

He fussed around, opening cabinet doors until he found cups. There was already coffee made, so all he had to do was pour it. A sugar bowl sat in the middle of the kitchen table, along with a little ceramic box that held packets of artificial sweetener. Joel got a carton of half-and-half from the refrigerator. His movements were brisk and his hands were steady. He had the sort of crisp assurance that most doctors demonstrated.

Within a few minutes, the four of them were sitting around the kitchen table, sipping coffee. Phyllis sensed that there was still a bit of a strain in the air, but that probably wasn't going to go away any time soon. The occupants of this house would have to get over Shannon's death first.

"I suppose you'd all like to know about the funeral," Joel said.

Actually, Phyllis hadn't planned on attending the funeral. She hadn't known Shannon that well. But she couldn't say that to Joel, not here and now, so she just nodded along with Carolyn and Marie.

"It'll be at Victory Baptist Church at eleven o'clock tomorrow morning," Joel went on.

Marie reached across the table and patted his hand. "Russ and I will be there," she said. Phyllis and Carolyn just murmured noncommittally.

"I'm thinking about establishing some sort of . . . memorial . . . in Shannon's name. I haven't decided what to do yet. Something for the school, maybe." Joel looked around the table. "Any suggestions you might have would be more than welcome."

"We'll think about it," Phyllis promised. "There are always a lot of things a school can use that aren't provided for in the budget."

Joel smiled again. "I know. Believe me, I know. Shannon preached that sermon to me many times. And I know she was right. I shouldn't have begrudged her the time and effort she spent on the . . . school." His voice began to break a little. "If I hadn't . . . then maybe we—we wouldn't have . . ."

He had to stop and draw in a deep breath as he struggled to control his emotions. Marie squeezed his hand and smiled sadly at him.

Phyllis couldn't help but feel sorry for the man. She knew that Shannon had been sincere about wanting to help the school, but at the same time, the question of her involvement with Russ Tyler still remained. Was it possible that she had piled so many jobs on Marie and kept her busy just so she would be out of the way and wouldn't notice that her husband was having an affair? It could have been that way, Phyllis decided.

"What about Kirk?" Marie asked in an obvious attempt to get Joel's mind on something else. "How's he doing?"

Joel shrugged and shook his head. "Who knows how

Kirk is doing? I've never been able to get a handle on that kid. Sometimes he seems pretty broken up, and sometimes he acts like he doesn't even care that Shannon is gone. They didn't get along very well, you know. I don't think he's ever forgiven her for sending him to military school when he was sixteen."

"She sent him to military school?" Carolyn said.

Joel nodded. "Yeah. She didn't have any choice, the way he was acting. Running with the wrong crowd, getting in trouble with the law, probably messed up on drugs . . ." He gave a heavy sigh. "Shannon thought the school could give him some discipline that she couldn't. I agreed with her. I'd tried to be a father to the kid, to help him grow up, but he wasn't having any of it. So I thought military school was worth a try." He laughed hollowly. "I guess it didn't take. Kirk came back as sullen as ever. Shannon convinced him to go to college, but he dropped out after a semester. He can't hold a job, and he started hanging out with the same bums who got him into trouble in the first place."

"We saw a young man leaving just as we got here," Phyllis commented.

"Yeah, that was Lane Erskine. He's actually not as bad as some of the others. He used to be pretty wild, but he's settled down some, I think, since he had a kid and got married . . . in that order, by the way. But I still wish Kirk would go back to school or try to get a decent job or—or something! I know it drove Shannon crazy thinking that she had raised a failure for a son."

Phyllis had seen the way Shannon treated Kirk, and it had been a dysfunctional relationship on both sides, as far as she was concerned. Joel didn't need to hear that right now, though. She said, "I'm sure that in time he'll straighten out. Nearly all children are vexations to their parents at times, but sooner or later they grow up and make us proud of them."

Joel grunted, as if to say that when it came to Kirk, he would believe it when he saw it.

Marie said, "I guess we'd better be going," and got to her feet. Phyllis and Carolyn stood up, too, as did Joel. Marie went around the table and gave him a hug. "If there's anything Russ and I can do to help, you just let us know," she told him.

Joel nodded and managed to smile again. "Thank you," he said. He looked over at Phyllis and Carolyn. "And thank you for the food, too. It's very kind of you."

"You take care, now," Carolyn told him. Phyllis just gave him a smile and a nod.

As they left the house, she noticed that the clouds had thickened even more. The sky looked like there might be rain before nightfall. That could ruin trick-or-treating for the kids.

But considering the atmosphere in the Dunston house, gloom was more than appropriate. . . .

Chapter 18

On the way back to Marie's house, Carolyn said, "I don't believe we'll be going to the funeral, if you think that's all right."

"Sure," Marie said. "It's not like you were all that close to Shannon, or even knew her for very long. I understand, and I'm sure Joel will, too, if he even notices that you're not there."

"How long did you know her?" Phyllis asked.

"Oh, gosh . . . since our kids were in preschool together? Yeah, I guess that's when I met her. She was a lot different back then, let me tell you. Still really . . . driven, you know, but not like she was later. She just wanted to do the best she could for her kids. She hadn't really gotten into the whole supermom thing yet."

"I guess you saw her a lot at school activities and things like that."

"Oh, yeah. Trips to the zoo and the museums and the Stockyards. And Girl Scouts for a while, until the kids got tired of it. And of course once the kids were all in regular school, there were PTO meetings. That's where Joel and Russ first met. They hit it off right away."

Phyllis wanted to ask how Russ and *Shannon* had hit it off, but she didn't think that would be a very good idea.

"Our families weren't really *close* close, you know," Marie mused, as Phyllis drove back toward her house. "But we saw a lot of each other for a while. We could tell that Shannon and Joel were drifting farther and farther apart. Russ was planning to have a talk with Joel, try to help him, you know, but he never did. Shannon and Joel separated before Russ got a chance to talk to him. And then the divorce went through quick after that. Poor Joel was like a deer caught in the headlights. Once Shannon made up her mind, he never had a chance."

"People ought to be able to get along," Carolyn said, "especially when they have children."

"Yeah. Why, if Russ ever told me we were getting a divorce, I'd kill his ass." Marie laughed. "Well, not really, of course. But I wouldn't ever let anything interfere with *my* marriage. It comes first. I guess Shannon never really felt that way."

I guess not, Phyllis thought.

And the way Marie had threatened to kill her husband just now was only a figure of speech. A rather tasteless one, under the circumstances, but clearly that hadn't occurred to Marie. She didn't really mean that she would commit murder to save her marriage.

Did she?

"Here we are," Marie said as Phyllis pulled up in front of her house. "Thanks for the ride. I appreciate not having to go over there by myself. It was easier with all three of us."

"We were glad to do it," Carolyn said. "I'll see you at church, dear."

"Yeah," Marie said as she got out of the car. The chilly wind whipped in through the open door. "Bye-bye."

She shut the door solidly and turned to go up the walk toward her house. As Phyllis pulled away from the curb, Carolyn said, "She's really a nice young woman. A little too salty in her language for my taste, but I suppose it could be worse. My goodness, some of the young people today swear like sailors—even the women!"

Phyllis knew that was true. She had heard stories from

some of the other retired teachers about kids as young as first and second grade coming to school and spewing obscenities that threatened to turn the air blue around their heads. And of course the only place they could have learned those words was at home. Or day care. But the filthy words had originated in *somebody's* home, that was for sure.

As they got back to the house and Phyllis pulled into the driveway, she saw Sam come out the front door and start toward his pickup. His long legs carried him quickly along the walk, and his face wore a concerned expression. Phyllis stopped the car in the driveway, opened the door, and stood up to call over the top of the Lincoln. "Sam! What's wrong?"

He stopped and looked around at her. He wore boots, jeans, and a denim jacket over a flannel shirt, and looked more like a weathered old cowboy than a retired basketball coach and history teacher.

"Got a call from the sheriff's department," he said.

Phyllis's heart leaped into her throat. Ever since Mike had become a deputy, she had hated those words for their potentially ominous portent.

"What is it?" she asked, her voice tight with the strain she felt.

"They've arrested Gary Oakley."

Phyllis frowned. "Who?"

"That custodian I knew up in Poolville. You met him the other day at the carnival, after all the uproar. You know, out in the parking lot."

Phyllis remembered the man now. She also remembered that Gary Oakley had been acting a little suspiciously that day, asking Sam to help him get away from there without being questioned by the deputies. He had told some story about needing to get home to feed his dogs, but at the time Phyllis hadn't been sure she believed him.

"What did they arrest him for?" she asked now.

"They think he killed Mrs. Dunston," Sam said.

"Dear Lord!" Carolyn exclaimed. She had gotten out of the Lincoln and was standing close enough to hear what Sam and Phyllis were saying. "You mean that nice man we talked to is a murderer?"

Sam started to shake his head, then stopped and shrugged instead. "That's what the sheriff thinks. I don't know whether I believe it or not, though. I knew Gary pretty well, and he never seemed like a killer to me."

"Why did he call you?" Phyllis asked. "Don't people who have been arrested usually call their lawyer?"

"Usually. Maybe he doesn't know any lawyers and wants me to find one for him. Or maybe he wants to borrow money to pay for a lawyer. I don't know. He just asked me to come see him, so I reckon I'll go."

That was so much like Sam, Phyllis thought. A friend called for help, and he answered without hesitation.

But in this case, the friend might actually be guilty of a very serious crime. If the accusation was true, would Sam be able to see that in time to protect himself from getting involved with Gary Oakley, or would his friendship blind him to the truth?

"Why don't I go with you?" Phyllis suggested.

Sam frowned slightly. "I think I can handle this—"

"Of course you can, but a lot of the deputies know that I'm Mike's mother, and so does the sheriff. I just thought it might make things go a little smoother if I was along."

Sam shrugged again and seemed mollified. "Well, sure, I'm always glad for your company, Phyllis."

"Just let me put my car away while you're warming up your pickup."

She knew that engines didn't have to be warmed up as much as they did in the old days, but it seemed like the right thing to say, anyway. Quickly, she finished pulling the Lincoln into the garage, and then got out to join Carolyn on the front lawn for a second.

"Be careful," Carolyn said. "If that man's really a murderer, there's no telling what he might do."

"We'll be in the middle of the sheriff's department," Phyllis pointed out. "I think we'll be safe enough."

At least, she hoped that was the case.

Sam had the pickup running. He started to get out and open the door for her, but Phyllis waved him back into his seat and opened the door herself. Such gestures were nice, but she was no shrinking violet who *required* them of the men around her. As she slid onto the seat beside Sam and closed the door, she thought how . . . *manly* the cab smelled. It wasn't any particular scent she could put her finger on, but rather a blending of aromas that served as a reminder of the fact that the person who spent more time than anyone else in this truck was male.

The closest route to the sheriff's department was along two sides of the square, out the old Fort Worth highway past the farmers' market, and over the railroad overpass. The sheriff's department and county jail were on the left just past the overpass. It didn't take long to get there, but Phyllis had time to ask, "Did Mr. Oakley say anything else besides telling you he'd been arrested?"

"Nope," Sam replied. "He sounded pretty shaken up. Asked me if I could come see him. I said I'd be right there."

"Remember a couple of days ago at the carnival how he wanted to catch a ride with you, because he thought maybe the deputies wouldn't question him as he left?"

Sam took his eyes off the road to look over at her, but only for a second. "What are you sayin', Phyllis?"

"It just struck me at the time that he seemed a little nervous, like he didn't want to talk to the deputies."

"Like he had something to hide, you mean?" Sam shook his head. "I don't want to believe that's true. But I remember now, he did mention that." His hands tightened on the wheel. "What do I do if the sheriff asks me about it?"

"You'll have to tell him the truth. You can't lie to the law."

As soon as the words were out of her mouth, Phyllis chided herself for being a hypocrite. She hadn't told Mike, Sheriff Haney, or anyone else in authority about seeing Shannon Dunston and Russ Tyler together in Fort Worth. That was withholding evidence, wasn't it? Even though she had what she felt was a good reason in trying to protect Marie's marriage. But at the very least it was a lie of omission. She had no business coming off so high and mighty with Sam.

"I'll talk to Gary first," Sam said. "Maybe he's got a good explanation for everything."

Phyllis found herself hoping that was true. She knew it would be a shock to Sam if it turned out that one of his friends was a killer. She'd been down that road herself a few months back, and she wouldn't wish that on her worst enemy, much less on a friend like Sam.

They turned left onto the side street that ran in front of the complex of buildings housing the sheriff's department and the jail. Phyllis saw the high fences topped by razor wire at the rear of the place, enclosing the jail section, and as always the sight of them gave her a little chill. She couldn't imagine being locked up, and was sorry some people made such bad choices that they had to suffer that fate.

A few tiny drops of rain came down as they walked from the parking lot into the building. Phyllis had been here several times before with Mike, so she knew where to go and what to do. She told the deputy at the front desk who they were and why they were there. The deputy was a young woman with blond hair pulled back into a short ponytail. "Why, sure, Miz Newsom," she said with a smile. "I was in your history class a while back, remember?"

Phyllis had always been good with names, and she got plenty of practice remembering them, because teachers were always running into their former students. "Debbie, isn't it?"

"Yes, ma'am, it was Debbie Collins then. Debbie Hall-wood, now."

"You married Mitch Hallwood?"

"Yes, ma'am." Deputy Hallwood stood up. "I'll go get Mike for you. I'm pretty sure he's back in Sheriff Haney's office."

She hurried down a corridor. Sam glanced over at Phyllis and said, "I reckon you were right about it being easier with you along. Remind me if I ever get arrested to be sure and call you."

"Oh, you'll never get arrested. You're too law-abiding."

He smiled. "You've just never seen my wild streak."

Phyllis found the idea that Sam Fletcher might have a wild streak oddly intriguing, but she put that thought out of her head a moment later when Mike came up the hall with a puzzled look on his face and said, "Mom? Sam? What are you doing here? Debbie said it was something about one of the prisoners . . . ?"

"Gary Oakley," Sam said. "He called me, said he'd been arrested."

"That's right." Mike frowned. "He called you? We don't listen in on prisoners, but when he refused to talk any more and asked for his phone call, we figured he was getting lawyered up."

"Cops really say that? *Lawyered up,* I mean. I figured it was just on TV."

Mike grunted. "Well, we probably say it more now than we used to . . . but, no offense, why did Oakley call you, Sam? What can you do for him?"

"Reckon I'll have to ask him. Maybe he just needed a friend to talk to, somebody who'll believe him when he says he's innocent."

Phyllis asked, "*Is* he innocent, Mike? Or do you have proof against him?"

Mike shook his head and said, "I can't really talk about that now."

"Can I bail him out?" Sam asked.

"He hasn't been charged yet, so bail hasn't been set. He's just being held for questioning right now. You can talk to him, but that's about all."

Sam nodded. "Guess it'll have to be enough."

"Okay. Come with me, then." Mike looked at Phyllis. "Mom, you can wait out here."

"I can't go with Sam?"

"I'm afraid not. One visitor only, and Sam's the one Mr. Oakley asked for."

Phyllis felt a flash of irritation, but she knew it wouldn't do any good to argue. Mike might bend the rules a little when it came to telling her about what was going on in the cases he worked on, but not with something like this. Jail regulations had to be followed right to the letter.

Sam looked over his shoulder at her and lifted a hand in farewell. "I'll be back in a little while," he told her.

"I'll be here," Phyllis said.

Then as Mike and Sam disappeared down the hallway, she sat down in a hard plastic chair to wait and tried not to sigh in frustration. She wanted to know what Gary Oakley was going to tell Sam.

She would find out soon enough, she supposed.

Chapter 19

Phyllis sat and watched through the glass door as the rain fell harder outside, spitting down from the gray sky and wetting the pavement of the parking lot. Neither she nor Sam had an umbrella or a raincoat, so it looked like they might get soaked when they left the sheriff's department. That is, unless the rain let up before then.

Which as it turned out was exactly what happened. After raining hard for fifteen or twenty minutes, accompanied by the occasional rumble of thunder, the storm began to taper off. Phyllis watched the drops hitting one of the puddles on the parking lot and could tell they weren't falling as hard or as fast as they had been a few minutes earlier. Soon it was just sprinkling outside as the clouds thinned and the sky grew lighter.

Then a shaft of sunlight burst through, lancing down brightly and making the clouds seem darker again. Phyllis wondered if she would be able to see a rainbow if she was outside. She had always liked rainbows.

The rain stopped completely a few minutes later, and it was then that Sam emerged from the rear of the complex. As Phyllis came to her feet and moved forward to meet him, he looked out at the sun shining on the parking lot and said, "Heard it thunderin' and was afraid we'd get poured on. Looks like it's about to clear up, though."

"What did you find out?"

Sam reached for the door. "We can talk about it in the

truck." His eyes held a worried look, and Phyllis had the feeling that the conversation with Gary Oakley hadn't gone very well.

Before Sam could open the door, Mike walked quickly up the corridor from the jail and called, "Mom, can I talk to you for a minute?"

Phyllis turned toward her son while Sam waited by the door. "What is it?" she asked.

Mike hesitated, as if unsure whether he wanted to proceed or not, but then he squared his shoulders determinedly and said, "The fact that you came here today with Sam doesn't mean that you're taking more of an interest in this case than you should, does it?"

Her chin came up a little. "Why don't you say what you mean, Michael? Your father and I taught you to speak your mind."

"All right, I will. You don't plan to investigate Mrs. Dunston's murder, do you? Because the sheriff wouldn't take too kindly to it if you did."

"There's nothing to investigate, is there? You've already arrested Mr. Oakley."

"Like I said, he's being held for questioning and hasn't been charged yet. So we don't really know—"

As Mike spoke, Phyllis saw something in his eyes, and it prompted her to interrupt him. "You don't think he's guilty, do you?"

"I don't have any idea. There was probable cause to bring him in, I can tell you that much."

"But you have your doubts," she insisted. "I can see that you do. I'm your mother, after all."

Mike looked even more uncomfortable now. "Everybody's considered innocent until proven guilty in a court of law. We just gather as much evidence as we can and turn it over to the district attorney. He's the one who decides whether or not to proceed with a case."

"But you form opinions, too," Phyllis said. "You can't help

but do that. And you're not convinced that Mr. Oakley killed Shannon."

Mike sighed. "Look, just talk to Sam, Mom. I'm sure he's going to tell you everything that Oakley told him, anyway."

"Even if he does, I can't turn around and come tell you what he said. That would be betraying a confidence."

"I'm not asking you to do that. I'm just saying talk to Sam and make up your own mind. Maybe we'll discuss it later. But just be careful, okay? This isn't like last time. If you start poking around in this case, you might put yourself in real danger."

"You mean besides annoying the sheriff?"

"I mean somebody stuck a knife in a woman's chest," Mike said bluntly. "If the killer's still out there, and he thinks somebody is threatening him, there's no telling what he might do. But it wouldn't be good, we can count on that."

Phyllis nodded. "I understand. And you don't have to worry about me, Mike."

"I hope not." He glanced past her. "Looks like it's clearing off outside."

That was true. There were even more breaks in the clouds now. The sky that showed through them was a deep, beautiful blue.

But the wind that was blowing as Phyllis and Sam left the sheriff's department and walked across the wet pavement of the parking lot was downright cold. "There's gonna be some chilly trick-or-treaters tonight," Sam said as he unlocked and opened the passenger-side door of the pickup. This time Phyllis didn't refuse the courtesy.

"That'll be better than if it was still raining, though," she said as she got into the truck.

"Oh, yeah. I expect a wet Halloween costume wouldn't be very comfortable."

As they drove away, Sam went on, "I suppose you want to know what Gary had to say to me. I heard Mike tell you to ask me about it."

"I don't think he believes that Mr. Oakley is guilty, but for some reason he can't come right out and say that."

"He can't come right out and say it because his boss the sheriff is convinced they've got the right man. And with what I found out about Gary today, even I've got to say it doesn't look too good for him."

"What did you find out?"

"He's got a record," Sam said. "He's what we used to call a jailbird."

Surprised, Phyllis asked, "But how could that be possible? He works at a school."

"Yeah, but when he filled out the job application he conveniently forgot to mention that he'd been convicted of three felonies and spent time in Huntsville. I guess nobody ever got around to checking that out before he was hired."

"What did he do? Why did he go to prison?"

"Burglary," Sam said.

"Oh. Well, that's not as bad as some—" Phyllis stopped short as she remembered something. "Wait a minute. There was a burglary at Loving Elementary a week or so ago."

Sam nodded. "Yep. And since there were no signs that somebody broke in, the burglar must've used a key."

"And Mr. Oakley *has* a key, since he works there."

"Right again. The way the sheriff has it worked out, Gary was responsible for the earlier burglary, and he was in the school office Saturday afternoon stealin' the PTO cash box from the secretary's desk when Mrs. Dunston came in and caught him at it."

"So he killed her to keep her from telling anyone?"

"That's what the sheriff says. I got to admit, given Gary's record, a jury might believe it, too."

Phyllis sat there in silence for a moment, thinking about everything Sam had told her. Then she asked, "What does Mr. Oakley say about it?"

"He claims he didn't do it. Says he's innocent and has gone straight ever since he got out of the pen."

"Then why was he trying to sneak away from the school Saturday afternoon before the deputies could talk to him? You don't believe he really just wanted to get home to feed his dogs, do you?"

"I asked him about that, flat out," Sam said. "He admitted he was lying about the dogs, although I think he really was a little worried about them. But he said he didn't want to talk to the deputies because he was afraid they'd run his name through the computer and find out about his criminal record. Said he was scared that if they did, he'd not only lose his job but also be considered a suspect in the murder." Sam sighed. "Looks like he was right about that."

"But they didn't arrest him until this morning," Phyllis pointed out.

"That's because when the deputies talked to him Saturday they just asked him a few questions, mostly about the school and had he seen anything suspicious during the afternoon. They didn't run his name at all. Gary said he was starting to breathe easier again, thinking maybe they wouldn't find out about him. But then this mornin' Mike and a couple of other deputies showed up at the school and took him into custody. I figure they must've put the names of everybody who was there through the computer over the weekend, and Gary's record got his name flagged."

"This is just a guess," Phyllis said, "but I'd be willing to bet that he wasn't the only one at the school that afternoon with a criminal record. Nearly every year I had at least one student in class who had a parent either in prison or one who had been in prison."

"Yeah, criminals' kids have to go to school like anybody else's, I reckon. But given the convictions that Gary had, and the fact that the school was burglarized not long ago, and the cash box being missing on top of everything else . . ." Sam shook his head. "He just had too many marks against him. The sheriff had to bring him in."

Again Phyllis mulled over what Sam had told her. They

were almost back to the house. She wanted to ask the most important question of all before they got there.

"What about you, Sam?" she said. "Do *you* think he did it?"

"The burglary or the murder?"

"Either. Both."

Sam took a deep breath and blew it out as he parked the pickup at the curb in front of the house. "The fella I knew at Poolville was always quiet but friendly, always got along with everybody, worked hard, and never caused a lick of trouble. I know people say those are the ones you got to watch out for. But no, I don't believe it. Gary Oakley's not a killer. Then again, I wouldn't have said he was a professional burglar, either, and for several years that's exactly what he was. So I don't know, Phyllis. I want to believe he's innocent. I really do. But I just don't know."

Phyllis could see how conflicted he was. Sam Fletcher was a straightforward sort of man who believed what he believed and had the strength of his convictions. It was unusual for him to be torn this way between his head and his heart.

"We need to talk about this again," she finally said. "There are some things you should know about—things that the sheriff isn't aware of."

Sam glanced sharply over at her. With a frown, he said, "Phyllis, have you been detectin' again? You know how Mike feels about that—"

"Hold your horses. I just happened to see something that I haven't told anyone about yet."

"Does it have any bearin' on the case?"

"It might. Or it might not. I'm not trying to be mysterious, truly I'm not. I just don't know yet."

"So tell me about it. You know I'll keep quiet if that's what you want."

She believed him. He had helped her look into those other murders, and she trusted him to keep her confidences. And if she was going to go ahead with her plans, she would likely need his help again.

Before she could say anything else, though, the front door of the house opened and Eve stepped out onto the porch. Phyllis thought she had seen the curtains in the living room flick aside a little as they pulled up, and she had no trouble believing that Eve had been watching and waiting for their return. *Sam's* return, rather. Eve wouldn't care that much about Phyllis's comings and goings.

As Eve came down the still-damp walk toward the pickup, Phyllis glanced over at Sam and said, "We'll talk more about it later, all right?"

He nodded. "Don't forget. If there's any way I can help Gary, I want to do it."

Phyllis wasn't as interested in clearing Gary Oakley's name as she was in simply finding out the truth about the murder of Shannon Dunston. But she didn't tell Sam that. If they worked together, they might be able to accomplish both goals.

"You two have been sitting out here for a long time," Eve said with a hard-edged smile as Phyllis opened the pickup door. "What exactly are you doing, necking? And in the middle of the day, at that?"

"Nope, just talkin'," Sam said as he got out of the truck. "Back in the days when I still did a little smoochin' now and then, I generally preferred a chilly night and a roarin' fire in the fireplace."

"Why, that sounds absolutely delightful, dear," Eve said as she took his arm and practically tugged him toward the house. "My, that's a cold wind blowing, isn't it? And I happen to know that there's a big stack of firewood out back by the storage shed. . . ."

Sam tossed a helpless grin over his shoulder at Phyllis, who stood there at the curb for a moment before she closed the pickup door with maybe just a little more force than was absolutely necessary.

Chapter 20

After lunch, Phyllis went upstairs to her bedroom, got the cordless phone from its stand on the bedside table, and sat down in an armchair next to one of the windows. As she gathered her thoughts, she looked out at the branches of a tree that grew next to the house. They waved back and forth in the wind, almost like someone waving good-bye.

Then she took a deep breath and called Information to get the number of the Lockheed plant over in Fort Worth. She hated to call Information anymore, since the telephone company charged for that service now, but she couldn't think of any other way to get the number she needed. It wasn't until she was finished and had written down the number that she remembered she might have been able to look up the information on the Internet. She supposed that option just didn't occur to her as naturally as it would to younger people.

She punched in the numbers and listened to the phone ringing on the other end for a moment before a woman answered. Phyllis said, "I need to speak to Russ Tyler, please." She had wondered if he might go by Russell at work, but since she had no idea, she went with what she knew.

"What department, please?"

Phyllis was ready for the question, having paid attention that morning while Marie was talking about her husband. "Engineering."

"Which engineering department?"

Phyllis's hand tightened on the phone. Maybe she wasn't as prepared as she had thought she was. Then she recalled something else Marie had said and took a guess. "Structural," she said.

"Just a moment."

Phyllis tried not to heave a sigh of relief into the phone.

More than a moment went by. It was several minutes before she heard a click and then a man's voice said, "Department One-eighty-four."

Phyllis hadn't heard Russ's voice all that many times, but she didn't think he was the man who had answered the phone. She said, "Russ Tyler, please."

"Hang on." This time, instead of the clicking noises that told her the call was being transferred, she heard a clunk as the phone was physically set down on something. The man's voice, more distant now, said, "Hey, Russ, phone."

Even more distant, Russ asked, "Who is it?"

"I dunno, some woman."

Footsteps approached the phone. It was picked up, and Russ said, "Marie?"

Phyllis said, "No, Mr. Tyler, it's Phyllis Newsom. We met at the school carnival the other day."

"Oh, yeah, Mrs. Newsom, hi." Russ sounded distracted, which came as no surprise since he was at work. But he didn't sound the least bit wary. He went on, "Listen, if this is something about school, you should call Marie, because she handles all that stuff—"

"It's not about school, Mr. Tyler," Phyllis broke in. She took a quick breath and plunged ahead before she lost her nerve. "It's about your lunch date in Fort Worth last week with Shannon Dunston."

Except for the sound of a sharply drawn breath, there was silence on the other end of the connection. Finally, Russ said, "I'm afraid I don't know what you're talking about. I don't believe I ever had lunch with Shannon Dunston, and certainly not last week."

"It was at an Applebee's in southwest Fort Worth, not far from Hulen Mall," Phyllis said. She told him the exact date, having looked it up beforehand. "I know what I saw. If either of you used a credit card to pay for lunch that day, I'm sure the authorities can subpoena those records to prove that you were there—"

"You told?" Now Russ sounded like he wanted to groan in dismay.

"Not yet," Phyllis admitted. "I wanted to ask you about it first."

"I can't talk to you now. I'm at work."

"You'd better talk to me soon," Phyllis said. "There have been developments in the case you don't know about." She felt bad about taking such a hard line with him, but it had to be done.

"I'll call you back in a few minutes. Give me your number."

Phyllis did so. She supposed Russ wrote it down, because he said, "I'll get right back to you."

"I'll be here," she told him. She pushed the button on the phone to break the connection, and then sat there holding the instrument in her lap. She felt a little shaky inside. Confrontation had never bothered her all that much; you couldn't be a teacher without learning pretty quickly how to stand your ground. But she didn't have much experience at confronting a possible murderer.

When the phone rang, the caller ID screen on it lit up and identified the incoming call as originating from a cellular phone. Russ had probably left Lockheed and gone out to his car to return her call. Phyllis answered, saying, "Hello?"

"What do you want?" Russ Tyler asked in a harsh voice, without any greeting. Before Phyllis could say anything, he went on, "Or rather, how much do you want?"

The question took Phyllis by surprise. "What are you talking about?"

"You want me to pay you to keep you from going to the cops, right?"

"What?" Phyllis was aghast. "You think I called you to *blackmail* you?"

"Why else?"

"To find out the truth," she said. "I like your wife, and before I go to the police and tell them you might have been having an affair with Shannon Dunston, I wanted to find out what you had to say about it. Once the sheriff's department knows about this, your wife *will* find out. You can count on that."

"All right, all right." Russ heaved a sigh. "Let me think a minute. . . . We need to get together and talk about this."

Phyllis had been expecting that. She said, "If you killed Shannon to cover up your affair with her, you can't expect me to just meet you somewhere, Mr. Tyler."

"Listen, I didn't kill Shannon and I wasn't having an affair with her, okay?" Russ's voice held an edge of exasperation and near-hysteria. "Just don't go running off to the sheriff until we've talked about this. I'll meet you someplace public, in broad daylight. There's a Waffle House down the road from here. How about that?"

Phyllis thought about it, then said, "That's fine. I'll be bringing someone with me."

"Somebody *else* knows about this?"

"You don't have to worry about him. He's trustworthy."

"To you, maybe. What about for me?"

"You don't really have much choice in the matter," Phyllis pointed out.

"Yeah, yeah. All right, that's fine."

"Tell me where to find this place."

Russ gave her directions. Phyllis knew the Waffle House wouldn't be difficult to find. "I can be there in about an hour," she said.

"That's fine." He paused. "Are you sure you don't just want money?"

"The truth, Mr. Tyler," Phyllis said again. "Just the truth."

* * *

When she went downstairs, she found Sam, Eve, and Carolyn in the living room. She said, "Sam, can I speak to you for a minute?"

"More secrets, dear?" Eve said.

"I don't recall having any secrets concerning Sam," Phyllis said, even though that was fudging the truth a bit. She was about to share a big secret with him.

Sam stood up and came over to join her. "What is it, Phyllis?" he asked quietly.

"Let's go out to the kitchen," she suggested.

Eve said, "See? It *is* a secret."

Phyllis swallowed her exasperation and forced a smile. She didn't trust herself to speak, though, as she led Sam into the kitchen.

"If this really is private, maybe we'd better go outside," Sam said in a half whisper as he nodded toward the hallway leading to the living room. Phyllis understood what he meant. Eve might be lurking out there in an attempt to eavesdrop.

"I just need to know if you'd be willing to take a drive over to Fort Worth with me this afternoon."

"This have anything to do with what we were talkin' about earlier?"

"It has everything to do with it," Phyllis said with a nod.

"Then sure, I'll go with you. I don't have any plans for the afternoon. But maybe along the way, you can tell me what this is all about."

"I will," Phyllis promised.

"When do we need to leave?"

Mentally, Phyllis estimated the time it would take to reach the Waffle House where she had agreed to meet with Russ. "In about fifteen or twenty minutes, if that's all right?"

He nodded. "I'll be ready." With a smile, he added, "What'll we tell Eve?"

Phyllis felt another flash of irritation. "I know that Eve

considers everything about you to be her business, but that's not really the way it is, is it?"

Sam looked a little surprised by the intensity of her reaction. He shook his head and said, "Nope, it's not. Reckon we just won't worry about that."

"Fine with me." Phyllis knew she shouldn't let Eve's flirtatious, possessive nature get under her skin like that, but sometimes she just couldn't help it.

With the temperature outside dropping, she went upstairs to get a jacket, as well as her purse. By the time she came down again, Sam was waiting for her in the kitchen. "Want to take your car or my pickup?" he asked.

"This is my errand," she said. "We'll burn my gas."

"Okay." He opened the door into the garage for her.

Phyllis got behind the wheel of the Lincoln as Sam settled into the passenger seat. The car was big enough so that there was room for his long legs. She backed out, drove past the courthouse, and headed east on the old Fort Worth highway, the same route they had followed in Sam's pickup that morning. As they passed the sheriff's department and jail, Phyllis glanced in the direction of the complex, wondering briefly if Gary Oakley was still in custody. She felt sure they would still be holding him for questioning. They could hang on to him for quite a while before they had to either charge him or release him.

Sam didn't say much until the old road merged with the interstate east of town. Then, as Phyllis accelerated onto the bigger highway, he said, "Maybe you'd better go ahead and tell me what's up. Where are we goin'?"

"To meet Russ Tyler. I called him earlier this afternoon and set it up."

"Marie's husband?"

"That's right."

Sam guessed, "This has somethin' to do with what you mentioned earlier, about how you saw somethin' that might be connected to the murder?"

"I saw Russ Tyler with Shannon Dunston in Fort Worth last week. They looked very friendly, if you know what I mean."

Sam listened intently as Phyllis filled him in on the details of what she had seen. When she was finished, he said, "If Tyler was foolin' around with Mrs. Dunston, that might give him a motive for killin' her. Maybe he wanted to break it off, and she threatened to tell his wife about it."

Phyllis nodded. "Yes, that's the first thing I thought of. But there could have been any number of reasons for a lovers' quarrel that ended badly."

Sam grunted. "*Real* badly. But here's somethin' you might not have thought of. Marie might've known about the affair already."

"And killed Shannon to protect her marriage," Phyllis said. "Yes, I thought of it, but I don't believe it. Marie just doesn't seem like the type of woman who would do something like that."

"Folks do things all the time that it doesn't seem like they would," Sam pointed out. "Like Gary Oakley bein' a burglar."

"You don't believe he's a killer, though. I feel the same way about Marie."

Sam nodded as he frowned in thought. "So you called Tyler and told him about seein' him and Mrs. Dunston. I'll bet he wasn't too happy about that."

"Actually, he accused me of trying to blackmail him."

"Sounds like a guilty conscience to me."

"I don't know," Phyllis said. "Even if he's telling the truth about not having an affair with Shannon, he could still be worried about Marie finding out there was anything at all between the two of them."

"I'm glad you had the sense to ask me to come along with you. If he *is* a killer, you could've wound up in a whole heap of trouble."

"That's why I insisted on meeting him in a public place."

Phyllis smiled. "And why I insisted on bringing a big strong man along with me."

Sam chuckled. "Yeah, that's me, all right. Just hired muscle."

That was hardly the way she felt about him, but she didn't say as much. Whatever was or was not developing between them, she wanted to keep it on the light side. She was much too old for anything more serious than that.

"This changes things quite a bit," Sam mused. "Both of the Tylers were at the carnival, and so was Mrs. Dunston's ex-husband."

"And all of them had just as many chances, if not more chances, to take the knife from the cafeteria," Phyllis pointed out as she swung north from the interstate onto the big loop that ran around Fort Worth. Russ had told her to take the first exit after she got on the loop, and to cross over the highway. In fact, she could already see the Waffle House sign up ahead on the left.

"You've got to tell Mike about this," Sam said. "Those extra folks with possible motives are enough to create reasonable doubt all by themselves. The district attorney might not charge Gary if he knew about it."

"I have to see what Russ says first," Phyllis said. "If I'm convinced that there wasn't any affair and that neither he nor Marie nor Joel had any reason to kill Shannon, I . . . I don't know what I'll do then."

"Tyler could lie to you," Sam said. "How are you gonna *know* he's tellin' the truth?"

"That's a problem," Phyllis admitted. "But if I decide to keep quiet about this, can I count on you to go along with me, Sam?" She knew it was an awfully big favor she was asking of him, considering that it was one of his friends who was currently under suspicion. She knew that she had been willing to do whatever was necessary to clear Carolyn's name when Carolyn had been suspected of murder, no matter who else might have been hurt.

Sam's forehead furrowed even more as his frown deepened. "The case against Gary's got a big hole in it, anyway, and Mike knows it. Whoever took that knife from the school cafeteria had to be plannin' to use it on Mrs. Dunston. That doesn't fit at all with the scenario the sheriff laid out against Gary. He wouldn't have had any reason to have the knife with him."

"That's right," Phyllis said. "I'll talk to Mike and make sure he points that out to Sheriff Haney. It's possible the district attorney may decide not to charge your friend at all."

Sam shook his head. "But even if he's not charged with murder, Gary's life is already ruined. Everybody knows about him bein' a jailbird now. He'll lose his job, and he'll probably be in trouble with the law for lyin' on his job applications."

"That's better than going to prison for a murder he didn't commit. And there's nothing you can do about any of that now, Sam. All you can do is try to save him from a prison term . . . or the death penalty."

Phyllis had exited from the loop, driven across the overpass, and pulled into the parking lot of the Waffle House by now. As she brought the Lincoln to a stop, Sam nodded grimly and said, "Yeah, you're right. Let's go see what this fella Tyler has to say for himself."

As they left the car and started into the restaurant, Phyllis thought that she didn't know what to hope for.

But one way or another, Russ's story could change the direction of this case completely.

Chapter 21

Phyllis had been in Waffle House restaurants before and knew that they usually stayed busy twenty-four hours a day. So she wasn't surprised that there were quite a few people in this one. The aroma of coffee was strong in the air as she and Sam went inside.

The counter was to the left, with booths along the windows on the right-hand wall. At the far end of the counter the booths continued on around to the left in an L. She spotted Russ Tyler sitting in a corner booth, as far back and inconspicuous as he could get.

The waitress behind the counter raised a coffeepot and smiled at them. "We're joining a friend," Phyllis told her and pointed toward Russ. "We'll just have coffee."

"Comin' right up, hon," the waitress replied.

Russ watched them warily as they came around the end of the counter and approached the booth. He had a cup of coffee in front of him, tightly clutched in both hands, even though he didn't seem to be drinking from it. Phyllis slid onto the bench seat across the table from him, and Sam sat down beside her. Even though she had a lot of other, more important things on her mind, she was aware of how close Sam was to her. It felt natural having him that close.

Russ wasn't saying anything, just looking at them, so Phyllis said, "Hello, Russ. This is my friend Sam Fletcher."

Sam nodded. "Howdy."

"Oh, God," Russ said in response to the greeting habitually spoken by Texas A&M students and graduates. "You're an Aggie, aren't you?"

Sam's eyes narrowed at the tone of scorn in Russ's voice. "Teasipper?" he asked, using the disdainful nickname his beloved Aggies pinned on anybody who went to the University of Texas.

Phyllis couldn't believe it. Even under these circumstances, the rivalry between A&M and UT reared its head. She said, "I don't think where any of us went to college has anything to do with why we're here."

Despite that, Russ and Sam continued to eye each other in an unfriendly fashion while the waitress brought coffee for Phyllis and Sam. Phyllis didn't particularly need the caffeine, but she put sweetener and cream in her cup, stirred it, and sipped from it, anyway.

None of the other booths back here were occupied. "All right, Russ," Phyllis said quietly, "you know why we're here."

"I wasn't having an affair with Shannon." His voice and expression were sullen. "I don't care if you believe me or not. It's the truth."

"I think you should care. I haven't gone to the sheriff yet, and what you have to say for yourself will determine whether I do or not."

"Yeah, you're a teacher, all right." His voice took on a mocking tone. " 'What do you have to say for yourself, Russell?' "

"Watch your mouth, son," Sam warned. "Show the lady some respect. I happen to know that the only reason she's givin' you the benefit of any doubt at all is because she's fond of your wife."

"Is that true?" Russ asked.

"I don't know Marie all that well," Phyllis admitted, "but yes, I do like her. She's a little rough around the edges sometimes, but I know she loves you and is devoted to you and your little ones. She deserves—"

"Better than me," Russ broke in. He stared down into his coffee cup as a look of misery came over his face. "I know that." He lifted his gaze to stare across the table. His arrogance and sullenness were gone. "But I didn't have an affair with Shannon. I just . . . thought about it. *She's* the one who wanted it."

"You mean Shannon?" Phyllis asked.

Russ nodded. "Yeah. For several years now, since we met each other because our kids went to school together, there's been a sort of . . . connection, I guess you could say, between us. We got along well together and enjoyed talking to each other. And I have to admit, there were times I . . . thought about her." His face flushed, and Phyllis realized that he was actually blushing. "Like that, you know? I wondered what it would be like . . . but that's all. It never went beyond that while she and Joel were married."

"While she and Joel were married," Phyllis repeated. "What about after the divorce?"

Russ finally drank some of his coffee. His hand shook a little as he put the cup back down on the table. "I ran into her at school one day. I had to take off work early and pick up the kids for some reason. I don't even remember why now. Marie usually picks them up. Anyway, I got there early and I was sitting out in the parking lot, and Shannon came over to talk to me. I asked her to get in the car. . . . I know, not a very smart thing to do. . . . Anyway, I asked her how she was doing. Just being friendly, you know?"

Phyllis nodded. So far, what Russ was saying wasn't incriminating. But she had a feeling it wasn't going to stay that way.

"She said she was fine, but that sometimes she missed . . . having a man around. She said that maybe . . . I could help her out with that."

Sam said, "Oh, come on! Sell that one to *Penthouse Letters*, amigo."

Russ bristled in anger. "It's true. I know it doesn't seem

like something Shannon would do, but think about it for a minute. When she wants something, she doesn't hesitate to come right out and say it. And she's not shy about asking somebody to take care of it for her, either. I mean . . . she *wasn't* shy about it. . . ." Unable to go on, he drew in a ragged breath and looked away for a moment.

Phyllis and Sam waited, and after a minute or so Russ continued. "When I looked surprised, she laughed and said she was just joking. But she wasn't, because the next time we were alone, she brought it up again. And that was at school, after a PTO meeting, for God's sake! She called our house, and if Marie answered, she'd pretend to be calling about school stuff. . . . Well, I guess it wasn't really pretending, because Shannon always had the other board members busy with projects for the school . . . but if I answered she would always ask me if I'd given her suggestion any thought, before she asked to talk to Marie. I didn't know what to do."

Sam said, "But I'll bet you liked the attention, didn't you?"

Russ glared at him. "Are you asking if I was flattered that a good-looking woman was pursuing me? Damn right I was. But that doesn't mean I was going to go along with what she wanted."

Phyllis said, "Marie's a very nice-looking woman—"

"It's not the same thing."

"He's right about that," Sam said. "It's not."

Phyllis just shook her head, having long since learned that there were nooks and crannies of the male mind that she would rather not explore.

"All right," she said. "So Shannon was . . . after you, I guess you'd say. What about that day I saw the two of you at Applebee's?"

"I agreed that I'd have lunch with her. That's all."

"You weren't on your way to or from a motel?" Sam asked. Phyllis was glad he was the one who put that question into words, so that she wouldn't have to.

"Absolutely not. I'll admit that I was thinking about it. Shannon had just about worn down my resistance—"

"Poor fella," Sam drawled.

Russ scowled. "Tell me you wouldn't even consider it," he snapped. "After months of some woman pretty much throwing herself at you, tell me you wouldn't think about giving in."

Phyllis thought about the way Eve had pursued Sam so diligently ever since the day he had moved into the house, and she waited with interest for his answer.

He didn't give one. Instead, he said, "We're talkin' about you, not me, friend."

Phyllis tried not to think about the way Sam had dodged the question. She said, "So you just had lunch with Shannon that day? That's all?"

"That's all," Russ said firmly.

"She didn't press you for an answer?"

"She did, but I told her I was still thinking about it. She said . . . she said I'd better make up my mind pretty soon. She said the offer wouldn't be on the table forever."

"And Marie didn't know that any of this was going on?"

"Good Lord, no. If she did, she would have blown her stack. There's no telling what she might have—" Russ stopped short and stared across the table, his eyes widening almost more than seemed humanly possible. "No! No, you can't mean . . . you can't think—"

His voice was rising. Sam cut in, "Settle down, son. You don't want to be drawin' attention to yourself."

Russ shook his head emphatically. "You've got the wrong idea. Marie didn't know, but even if she had, she wouldn't have done anything to hurt Shannon. They were friends."

"Friends or not, Shannon was trying to have an affair with you."

"Oh, Lord." Russ closed his eyes for a second and rubbed vigorously at his temples with both hands. "If Marie had found out, she would have yelled at me for even *thinking* about it. She would have yelled at Shannon and probably refused to have anything more to do with her. But that's it. She would never hurt anybody. I thought you were trying to pin the murder on me, but it was Marie you were after all along, wasn't it?"

"We're not *after* anybody," Phyllis told him. "We don't have any legal authority. I just wanted to know the truth about what I saw that day."

"I've told you the truth." Russ leaned forward over the table. "Please don't say anything to anybody else, Mrs. Newsom. Nothing happened between me and Shannon. I swear it. We just had lunch together that one time. That's all."

"Well . . ."

"Please," he said miserably. "If Marie finds out that I was even considering cheating on her . . . Wait a minute. I didn't mean that the way it was starting to sound again. I just don't want anything to threaten my marriage."

Sam said, "You've got a funny way of showin' it."

Anger flared briefly in Russ's eyes. "I didn't—" He subsided and took a deep breath. "You're right. I should have put a stop to it as soon as Shannon brought the subject up. I wish I had. But I didn't, and there's nothing I can do now to change that." He looked at Phyllis. "All I can do is hope that you'll keep this to yourself, for Marie's sake."

She knew he was looking for a promise from her. She couldn't make that commitment—not as long as the case was still unsolved—but at least now she was inclined to believe him.

"I'll have to think about it," she hedged. "My son is a deputy sheriff, you know, and by not telling him, I'm withholding evidence. Not only that, but now I've made Sam here an accessory to that, too."

"Don't worry about me," Sam told her without hesitation. "You just do whatever you think is right, Phyllis. I'll back you all the way."

She smiled at him. "Thank you." She looked at Russ again.

"I'm not going to say anything . . . for now. But you know what you need to do?"

"What?" he asked warily.

"You need to tell Marie about it yourself."

"I couldn't do that. I just couldn't."

"Why not, if you didn't do anything wrong?"

Russ didn't have an answer. He slumped back against the seat and muttered something.

"I know you don't want to hurt her," Phyllis said, "but if this comes out, she'll be a lot more hurt by knowing that you lied to her."

"I didn't lie to her. I never told her anything, one way or the other."

"It's the same thing as lying."

He sighed and shrugged. "I'll think about it."

Phyllis reached for her purse. They were done here. When she opened it and took out some bills, Russ said, "No, I've got the coffee. Since you're not blackmailing me, it's the least I can do."

"You've still got too big a mouth on you, Teasipper," Sam said.

Russ didn't say anything, and Phyllis and Sam slid out of the booth and left him sitting there, staring dispiritedly at the table.

"What do you think?" Phyllis asked when they were back in the car and heading toward Weatherford again. "Was he telling the truth?"

"About what part of it?" Sam said.

"Any of it. Was he having an affair with Shannon or not?"

Sam considered for a moment, then said, "Hard to be sure either way. He strikes me as a fella who's not just real good at resistin' temptation. But he *could've* been tellin' the truth."

"It's hard to believe that Shannon would chase after him like that."

"Now that part of it, I reckon I believe. More than once

when I was coachin', the mama of one of my players would come up to me and flat-out proposition me."

Phyllis glanced over at him. "You're kidding. I can't imagine a woman acting that way."

He nodded solemnly. "It happens. Lucky for me I was a happily married man."

And that happy marriage had continued right up until the day that cancer had claimed Sam's wife, Phyllis knew. Once in a while she caught glimpses of the pain that still lurked in his eyes.

"What do we do now?" she asked. "If there was no affair, would Russ or Marie or Joel Dunston have any motive for killing Shannon?"

"What if Shannon was gettin' tired of Tyler puttin' her off?" Sam suggested. "What if she told him to either go along with what she wanted, or she'd tell Marie they'd been doin' it anyway?"

"Russ really didn't want Marie to find out about it." Phyllis nodded slowly. "Shannon had a history of doing whatever was necessary to get what she wanted. I wouldn't put it past her to threaten Russ like that."

"So there's your motive again," Sam said. "Or maybe Shannon's ex-husband found out what she was up to and *thought* that she'd been carryin' on with Tyler all along, even when they were still married. There's another one."

Phyllis sighed in exasperation. "So even if everything Russ told us is true, we didn't really eliminate anyone as a suspect, did we?"

"Not as far as I can see."

"Then what, exactly, did we accomplish?"

"Well, we annoyed a Teasipper," Sam said. "That's always worth somethin'."

Chapter 22

Late that afternoon, Mike stopped by the house. "I can't stay very long," he said as he took off his hat and sat down in the living room with Phyllis and Sam. "Tonight's Halloween, and I want to get home in time to take Bobby trick-or-treating. He was too young to go last year, but he ought to enjoy it this year."

Phyllis thought that her grandson was probably still too young to know what would be going on, but she figured Mike was enthusiastic enough that it wouldn't matter. Tonight was more for him than it would be for Bobby. And for the cute pictures to put into the family photo albums, of course.

"Bring him by here if you get a chance," she said with a smile. "I want to see him in his costume."

"Okay." Mike turned his hat over a couple of times, and Phyllis knew he was about to get to the real reason for his visit. "We got a search warrant for Gary Oakley's house and had a good look around. He rents a place out on Peaster Highway."

"What did you find?" Sam asked.

"Well, we were looking for that PTO cash box, or any of the things that were stolen from the school in that earlier burglary. The sheriff figured that if we found any of that stuff in Mr. Oakley's possession, that would be the last bit of evidence we needed to convince the DA to charge him with murder."

"Loot from the previous burglary wouldn't establish that he was in the school office on Saturday and took that cash box," Sam pointed out.

"That's right, but it doesn't really matter."

"Because you didn't find anything," Sam guessed.

"Not a thing," Mike admitted with a sigh. "There were specific items we were looking for that were listed on the warrant, but we tossed the place pretty thoroughly, of course, just in case he had anything else he shouldn't have. The place was clean. No guns, drugs, or anything else that an ex-convict shouldn't have. Based on that search, we couldn't even charge him with animal cruelty, because those three dogs of his are all healthy and well cared for. Their vaccinations are even up to date."

"So it looks like Gary was tellin' the truth when he said he's gone straight since he got out of prison."

Mike nodded. "So it appears. Other than lying on his job applications. That can be prosecuted as a felony."

Sam sat up in his chair and frowned. "Will he go back to prison for that?"

"It's possible," Mike replied with a shrug. "Depends on how good a lawyer he gets, and what sort of mood the judge is in. It helps that he's lived a good clean life for the past several years."

"What about the murder charge?" Phyllis asked.

"The sheriff's not happy about it, but I don't think there's going to be one. There's just not enough evidence for the district attorney to proceed . . . even though he might be able to get a conviction just from the fact that Mr. Oakley lied about being an ex-con and was working at an elementary school. A jury wouldn't like that, and would be eager to believe the worst about him. So there's still a chance the DA might decide to go ahead with it. We can keep Mr. Oakley in custody until tomorrow for questioning."

"That's not the right thing to do," Sam said. "You know he didn't do it. What about the knife?"

"He was in and out of the cafeteria all day. He would have had plenty of chances to pick it up without anybody noticing."

"But why would he do that?" Phyllis asked. "What reason would anybody have to steal a knife from the cafeteria unless they were planning to use it to commit a murder?"

"You're looking at the question from hindsight," Mike pointed out. "We know the knife *was* used to kill Mrs. Dunston, so we think the murderer must have planned it that way all along. But we can't be sure of that. Maybe the killer took the knife for some other reason and just happened to have it on him when he decided to use it as a murder weapon."

Phyllis leaned back in her chair and shook her head. "That seems awfully far-fetched to me," she said. "Look at the way the killer also wiped the knife clean and then brought it back to the cafeteria. The whole thing was premeditated, Mike. I'm sure of it."

"I think you're right," he agreed, "but there's still a matter of proving it."

Sam clasped his hands together between his knees as he said, "All right, so where it stands now is that you don't have any real evidence against Gary for the murder or the burglary, and you're probably gonna have to let him go."

"You didn't hear it from me . . . but yeah, that's about the size of it."

"So you're no closer to finding the real killer?"

"Not as far as I can see," Mike admitted. "But again, you didn't hear it from me. The sheriff wouldn't want me to be here even talking to you about the case."

Phyllis said, "Maybe you'd better stop doing it, then. I don't want you to get in any trouble on your job."

Mike shrugged. "I'm off duty," he said, "and besides, it doesn't hurt anything to run all this past you, Mom. You sometimes notice things that I don't."

"That's because I was a history teacher for all those years. History is nothing but cause and effect, and you see the same patterns being repeated over and over."

"Well, if you can see a pattern in this, I'd be glad to hear about it."

Phyllis and Sam exchanged a glance. She knew he was thinking about their conversation with Russ Tyler earlier in the afternoon. Phyllis wrestled with her conscience. She had hoped that talking to Russ would help her make a decision about how she should proceed, but instead it had just muddled things even more.

Finally, in response to Mike's comment she said, "I'll mull it over, and if anything occurs to me I'll let you know."

He stood up. "Thanks, Mom. I'll be back this evening with Sarah and Bobby."

"What's his costume going to be?"

Mike smiled. "Wouldn't you rather wait and be surprised?"

"Oh, I suppose so," she said with a laugh. "I'll see you later."

After Mike was gone, Sam looked over at Phyllis but didn't say anything. "I appreciate what you did," she said. "Keeping quiet about Russ and Shannon, I mean."

"I knew what you meant," he said. "Just because we didn't say anything doesn't really change the situation, though."

"I know. If Russ goes to Marie and tells her himself about what Shannon was doing, then maybe I can tell Mike. That way I won't be responsible for whatever happens with Russ and Marie's marriage."

Sam grunted. "Russ isn't gonna tell her."

"But I pointed out to him that he ought to."

"Doesn't matter," Sam said with a shake of his head. "He's not gonna paint a big target on his back like that. Shoot, if a man told his wife every time he *thought* about carryin' on with another woman, he'd be in the doghouse all the time."

"Really?"

Sam nodded solemnly.

"Men think about it that much?"

"I reckon most do. A fella learns real early that when it comes to women, he'd best worry more about what he *does,* not what he thinks. Any other way lies madness."

"Well, being around you is certainly an education in the male psyche, Sam. What other deep dark secret thoughts are you hiding in that brain of yours?"

"You don't want to know," he said as he stood up.

That was the problem, Phyllis thought. She *did* want to know.

True to his word, Mike brought Sarah and Bobby by the house that evening, after they had gone trick-or-treating in their own neighborhood. When he walked in carrying Bobby, Phyllis smiled at the hat, vest, chaps, and boots her grandson was wearing. "He's a cowboy!" she said. "And he's just adorable."

"The old classics never go out of style, I reckon," Sam added with a grin. "Did you make a big haul, pardner?"

Bobby shook the treat bag he was carrying and burbled, "Candy!"

"Yes, I know." A few trick-or-treaters had come by the house earlier, and Phyllis still had a bowl of candy by the door. She picked it up and held it so that Bobby could see it. "What do you say?"

The little boy made a grab for a lime sucker with a safety loop instead of a stick. "Want candy!"

Mike gently pulled him back. "No, no, what are you supposed to say?"

Sarah leaned over to whisper in her son's ear. Bobby yelled, "Trickertreat!"

"That's it," Phyllis said. She picked up the green lollipop and held it out so that Bobby could grab it.

Mike prodded him, "Now what do you say?"

Bobby looked like he wanted to cram the sucker in his mouth, wrapper and all, but he mumbled, "Tankoo."

"You're welcome," Phyllis told him.

Sarah said, "We're perpetuating archaic stereotypes and outdated traditions, you know."

Mike grinned. "Yeah. Ain't it fun?"

It was an enjoyable visit, and Phyllis was glad she could spend the time just being with her family and friends, rather than thinking about murder and the moral dilemma she faced. As Mike was about to leave, she started to grab his arm and tell him she needed to talk to him for a few minutes in private, but she stopped herself before she could do that.

Let it go until morning, she told herself. That would give her a chance to sleep on it. No harm could come of waiting a little while longer.

The phone rang right after breakfast the next morning. When Phyllis answered it, she heard Marie Tyler's voice on the other end. Marie sounded upset, and Phyllis thought, *Sam was wrong. Russ told her about Shannon after all.*

But Marie's news took Phyllis completely by surprise. "The sheriff has arrested Lindsey," she said.

"Lindsey?" Phyllis repeated. "You mean Lindsey Gonzales? What in the world for?" Even as the question left her mouth, she realized that she probably knew the answer.

"Someone said they saw her having a terrible argument with Shannon not long before she was killed. Now they think . . . Lord, I can hardly bring myself to say it. They think Lindsey might have killed her."

Phyllis remembered the pain and the anger she had seen in Lindsey's eyes at that board meeting when Shannon had laced into her about the posters. From what she had heard, it wasn't unusual for Shannon to treat Lindsey like that. And evidently Lindsey accepted that abuse because she was afraid of Shannon.

But afraid or not, when people were mistreated, sooner or later they would turn on their abusers. And often, the longer the situation went on, the more extreme the inevitable outburst finally was.

Once again, though, Phyllis was faced with the feeling that a suspect in Shannon's murder just wasn't the sort of person who could kill anyone. She didn't know Lindsey well at all, she reminded herself. She couldn't really say what the woman might be capable of.

"What are we going to do, Phyllis?" Marie was saying. She hadn't asked to speak to Carolyn. Evidently she had gone from being Carolyn's friend to considering Phyllis one as well.

"I don't know that there's anything we *can* do," Phyllis told her. "How did you find out about it?"

"I saw the whole thing," Marie said, her voice shaking slightly. "A couple of deputies were waiting for Lindsey when she came out of the school this morning. She had just dropped her son off. I guess the deputies must have gone to her house, and when they didn't find anybody at home, they decided she was at the school and went there to wait for her."

"They didn't put her in handcuffs or anything like that, did they?" Phyllis remembered Mike's description of how he and the other deputies had been forced to subdue Gary Oakley and take him out of the school in cuffs.

"No, she just went with them. I had just gotten there with Amber and Aaron, so I sent them on into the school and hurried over to see what was going on. One of the deputies told me Lindsey was being taken in for questioning."

"See, she hasn't really been arrested," Phyllis said, searching for something positive in this news. "They're just talking to her."

"It was more than that," Marie said heavily. "I could tell by the deputies' expressions. And Lindsey was scared, too—really scared." She paused, then asked, "Do you think she could have done it?"

"You know her a lot better than I do," Phyllis said. "But I wouldn't think so."

"I hope she's got a good lawyer. Even when you're innocent, you need a really good lawyer these days when the cops go after you. No offense. I know your son's a deputy."

Phyllis wondered if Mike had been one of the deputies who took Lindsey in for questioning. She would find out later, she supposed.

"I guess I knew there's really nothing we can do," Marie went on. "I just had to talk to somebody about it, and I didn't want to bother Russ at work. There's just been so many bad things happening lately, what with Shannon being killed and all, and now this. . . ."

"What about at home?" Phyllis asked.

"What?" Marie sounded surprised and confused. "What do you mean? Everything's fine at home. Thank God for that. With everything else that's going on, I don't need any family uproars."

Sam must have been right after all, Phyllis thought. Russ hadn't told Marie about the way Shannon had tried to pressure him into having an affair with her. Phyllis was a little disappointed in Russ. He should have done the right thing.

She could take care of that for him, if she wanted to.

But even as the thought crossed her mind, she knew she wasn't going to say anything to Marie about it. Marie was right; she had enough on her mind right now. Anyway, Phyllis reminded herself, it was really none of her business. What went on between Marie and Russ was personal.

At least, it would have been if it didn't have any possible bearing on a murder case.

"On top of everything else," Marie went on, "the money that was stolen during the carnival is still missing. Sometime we all need to get together and talk about how we're going to deal with the shortfall in funds for the rest of the school year."

"That's something for you and the rest of the board to discuss," Phyllis said. "Are you taking charge of it now that Shannon is . . . gone?"

"I guess so. According to the bylaws, the fund-raising chairman is also the vice president. But if anybody else wants the job, they can have it." Marie laughed hollowly, without any real humor. "Yeah, like that's gonna happen."

"I wish you the best of luck with it—"

"Maybe you and Carolyn could come to the next meeting?" Marie broke in. "I hate to ask such a big favor of you, but we're going to need some advice from older and wiser heads. No offense about the older part."

"None taken. But we're not members of the board. We're not even members of the PTO. It just wouldn't be proper for us to horn in—"

"Consultants," Marie said. "That's what you'd be. Businesses hire consultants all the time. There's no reason why the PTO board shouldn't do the same thing. Although we can't actually hire you, of course. You'd have to volunteer." She paused. "Come on, Phyllis. I could sure use a hand."

"Well . . . I'll talk to Carolyn." Marie was more adept at this than she thought, Phyllis mused. Already she was learning how to talk people into doing what she wanted and helping her. "I can't make any promises, though."

"That's fine. I'll be in touch and let you know when we're getting together. Maybe by then we'll know more about what's happening with Lindsey."

Phyllis was curious about that herself. If Lindsey Gonzales was the killer, there was a chance this whole horrible experience would soon be over, and she could stop worrying about what she should—or shouldn't—tell the authorities.

Chapter 23

One last time, Mike was going over the inventory of items that had been found during the search of Gary Oakley's house, searching for *anything* that the sheriff could use to justify holding the custodian longer.

Former custodian, Mike supposed he should say, since it was a foregone conclusion that Oakley would be terminated from his job at Loving Elementary, if he hadn't been already. He would be lucky just to keep his freedom. Being charged with a felony could result in the revocation of his parole and mean that he would have to go back to Huntsville to serve out the remainder of his original sentence for the prior burglary conviction.

Sheriff Haney would have preferred sending Oakley to the penitentiary for murder, though, so he had ordered Mike to go over the results of the search again. Although Mike didn't know for sure, he suspected that the district attorney had told Haney to either come up with more evidence right away or else let Oakley go.

It looked like the sheriff was going to be disappointed, because for the life of him, Mike couldn't see anything in the report to indicate that Oakley was guilty of anything.

The door into the office where Mike was working swung open, and when he glanced up he saw Sheriff Haney standing there. "You've been part of this investigation all along, Mike," the sheriff said. "Come with me."

Mike pushed the papers aside and got to his feet. "Has there been some new development, Sheriff?"

"You could say that." Haney gave him a smug grin. "We've brought in another suspect for questioning."

Mike couldn't stop his eyebrows from lifting. He hadn't heard anything about another arrest being imminent, even if it was just someone being brought in for questioning.

Haney didn't pause to explain. He strode down the hall toward the interrogation room with Mike following closely behind him. They went into an observation room. On the right-hand wall was a sheet of one-way glass. Mike looked through it and saw a young blond woman sitting at the table in the adjacent interrogation room, looking scared and panicky. She was familiar to Mike, but he couldn't recall her name.

Sheriff Haney supplied it without being asked. "Lindsey Gonzales," he said. "She's one of the members of the PTO board at Loving Elementary."

"The one who found the body," Mike said, remembering Lindsey now.

"That's right. And mighty convenient that she did, too, since we know now she had an argument with the murdered woman not long before that."

Mike frowned and said, "Sheriff, I hate to point this out, but there could be a lot of people who had arguments with Mrs. Dunston that day. She ran roughshod over most folks she dealt with."

"She's the only one where we have eyewitness testimony that she screamed at Mrs. Dunston and threatened to kill her."

Mike had to admit that was a pretty good point, and probably reason enough to ask Lindsey some questions. But he was still curious. "How come we didn't know about this eyewitness until now? If somebody saw that happening on Saturday, shouldn't they have said something about it when we questioned everybody that day?"

"Yeah, but the guy didn't come forward until this morning. You know how people are, Mike. They don't want to get involved, or they don't think that what they saw or heard could really be important. In this case, the guy who saw the argument has a little girl in the same kindergarten class as Mrs. Gonzales's son. So he knows her and didn't think she would kill anybody. But he kept worrying about it and finally decided he'd better talk to us. I took his statement myself."

"What was the argument about?"

"The witness didn't have any idea. He just saw the two of them yelling at each other in that hallway, near the place where the Dunston woman's body was found a short time later. He claims Gonzales was saying that she wasn't going to take Dunston's crap anymore and that she was tired of getting all the blame for everything. She told Dunston to lay off or she'd kill her."

"And then Mrs. Gonzales was the one who found the body."

"Yeah," the sheriff said. "She never really explained what she was doing up at the end of that hall, either. She said she was just wandering around the school because she wanted to get away from the noise of the carnival for a little while. I think what she really wanted to do was make sure she was the one who stumbled over the body, so nobody would think that she had anything to do with it."

It could have been like that, Mike thought, but he reminded himself that only a day earlier Sheriff Haney had been just as convinced that Gary Oakley was guilty. He wanted to hear what Mrs. Gonzales had to say before he made up his mind one way or the other.

"What are we waiting for?" he asked.

Haney nodded toward the one-way glass and the scared woman on the other side of it. "She refused to answer any questions without her attorney being present." He nodded solemnly. "Lawyered up."

Mike couldn't stop himself. "Sheriff, did you ever say that before all the police procedural shows on TV?"

"What?" Haney frowned at him.

"*Lawyered up.* It just sounds like something they'd say in New York, not Weatherford."

"What the hell are you—"

A knock sounded on the door of the room before the sheriff could go on. The door opened as he and Mike turned toward it, and a deputy stuck his head in to say, "The lady's lawyer is here, Sheriff."

"Tell him we'll be there in a second," Haney said.

"He's a her," the deputy replied. "Juliette Yorke, with an E."

"Whatever."

Wisely, Mike refrained from asking the sheriff if he used to say *whatever.*

They left the observation room. A woman in her forties stood beside the door of the interrogation room where Lindsey Gonzales waited nervously. The attorney wore a dark brown suit and sensible heels, and had her light brown hair pulled back into a ponytail. She held an inexpensive briefcase in her left hand. Silver-rimmed glasses perched on her nose. Intense green eyes peered through them.

"Sheriff Haney," she said as she put out a hand, "I'm Juliette Yorke. With an E."

"Pleased to meet you, Ms. Yorke," Haney said as he shook hands with her. "I don't believe we've run into each other before."

The attorney shook her head. "No, I haven't been practicing in Weatherford for very long. I moved down here a short time ago from Pennsylvania."

The sheriff frowned slightly and said, "You're not Ms. Gonzales's regular attorney?"

"No, I've never met her. I assume she doesn't have a regular attorney."

"Then, no offense, why did she call you?"

"I have no idea." Juliette Yorke was all business. "Can you get me up to speed on this case, Sheriff?"

"Yeah, sure." Haney glanced over his shoulder and seemed to remember that Mike was there. "Uh, this is Deputy Mike Newsom. He's one of the investigators heading up my team."

That was the first time Mike had known that he was heading up anything. He nodded politely and said, "Ms. Yorke."

Curtly, Yorke returned the nod, then swung her gaze back to Haney. "What's my client being charged with?"

"She's not being charged with anything yet. We brought her in for questioning in the murder of Shannon Dunston."

For the first time in this conversation, Juliette Yorke's expression changed from a cool blank. She frowned slightly and said, "The woman who was killed at that school carnival a few days ago?"

"That's right. You read about it in the paper?"

"Yes, I did. I didn't realize this was in relation to a murder case."

"Well, it is. That gonna be a problem?"

Yorke shook her head. "No, of course not. You believe my client is the killer?"

Confidently, Haney said, "We have a statement from a witness who saw Ms. Gonzales having a violent argument with the victim a short time before the murder took place. Not only that, but Ms. Gonzales was the one who 'found' the body."

Yorke picked up on the emphasis the sheriff put on the word. "The person who discovers a body isn't necessarily a suspect," she said.

"But it's funny how it works out that way a lot of the time, isn't it?"

Yorke didn't reply to that. She said, "Have you questioned her at all? Was she advised of her rights?"

"Absolutely she was," Haney declared. "When you've been around here for a while, you'll know that we're not slipshod about procedural matters, Ms. Yorke. Mrs. Gonzales requested that we not ask her any questions until she had legal counsel present, so we waited to talk to her. Now that you're here"—he leaned his head toward the door of the interrogation room—"why don't we go see what she has to say?"

"Of course. I'll want a moment alone with her first, though."

Haney's mouth tightened a little, but he didn't hesitate before nodding and saying, "Sure. That's her right. Just don't make it too long."

"We'll try not to delay your interrogation too much, Sheriff," Yorke returned.

Mike could tell that Haney didn't like that much, either, but he just opened the door of the interrogation room and held out a hand for the attorney to go right ahead. Yorke went inside and Haney pulled the door closed. "I hope she tells the woman it'll go easier on her if she cooperates with us."

"Unless Mrs. Gonzales didn't have anything to do with the murder," Mike said.

Haney shook his head. "Not likely. But we don't rush to judgment around here."

It seemed to Mike that was exactly what Haney was doing yet again, after jumping to the conclusion that Gary Oakley was guilty. But he knew what the sheriff meant. Under normal circumstances, Royce Haney was a solid, more than competent lawman. He had to be feeling a lot of public pressure, though, because a murder being committed in an elementary school—in the middle of a school carnival, at that—really got people's attention.

They stood there in the hall waiting for several minutes before the door opened again and Juliette Yorke said, "My client is ready to talk to you now, Sheriff."

Haney went into the room, followed by Mike. They all sat down, the two lawmen on one side of the table, Lindsey Gonzales and her attorney on the other. The sheriff started the tape rolling in the recorder and announced the details of the interrogation. Then before he could ask any questions, Yorke said, "My client would like to make a statement."

Haney leaned forward eagerly. Mike knew he was antici-
pating a confession. "All right. Go ahead, Mrs. Gonzales."

Lindsey still looked pale and scared, but her voice was relatively strong as she cleared her throat and said, "I did not
kill Shannon Dunston. I had nothing to do with her death."

Haney's expression hardened. "We have eyewitness testimony that you were engaged in an argument with her not
long before her death and even threatened to kill her. Then
you were the one who found the body and started screaming
your head off so everyone would know you found it."

Lindsey took a deep breath and said, "I did not kill Shannon Dunston and had nothing to do with her death."

Haney's expression was darkening with anger as he
switched his gaze to Juliette Yorke and said, "Counselor, you
should advise your client that it would be wise to answer our
questions."

"You haven't actually asked her any questions," Yorke
pointed out. "You've simply made a statement, Sheriff, and
so has my client. One that covers things sufficiently, I believe."

Haney sat back in his chair, looking stunned. "What do
you mean?"

"I mean that Mrs. Gonzales has denied any involvement
with Ms. Dunston's murder, and she won't be making any
further statements or answering any questions. Since that's
the case, I suggest that unless you have any actual evidence
against her, you release her now."

"But . . . but we have a witness's testimony—"

"That an argument took place. Does your witness claim to
have seen my client kill, attack, or otherwise harm the victim
in any way?"

"Well . . . no."

"Do you have any physical evidence to link my client to
the actual crime?"

"No," Haney snapped. "But I have a history of ill feeling
between the victim and your client, and I have the testimony

regarding that argument . . . which I notice your client hasn't denied." A note of stubbornness came into his voice. "That's probable cause to bring her in for questioning."

"We're not denying that. But Mrs. Gonzales has cooperated with your investigation and now has nothing more to add."

"Damn it, stonewalling's not going to get her anywhere!"

Juliette Yorke didn't appear to be fazed by the sheriff's frustrated outburst. She said, "On the contrary, it's going to get her out of here . . . unless, as I said, you have some other evidence against her."

With a visible effort, Haney brought his anger under control. He turned to Lindsey and said, "Mrs. Gonzales, did you see anyone attack Shannon Dunston on the afternoon of the carnival at Oliver Loving Elementary School?"

Lindsey glanced over at Yorke, who nodded. Lindsey swallowed and said, "No, I didn't."

"Just before you discovered her body, did you see anyone leaving the area?"

Lindsey shook her head. "No."

"You walked up that hall, didn't see anyone around, went around the corner, and found Ms. Dunston's body?"

A little shudder went through Lindsey's body as she closed her eyes, obviously remembering the scene. "Yes," she replied in a half whisper.

"And when you saw the body you started screaming?"

Lindsey nodded. "Yes." She glanced at Yorke, who gave her a tight but reassuring smile.

"Do you know of any reason why someone would want to kill Shannon Dunston?" Haney asked.

"No," Lindsey answered without hesitation. She added, "A lot of people didn't get along with her, including me, but I don't know anyone who wanted her dead."

Mike saw a flash of irritation in Juliette Yorke's eyes, as if the attorney wished that Lindsey hadn't added that last comment, but Yorke didn't say anything.

Haney turned toward her and said, "*Now* your client has cooperated with our investigation."

"So you're going to release her?"

"Wait here," Haney said as he got to his feet. He didn't have to tell Mike to come with him. They stepped out into the hall and closed the door behind them.

"Are you going to let her go, Sheriff?" Mike asked.

"We can hold her for a while without charging her—" Haney stopped and shook his head. "But what would be the point? That woman's not gonna let her say anything else, and the evidence we have now isn't strong enough to get the DA to bring charges."

Mike was glad to see that the sheriff was going to be reasonable about this. He knew that Haney wasn't really a vindictive man by nature. Clearly, the sheriff didn't like Juliette Yorke very much, but he was professional enough not to let that influence his decision.

Haney nodded as he made up his mind. "Go back in there and tell them they can go," he said. "Warn Mrs. Gonzales not to leave the area without letting us know, though."

"Sure."

Mike waited until Haney had gone back down the hall to his office; then he opened the door of the interrogation room again. Lindsey looked up anxiously from the table.

"The sheriff said for me to tell you that you're free to go, Mrs. Gonzales, and he also thanks you for your cooperation," Mike said. Haney hadn't said any such thing as that last part, but Mike figured it wouldn't hurt anything to add it. "Please don't leave the area without letting us know first, though."

"Does that mean I'm still a suspect?"

"We just, uh, might want to ask you a few more questions."

Juliette Yorke got to her feet and picked up her briefcase from the table. "I assume that the sheriff won't be unreasonable about this matter?"

"No, ma'am."

Lindsey said, "I know your mother, you know."

"Yes, ma'am," Mike said. Lindsey's comment struck him as odd. It was the sort of thing a grown-up would say to a child, and she probably wasn't more than two or three years older than he was.

"Ask her if she thinks I'd kill anybody," Lindsey said. She was starting to look angry now, and she might have gone on to say something else if Yorke hadn't touched her arm and murmured that they should be going.

Mike couldn't really blame Lindsey for being mad, he thought as he perched a hip on the table and watched the two women leave the interrogation room. Somebody who was innocent never liked being accused of a crime. Their first reaction was usually fear, as Lindsey's had been, but once that started to wear off, they began to get angry that anyone could believe such a thing of them. Law enforcement officers saw similar reactions all the time. In this case, Lindsey's anger tended to make Mike think she was telling the truth.

Or maybe she was just a good liar and actress. Maybe she really had gotten mad enough to stick that knife in Shannon Dunston's chest.

Haney appeared in the doorway. "They gone?"

"Yes, sir."

"Find out everything you can about that woman. And about all the other members of the PTO board, too. And everybody else who had any possible connection to Ms. Dunston." Haney shook his head. "That woman," he said again.

"Mrs. Gonzales, you mean?"

"The lawyer," Haney said.

Mike couldn't tell what he heard more of in the sheriff's voice—anger or admiration.

Chapter 24

The call from Marie came sooner than Phyllis expected. "We're getting together at the school this afternoon," the younger woman said. "Can you and Carolyn make it?"

Phyllis had already talked to Carolyn, who was reluctant to continue their involvement with the PTO board, but felt like they could do some good by helping out. "We'll just give them some advice and let that be it," she had said when Phyllis told her about Marie's earlier phone call.

Now Phyllis told Marie, "All right, this one time. But really, you and the other members of the board will have to decide what to do."

"Sure, we know that," Marie said. "We'll see you at one thirty."

Phyllis went upstairs and told Carolyn about the meeting. Carolyn said, "I'm starting to believe Marie thinks of you and me as surrogate mothers. She wants us to tell her how to fix things."

Phyllis nodded. She had a feeling that Carolyn was right. Marie was in over her head these days. Unfortunately, things were even worse than Marie thought they were, because she didn't even know about her husband's involvement with Shannon.

Nothing had really happened between Shannon and Russ, Phyllis reminded herself. At least, that was what Russ had claimed. And Phyllis was going to make herself believe it until she had evidence to the contrary.

Carolyn asked, "Did Marie say anything else about Lindsey?"

Phyllis shook her head. "I guess she hasn't heard anything more. It can take quite a while when someone is brought in for questioning, I suppose."

But to her surprise, when she and Carolyn walked into the meeting room at the school that afternoon, Lindsey Gonzales was sitting there at the table with the other members of the PTO board. Lindsey's face was pale and drawn, as if she'd been through an ordeal, but otherwise she seemed to be all right.

Of course she was all right, Phyllis told herself as that thought crossed her mind. It wasn't like members of the sheriff's department shone bright lights in the eyes of suspects and beat them with rubber hoses. Things like that only happened in old black-and-white movies.

Phyllis noticed how Lindsey looked away from her as she and Carolyn sat down. An awkward silence had fallen on the room as they entered. She said, "I'm sorry. If you'd like for Carolyn and me to go, or just me—"

"Of course not," Marie said quickly. "We need you here. Isn't that right, Lindsey?"

"Yes." Lindsey met Phyllis's eyes and went on, "We were just talking about it, so we might as well go ahead and get it over with. Clear the air. I'm not mad at you, Mrs. Newsom, or your son. He was there, but he was just following the sheriff's orders, I'm sure. I don't think he really believed I was guilty."

"Mike's always prided himself on doing his job properly."

"Well, you can tell him for me that I didn't kill Shannon. That's about all my lawyer will let me say."

"They didn't charge you?" If Lindsey was willing to talk about it, Phyllis certainly was, too.

Lindsey shook her head. "No. They didn't have any real evidence against me, just somebody who said they saw me arguing with Shannon earlier that afternoon. And that part was true." A note of defiance came into Lindsey's voice. "I finally got fed up with the way she treated me all the time and told her to stop it."

Kristina Padgett said, "Good for you. It was about time somebody stood up to her."

Holly Underwood looked around the table and said, "I think all of us here probably wanted to tell Shannon off more than once."

"I would have," Irene Vernon said, "if I hadn't been afraid that it would just make things worse."

"Look," Abby Granger put in. "Shannon was a bitch, no two ways about it. All of us knew it, none of us liked her, and I don't mind saying it now." She looked at Phyllis. "But none of us would have killed her. No way. You should tell your son that."

Phyllis began to feel a little irritated. "I'm not here working as a spy for the sheriff's department, if that's what you're all thinking. Marie asked Carolyn and me to come to this meeting."

"That's right. I did," Marie said. "Please don't get mad, Phyllis. We're all just shaken up by what's happened." She looked around the table and went on, "Why don't we put the tragedy aside for now and get down to business? The carnival was a major fund-raiser, and it looks like most of that money is gone for good. How are we going to replace it?"

"I don't know that we can," Holly said. "The parents won't sit still for it if we try to hold some other fund-raising event right away. They'll be sorry about Shannon, of course, and sorry that the money got stolen, but they feel like they've already done their part for a while."

Marie said, "Surely they would understand—"

"I've had four kids go through the school system," Holly stopped her. "When you're already struggling with taxes and credit card debt and house payments, you get tired of the PTO coming around with their hands out for more money, even though you know it's for a good cause. There's *always* a good cause that needs money."

A couple of the other women nodded in solemn agreement. Kristina shrugged and said, "Maybe we just won't do as much for the school this year as other boards have. It's not our fault."

"We can have something else in the spring," Abby suggested. "A pancake supper or spaghetti supper or something like that. That'll replace some of the money. But for now I think we just have to let it go."

Marie looked disappointed. Clearly she had hoped for a more enthusiastic response. She turned to Phyllis and Carolyn and asked, "What do you ladies think?"

Carolyn said, "Holly's right about the constant fundraising from all the different groups. We saw it as teachers. We always bought the PTO candy, too."

"It's true that the school relies on the PTO to provide things that the budget just doesn't have room for," Phyllis said. "But nobody's going to blame you if you just don't have the money. Like Christina said, it's not your fault."

"No, it's the fault of the son of a bitch who stole that cash box," Marie snapped. "And because of that, we're going to wind up letting Shannon's memory down."

She might not be so worried about Shannon's memory, Phyllis thought, if she knew that Shannon had been trying to get Russ to have an affair with her.

Something else was nudging at Phyllis's brain. She said, "You were collecting the money during the carnival and locking it up in the cash box, weren't you, Marie?"

"That's right," Marie said with a nod. "What about it?"

"It's just that Shannon's daughter heard her say something about the cash box not long before . . . well, before what happened. That's why the sheriff thought that maybe Shannon caught the thief in the act. But why would she have been going into the office if you were the one responsible for collecting the money?"

"Oh, it wasn't really that formal," Marie said. "Maybe somebody at the ticket booth or the concession stand thought they were getting too much cash on hand and gave some of it to Shannon to deal with. Or maybe she just wanted to check and see how we were doing. She was the president, after all. There wouldn't have been anything un- usual about her doing a quick count of the take."

Phyllis nodded, feeling a little disappointed. She had thought there might be something unusual about Shannon's involvement with the cash box that would point in the direc- tion of the murderer. But instead, it was just business as usual. Shannon had had every right to go to the office and check on the money.

"I heard that Mr. Oakley, the custodian, was a criminal," Irene said. "Wasn't he arrested here at the school?"

"Yeah, but they let him go," Abby said. "They must not have had any real evidence against him."

Marie said excitedly, "Wait a minute. I just thought of something. If whoever took the money killed Shannon, then maybe if we could find the murderer we might be able to get at least some of that money back!"

The other board members stared at her. Kristina said, "Are you saying that *we* should investigate the murder? We're not detectives."

"Phyllis is." Marie pointed at her.

"Hold on," Phyllis began.

"Carolyn told me how you solved that murder at the Peach Festival last summer," Marie went on. "And your son's a deputy sheriff. You could tell us how to go about in- vestigating a crime."

Phyllis looked over at Carolyn, who shrugged and said, "I know there was nothing in the paper about your involve- ment with solving those other cases, but I didn't see what harm there would be in mentioning it. After all, you saved *me* from being arrested. I was grateful."

It was too late to worry about such things now. The damage was already done. But it could get worse, Phyllis realized. The sheriff really *would* be unhappy if a whole group of PTO moms started poking their noses into an active murder investigation.

Better if only one amateur detective did that, she thought wryly—or two if you counted Sam Fletcher.

"Look, I'm sure the sheriff's department will find the killer," Phyllis said, "and maybe when they do, if the same person was responsible for stealing the cash box, maybe you'll get some of the money back. But in the meantime, you don't need to get involved with the case."

Lindsey said, "We're already involved. I was *arrested,* for God's sake. And the sheriff probably still suspects me. If we're taking a vote, I say we try to find the real killer."

"We're not taking a vote," Marie said quickly.

Thinking rapidly, Phyllis said, "How about this? Let's go over everything that happened Saturday afternoon and see if we can come up with anything that we haven't thought of so far. If we do, I can pass along the information to my son."

That brought nods and mutters of agreement from the assembled women. Phyllis went on, "Let's start by all of you figuring out the last time you saw Shannon that afternoon, what she was doing, and whether or not anyone was with her."

"That's easy," Lindsey said. "I saw her about thirty minutes before I . . . I found her body. That's when I argued with her. But after that I was so upset I spent the next half hour just wandering around the school, trying to get over being mad." She sighed. "I don't like being mad. I'd rather get along with people."

"What brought you back to the end of the hall where you found Shannon?" Phyllis asked.

"Actually, I was looking for her. I wanted to apologize, and that was the last place I'd seen her."

"Did you tell that to the deputies?"

Lindsey shook her head. "Not really. I . . . I didn't want to tell them that I'd been arguing with Shannon. I was afraid they would think . . . what they wound up thinking anyway." Her forehead creased in a frown. "I wish I knew who it was that told them about seeing me with her. I didn't think anybody was around just then except a little girl who came wandering out of the boy's bathroom down there."

"The boy's bathroom?" Abby said.

"Yes, but she wasn't more than four or five." Lindsey couldn't help but smile. "She was so cute in her little Elmo shirt. She must have just gone in the wrong bathroom."

Carolyn nodded. "When they're that young, it's a common mistake."

Phyllis looked around the table. "What about the rest of you? When was the last time you saw Shannon?"

"It must have been before that," Holly said. "Irene and I were working at the concession stand. Do you remember seeing her in that last half hour or so, Irene?"

"No, but she could have come through the cafeteria, I suppose," Irene said. "We were busy, so I might not have noticed her."

"Carolyn and I didn't see her, either," Phyllis pointed out. "That means there were four of us in the cafeteria, and none of us saw Shannon there toward the end of the carnival. Not only that, but her ex-husband came through looking for her, and he didn't find her in there, either. So I'd say there's a pretty good chance she was somewhere else in the school during that time."

"I was working at the face-painting booth," Kristina said. "I don't recall seeing her except during the early part of the afternoon."

Abby said, "Same here. I was helping keep the kids in line while they were waiting to get in the bounce house. I remember seeing Shannon. . . ." She shrugged. "But I couldn't tell you when."

"My friend Eve saw her outside with her son," Phyllis recalled. "That must have been around the time of her argument with you, Lindsey, either right before or right after. Do all of you know Shannon's son by sight?"

"Kirk is hard to miss," Abby said dryly, "what with the tattoos and piercings and all."

"I saw him at the carnival," Kristina put in. "He was walking around with a friend of his."

Phyllis thought of something else. "Shannon was married twice. Did she ever talk about her first husband? Does he still live around here?"

"Goodness, no," Marie said. "Roy moved away years ago. I think Shannon said one time that he lives in Oklahoma now."

"So he wouldn't have been at the carnival?"

Marie frowned. "I can't think of any reason why he would have been. He didn't hang around much even when his son was still a kid, and Kirk's a grown man now. I don't think Shannon saw anything of him for years except the child-support checks, and those stopped coming when Kirk turned eighteen."

So they could just about cross off that angle, Phyllis thought. Even if Shannon's first husband had been nursing a grudge against her for years, it was highly unlikely he would have driven down from Oklahoma to murder her at a school carnival.

"So we don't really know where Shannon was or what she was doing during the last half hour or so of her life," Phyllis summed up. She turned to Lindsey. "One other thing. Did the two of you argue about anything in particular, or was it just because of the way she always treated you?"

"I guess it had been building up for a long time," Lindsey said, "but what really made me lose it was when she tore into me again about those posters. She said we weren't

doing as well as she had expected, and it was all my fault because the posters didn't get put up in the stores in time to ad-
vertise the carnival properly."

Phyllis felt her pulse speed up a little as Lindsey spoke.
Something important was in those words, and Phyllis's brain
quickly isolated it.

"Shannon said that the carnival wasn't doing as well as
she had expected?"

"Yeah, that's right."

"She had to be talking about the money, didn't she?"
Phyllis asked.

Marie said, "How else could anybody judge whether or
not the event was a success? It was a fund-raiser, after all."

"So when Shannon said that, she had to have a pretty
good idea how much money had been taken in," Phyllis said.
"That means she'd already checked the cash box."

Carolyn and the board members nodded as they saw
Phyllis's point. "If she checked the cash box *before* the
argument she had with Lindsey," Carolyn said, "that
means she didn't walk into the office and catch somebody
stealing it."

"Well, we can't *know* that," Phyllis said. "But it makes
sense. If Shannon had already looked in the box and done a
quick count of the money, it's not very likely she would have
gone right back there after arguing with Lindsey."

"But how does assuming that help us figure out who
killed her?" Marie asked. "All it does is take away a possible motive."

Phyllis said, "Every motive that can be eliminated helps.
Sooner or later there'll only be one left. And with any luck,
that one motive will point straight to the killer."

A shudder went through Lindsey. "I hate that we're sitting around discussing motives and murder. Why do people
have to kill other people, anyway?"

"Unless you're talking about someone who's psychotic,

there's always a reason," Phyllis said. "It's probably not a good reason, but it seems like one to the killer."

And in the back of her mind a feeling stirred, a vague sense that around this table today, something important had been said, something that perhaps wouldn't solve the mystery by itself, but that could point her in the right direction.

Whatever the thing was, though, it proved elusive. She couldn't grasp it.

But she knew it was there now, and she swore to herself that she wouldn't give up until she had captured it.

Chapter 25

Mike came by Phyllis's house late in the afternoon, on his way home after his shift was over. He came in wearing his uniform jacket, because the temperature was even chillier today than it had been the previous day after the cold front blew through.

"I hear that you helped interrogate Lindsey Gonzales," Phyllis said to him as they sat down in the living room with Sam, Carolyn, and Eve.

Mike raised his hands in a gesture of surrender. "That was the sheriff's idea, not mine," he said. "He did just about all the talking, too. Except for when that lawyer lady was talking."

"Lindsey's lawyer?"

"Yeah. An attorney who's new in town, named Juliette Yorke. With an E. She got under Sheriff Haney's skin pretty good. He thought Mrs. Gonzales was about to confess, and all he got was a statement denying any involvement in the murder."

"But he didn't have any real evidence against her, just someone saying that they saw her arguing with Shannon."

Mike grunted. "Word of that got around, eh?"

Carolyn said, "We saw Lindsey at the school this afternoon, along with the other members of the PTO board."

Mike glanced at Phyllis and asked, "What was that about?"

"It was a special meeting to decide what to do about the money that was lost when the cash box was stolen. Marie Tyler asked Carolyn and me to attend, even though we're not members. Consultants, she called us."

"She's scared she's not going to be able to hold everything together, if you ask me," Carolyn said.

"And Mrs. Gonzales came to the meeting?" Mike asked with a frown. "She seemed pretty shaken up this morning. I'm a little surprised she was there."

"Wouldn't you be shaken up if you were accused of a murder?" Phyllis said.

"She wasn't actually *accused*. . . ."

"You said yourself the sheriff was convinced she was guilty. I'm sure Lindsey knew that."

"Yeah, he didn't make any big secret of it," Mike agreed. "Anyway, with nothing but that witness statement to go on, we had to release her. It's not like the witness actually saw her kill Ms. Dunston or anything."

"Who was the witness?"

Mike shook his head. "I couldn't reveal the person's identity . . . but to tell you the truth, I don't actually know. I'm sure it's in one of the reports, but I've been so busy with other things all day I never saw it."

"The reason I asked was that Lindsey didn't see anyone else in that area except a little girl, and I don't think Sheriff Haney would put much weight behind a statement given by a kindergartner."

"Well, somebody must've been there, whether Mrs. Gonzales saw them or not."

"You said you'd been busy all day," Phyllis said. "Doing what?"

Mike hesitated, then said, "Background checks."

Carolyn asked, "On who?"

"All the other members of the PTO board. Both of Ms. Dunston's ex-husbands. The rest of the faculty and staff of the school." Mike flexed the fingers of his right hand. "I've been on the computer so much I'm gonna get carpal tunnel."

"Find out anything interestin'?" Sam asked.

"Just that the PTO board is a pretty clean-living bunch. A couple of them have gotten speeding tickets, but that's the closest any of them have ever come to being in trouble with the law."

"What about Shannon's ex-husbands?" Phyllis asked.

"Joel Dunston you know about," Mike said. "He's a well-respected doctor, has a good practice here in town, and is on the staff at Campbell Memorial. Ms. Dunston's first husband, Roy Warren, lives in Tulsa and owns a concrete business there. Builds septic tanks, mostly. He's remarried and has another family up there."

"Has he ever been in trouble?"

Mike shook his head. "His record's clean. I called the Tulsa PD and asked them to check on him. He was home with his wife and kids all weekend except when he was playing golf in a pro-am tournament with a couple of hundred people around all the time. If you're thinking he could have snuck down here to kill Ms. Dunston over some old grudge, you can forget about that possibility."

Sam said, "What about the other folks who work at the school? Anybody else like Gary Oakley crop up?"

"Convicted felons, you mean?" Mike shook his head. "One of the lunchroom ladies had a DUI conviction five years ago. That was the worst thing we found." He smiled. "You schoolteachers are a pretty mild bunch."

"We have our moments, dear," Eve said. "We're just discreet about them, that's all."

"I'll take your word for that, Ms. Turner." Mike looked at Phyllis and went on, "Did you think of anything else that might help, Mom?"

Phyllis shook her head. "Not yet." She hated to stretch the truth, but she was still hesitant to drag Russ Tyler into this, considering how shaken Marie already was. And she still hadn't been able to figure out what it was she had heard during the meeting at the school that had tickled at her brain for a moment.

Mike reached for his hat. "I guess I'd better get on home, then," he said. He stood up and nodded politely as he put his hat on. "Ladies." Then he added, "See you later, Mr. Fletcher," as he went out.

Phyllis was distracted all through her preparations for supper and then during the meal itself. Sam offered to help her clean up afterward, and when they were alone in the kitchen, he said, "Something's botherin' you, isn't it, Phyllis?"

"It's this case," she replied quietly. "When you look at it, it seems like there are plenty of motives and suspects, but those motives gradually get weakened or wiped out entirely, and then there are no suspects left."

"There's got to be one left, because somebody sure killed that poor woman. We just haven't figured out the whole story yet."

Phyllis nodded. "Yes, I have that feeling, too. There's something we don't know about, or something we've overlooked."

"You realize," Sam said, "that it's not your job to figure it out. I know Mike sort of keeps you filled in and all—"

"You think he's just trying to placate his nosey, meddling mother?"

"Now, I didn't say that," Sam replied. "I think he believes you're a pretty smart woman—and he's right about that, by the way—and he likes to run the facts by you because that helps him keep 'em straight in his own mind. And there's always the chance that you'll notice something he doesn't. But my point is, you can walk away from this whole thing any time you want to, and nobody's gonna think any less of you for doing it."

"I'm not trying to figure it all out because of what anybody will think of me if I don't," Phyllis said. "Despite her faults, Shannon didn't deserve what she got. And if I can help Mike bring her killer to justice, I'm going to."

Sam nodded, but she thought she saw a faint gleam of skepticism in his eyes. She wondered if he believed she got mixed up in murder investigations for the thrill of it. In truth, she had pondered that same question herself. She told herself that wasn't the way it was, but at times, doubt nibbled at her mind. Maybe she liked playing detective a little too much. . . .

She put those thoughts out of her head and said, "Are you busy tomorrow?"

"What'd you have in mind?" Sam asked.

"I want to talk to Joel Dunston. I don't know if he'll see me or not, but I'm going to give it a try."

"What do you think he knows that you don't?"

"I'd like to find out just how much, if anything, he knew about what was going on between his wife and Russ Tyler."

"Ex-wife," Sam reminded her.

"Of course. I'm not sure he really thought of her that way, though. When he was looking for her during the carnival, he called her his wife. Maybe he thought they'd eventually get back together. Maybe he wouldn't like it if he knew about Russ's involvement with Shannon. After all, he considered Russ his friend."

"In other words, you think *he* might be the killer." Sam nodded. "You're not goin' to talk to him alone, that's for sure. Just let me know when you're ready to go, and I'll go along with you."

"Thank you, Sam." Phyllis patted his arm. "I knew I could count on you."

"You always can," he said, and Phyllis found herself looking into his eyes for a few seconds longer than she'd intended to before she turned away and forced her mind back onto simpler things—like murder.

*   *   *

Early the next morning, Phyllis called Joel Dunston's office to see if she could make an appointment to see him that day, claiming to suspect that she had a sinus infection. She hated to do anything under false pretenses, but it didn't seem likely he would agree to see her if she admitted she wanted to question him about his ex-wife's murder.

The receptionist at Joel's office informed her that he wasn't in the office that day and wouldn't be for the rest of the week.

"There was a death in the family, you know," the woman said. "Dr. Dunston is taking a little time off."

"Well, that's probably for the best," Phyllis said.

"Would you like to make an appointment to see him when he's back in the office?"

Phyllis continued the fiction she had started with, saying, "No, thanks. I'll have to have this problem looked at before then."

She hung up the phone and frowned as she tried to figure out what to do next. A couple of days earlier, Joel had been at the house he had once shared with Shannon, looking after his daughter. Becca might be back in school by now, but it was likely that Joel was still staying at the house. He might move back in permanently now that Shannon was gone.

She found Sam upstairs and said, "Joel Dunston isn't in his office today, so we're going to see him at his house."

"You know for sure he's there?"

Phyllis shook her head. "No, but I don't know where else to look for him."

"Let me get my jacket," Sam said with a nod.

He shrugged into his denim jacket while Phyllis fetched her purse and a lightweight coat from her room. As they went downstairs together, Phyllis hoped they could avoid running into Eve, who would certainly want to know where they were going if she saw them leaving together. Phyllis was getting tired of fibbing to people, even for a good cause.

They were lucky and were able to get out of the house

without being noticed. Getting back in might be a different story.

"Let's take my pickup this time," Sam suggested. Phyllis was about to say that they could go in her car instead, but then she decided to go along with Sam's suggestion. He was a man, after all, and she knew how men were about driving. Anyway, it didn't really matter how they got there.

"That's fine," she said. "I can tell you how to find the place."

As they headed out South Main Street toward the interstate, Sam said, "What are you plannin' to say to the doc?"

"I thought I'd try to find out—subtly, of course—if he had any idea there was something going on between Shannon and Russ Tyler. I'm not sure how I'll go about it."

"Can't just come right out and ask him, I reckon."

"No, probably not."

Sam looked over at her. "Mike could, though, if he knew about what was goin' on."

Phyllis frowned. "Sam, you're not scolding me for keeping this to myself, are you?"

"Me, scold you? Nope. I figure you know what you're doin'."

"I don't want to ruin Marie's marriage if I can avoid it."

She realized that she had made that statement several times over the past few days, and she wondered if that was really her motivation or if she just didn't want to give up the one piece of evidence she had. She wanted to think that she was just trying to save the Tylers' marriage, but she was coming to doubt that more and more.

The solution was to get to the bottom of this, to figure out exactly what it was she had heard or seen or both that would give her the answers she was looking for. As Sam drove, she cast her mind back to the day several weeks earlier, during the bake sale at Wal-Mart, when she had met Marie and first gotten involved with the PTO board from Loving Elementary.

Phyllis tried to take it day by day, event by event, conversation by conversation. . . .

"Now where do I go?" Sam asked, breaking into her train of thought. Phyllis blinked, looked up, and realized that they had reached the interstate.

"Oh," she said. "Turn left and get on the highway. You'll get off again a couple of exits up."

"Okeydoke." Sam wheeled the pickup into the turn.

Phyllis knew that he hadn't meant to intrude on her thoughts, but she was frustrated anyway. She had felt like she was closing in on something, but it was still incomplete, like a painting without all the details filled in. And there wasn't time now to get back into that state of concentration. She had to pay attention to finding the Dunston house again and giving Sam directions for how to get there.

She realized that she would have to start from Marie's house, because that was the way she had gone before. "Take the next exit and turn right," she told Sam. "It shouldn't be much farther."

The twists and turns of the housing development south of the interstate were confusing, but they found Marie's house without too much trouble. From there, Phyllis was confident she knew where they were going. She looked over at the Tyler house as they drove past it, but didn't see Marie anywhere. That wasn't surprising on a chilly day like this one. She was probably inside, and Russ was at work in Fort Worth.

Unless he was off meeting some other woman for lunch.

Phyllis told herself she had no reason to think that. With Shannon gone, maybe there wouldn't be any more threats to the Tylers' marriage. Although, as Sam had said, Russ didn't seem to be the sort of man who was good at resisting temptation. . . .

"Take this left and then the next right."

"Got it," Sam said.

A minute later, after Sam had made the turns, Phyllis

said, "That's the house on the left. You can pull up at the curb."

There were no vehicles parked in the driveway. Both doors of the two-car garage were down, and Phyllis couldn't tell if there were any cars inside or not. They would find out soon. She had decided that if Joel was here, she would ask him about the casserole dish she had left a couple of days earlier. She'd told him then there was no hurry about getting it back, but she could tell him that something had come up and she needed it. Yes, a casserole emergency. Happened all the time, didn't it? Actually, it didn't, but Joel probably wouldn't know that.

Sam eased the pickup to a stop at the curb. They got out, Phyllis opening her own door rather than waiting for Sam to come around and open it for her. When they reached the front door, Sam stood back and let Phyllis take the lead. She pressed the doorbell and heard it chiming somewhere in the house.

A moment later the door swung open. Becca Dunston stood there in jeans and a sweatshirt. Her brown hair was in braids that hung over the front of her shoulders. She looked surprised and worried as she said, "Oh, hi. I thought you were somebody else. That's why I opened the door."

To make sure the little girl didn't close the door in their faces, Phyllis said quickly, "You remember me, don't you, Becca? I was working at the carnival the other day, in the cafeteria."

"Oh, yeah, you were the lady with the cakes and the snacks and that stuff." Becca seemed to relax a little. "My dad doesn't like for me to open the door when he's not here, but I saw that pickup through the picture window and thought it was Lane's."

Phyllis thought back to her visit to the Dunston house a couple of days earlier, recalling the name of the young man she had seen there with Kirk. "Lane Erskine, you mean?"

"Yeah, Kirk told me he was coming by to pick up some

stuff from the shed in the backyard. I thought maybe he'd bring Nicole with him."

"Who's Nicole?" Phyllis asked. Becca hadn't asked them in yet, so she wanted to keep the girl talking. From what Becca had said, Joel wasn't here right now. Phyllis wasn't sure how much information she could get out of Becca, but the possibility seemed worth a try. She was a little troubled, though, by the thought that she was trying to question an innocent child who had just lost her mother.

"She's Lane's little girl. We play together sometimes. She's so cute and adorable." The superiority of being three or four years older was plain to hear in Becca's voice. "She goes everywhere with him when he's got her." Becca adopted a confidential tone. "Lane doesn't live with Nicole's mother, you know. But he has her on weekends, and other times, too. Her mother's not a good person."

Phyllis wouldn't know about that, but it didn't surprise her. So many people had children these days who really shouldn't.

"But of course Nicole's in school today," Becca went on. "She's in kindergarten. I didn't think about it being a school day because I'm still home, since . . ."

Her voice trailed off as sorrow appeared in her eyes. Phyllis knew she was remembering *why* she was home from school. To distract her from that, Phyllis asked, "What was your brother's friend supposed to pick up?"

"Oh, I don't know. Just some stuff. Kirk keeps it covered up with a tarp. He won't let me look at it. Daddy doesn't know it's out there in the shed."

"We came to talk to your daddy. Did you say he's not here?"

"He's gone to the store. He asked me to come, too, but I didn't feel like it. I had a stomachache earlier."

"I'm sorry to hear that. Do you think he'd mind if we came in and waited for him?"

"I dunno. . . ." Becca looked rather suspiciously at Sam.

"Oh, this is my friend, Mr. Fletcher," Phyllis said. "He used to be a teacher, too."

"And I coached basketball," Sam put in. "You ever shoot hoops, Becca?"

"Sometimes." She started to step back. "I guess it would be okay—"

At that moment, a car pulled into the driveway from the street and one of the garage doors started to rise, its opening mechanism no doubt triggered by a remote control in the car. The driver stopped before pulling into the garage, though, and quickly got out of the vehicle. Phyllis heard anger in Joel Dunston's voice as he demanded, "What's going on here?"

Chapter 26

Joel came around the front of the car toward them. His movements were stiff and his eyes were intense behind his glasses. But after a couple of steps he slowed and the frown on his face went away. "Oh, it's you, Mrs. Newsom," he said. "I didn't notice you at first. I just saw this fellow standing there, and I've told Becca not to answer the door when I'm not around, or talk to strangers—"

Sam moved along the walk that ran from the driveway to the front door and stuck out his hand. "Sam Fletcher. I'm a friend of Phyllis's. Pleased to meet you, Doctor."

Joel shook hands with him and smiled a little. "Sorry I almost overreacted there." He switched his gaze to Becca for a second. "Although you and I will have to have a talk about following the rules, young lady."

Becca began, "I thought—" then stopped short. Phyllis knew she'd been about to say that she had thought Sam's pickup belonged to Kirk's friend Lane Erskine. But Becca had caught herself in time, realizing she couldn't tell her father that because he wasn't supposed to know about whatever it was in the shed that Lane was coming by to get. Instead, Becca finished by saying, "I remembered Mrs. Newsom from the carnival the other day."

"Well, you can never be too careful." Joel gestured toward the open door. "You folks go on inside. I'll just pull the car in and unload the groceries, and I'll be right with you." He looked at Becca again. "Where's Kirk?"

"Up in his room asleep."

"Of course he is. It's only eleven o'clock in the morning. Go get him up and tell him to come down and help me with the groceries."

"He won't like that," Becca warned.

"I don't care whether he likes it or not."

Becca nodded and vanished back into the house. Phyllis and Sam followed her as Joel turned around and went back to his car in the driveway. Sam closed the front door behind them.

A living room that looked like it wasn't used very much was to their left. They went into it and sat down on a sofa. As they sat there quietly, Phyllis heard a door open and shut, and assumed that Joel had come into the house through the garage. A moment later she heard footsteps coming down the stairs. Kirk muttered in a sleepy, resentful voice, "This is a bunch of crap, man," and went on out to the kitchen without Phyllis ever seeing him.

Becca appeared in the opening between the living room and the foyer. "My dad said to ask you if you'd like some coffee or something else to drink."

Sam shook his head, and Phyllis told her, "We're fine, dear."

"Okay." The little girl disappeared again, with a wave and a look that said she was grateful she didn't have to stay and entertain a couple of adults who must have seemed positively ancient to her.

Joel came into the living room a few minutes later. "Now, what can I do for you?" he asked with a smile that said he was trying to be friendly but also that he was baffled about why they were here.

"I wanted to see how you were doing," Phyllis said, "and Sam offered to come along with me."

Joel sat down on a straight-backed chair and laced his

fingers together as he clasped his hands between his knees. "About as well as can be expected, I guess. We all are. The funeral was yesterday morning, you know, and it was pretty rough. I thought maybe Becca might want to get started back to school today, but she said she didn't feel good and wanted to stay home one more day." He shrugged helplessly. "I couldn't tell her no."

"Of course not," Phyllis agreed. Joel hadn't mentioned the fact that she and Carolyn hadn't attended Shannon's funeral, and she wasn't going to bring up the subject, either. She went on, "I was wondering, too, if you happened to be done with that casserole dish I brought over the other day. I didn't expect to need it back so soon, but . . ."

"Oh. Sure." Joel nodded. "As a matter of fact, we ate the last of those sweet potatoes last night. They were really good. Thank you." He unclasped his hands and put them on his knees, poised to push himself to his feet. "The dish is clean, I'll go get it—"

"There's no hurry," Phyllis broke in. As soon as the dish was in her hands, she and Sam no longer had any reason to stay. Even though she already knew the answer, she asked, "Are you taking some time off from your practice this week?"

Joel sat back and nodded. "That's right. I feel kind of bad about it because I'm letting down my patients, but I . . . I just wasn't ready to go back to work yet."

"I don't reckon anybody could blame you for that," Sam said.

"Yes, even though you and Shannon weren't together anymore, it's easy to see that you still cared a great deal for her," Phyllis said.

Joel took his glasses off and held them in his right hand while he used the left to rub wearily at his eyes. He sighed, then put the glasses back on and said, "That's true, you know. I didn't really want us to split up. It just sort of . . . happened."

Sam nodded and said sympathetically, "Things have a way of doing that."

"I wouldn't have made it through that whole ordeal if it hadn't been for the support of my friends. They've really been there for me now, too. Russ Tyler's been like a rock."

Phyllis couldn't stop her mouth from tightening a bit at that comment, but she didn't think Joel noticed, and she quickly controlled the reaction. "Russ and Marie seem to have a good marriage," she said.

"The best," Joel agreed with a nod. "I just wish that Shannon and I could have been as successful at it as those two are."

Either he was an absolutely magnificent actor, or else he had no idea that Russ had been contemplating having an affair with his ex-wife. Phyllis couldn't detect an iota of insincerity in his voice or his expression.

Joel took his glasses off again, and this time when he rubbed at his eyes, Phyllis saw that they shone with unshed tears. He went on, "I had hopes that, you know, someday things might change. I know that when a relationship is over, you . . . you're supposed to move on, but I thought that when Becca got a little older . . . maybe Shannon would see that she didn't have to spend all her time at the school. Maybe she would be willing to give our marriage a try again." He shook his head. "Now there won't ever be a chance for that."

He placed the glasses on a little table beside the chair where he sat and covered his face with both hands. He didn't sob out loud, but his back shook from the power of the emotions going through him.

There was no way he had killed Shannon, Phyllis told herself. He was still deeply in love with her, whether he wanted to admit it or not.

"I'm sorry," she said. "We didn't mean to upset you by coming by. I realize now it was a terribly insensitive thing to do. . . ."

Joel took his right hand away from his face and gestured vaguely with it. "No, no, that's fine. You didn't cause this. I've been holding it together for Becca's sake, but it's hard. I need to let some of it out." He lowered his other hand and drew in a deep breath. "I'm going to move back in here, you know. We're going to be a family again, as much as we can. Even Kirk. We're going to make it work, one way or another."

"I hope you do," Phyllis said, and meant it. She got to her feet. "Why don't I get you a glass of water?"

Joel sniffled and nodded. "That would be nice. The kitchen—"

"I remember where it is." Phyllis glanced at Sam as she left the living room. He looked a little uncomfortable at the prospect of being left there alone with a grief-stricken Joel, but Sam was nothing if not a trouper. He gave Phyllis a tiny nod of encouragement that told her to go on.

She went into the kitchen, found a glass in one of the cabinets, and ran it full of water at the sink. As she turned away, her gaze moved over the refrigerator and she stopped short as she looked at the photographs of Becca, attached to the door with little round magnets.

In the old days, she told herself with a smile, those would have been Polaroid photos on the refrigerator door, but these pictures has probably been shot with a digital camera and printed out on some fancy printer. Probably by Shannon, Phyllis thought. She leaned closer to look at a photo of Becca in happier times, standing in front of a swing set in a sun-dappled backyard with another little girl beside her, both of them grinning for the camera. . . .

"Oh, my," Phyllis said as the glass of water almost slipped out of her hand. She tightened her grip on it as she stood there for a moment longer. Then she turned and carried the glass back to the living room.

"Thank you," Joel said as she handed it to him. He drank part of it, then sighed.

Phyllis reached for her purse and nodded to Sam. "We really have to be going," she said to Joel.

"Wait a minute," he said as he set the glass on the table and stood up. "You don't have that casserole dish."

"I should have gotten it while I was in the kitchen. I swear, I'd forget my head if it wasn't attached."

"I'll get it for you," Joel said. "Just a minute."

He hurried out of the room. While he was gone, Sam looked at Phyllis and asked, "Are you all right? You look a little shaky."

"I'm fine," she assured him. "I'm just ready to get out of here."

Sam frowned but didn't say anything else. Joel came back a moment later with the casserole dish, handed it to her, and said, "Thanks again. You've been awfully nice."

Phyllis smiled and nodded. "Good-bye now," she said as she and Sam walked into the foyer.

From the top of the stairs, Becca called, "Are you leaving?"

Phyllis turned to smile up at her. "Yes, dear."

Becca waved. "Bye-bye. Come back to see us sometime."

Joel came into the foyer behind them and said, "Becca, go put on some nicer clothes and tell Kirk to get cleaned up, too. We're all going out to eat lunch together. We're going to start doing more things as a family."

"Really?" The little girl sounded excited. "Can we get pizza?"

"Sure, whatever you want," Joel told her. Phyllis could tell that he was forcing the smile on his face, but he was making a valiant effort of it.

Becca turned and ran along the upstairs hall, calling, "Hey, Kirkie, we're gonna get pizza!"

Sam opened the door and stepped back for Phyllis to go out first. As she stepped into the chilly air, she saw another pickup swinging toward the curb as if to park, but the driver looked at her and Sam and then Joel Dunston as Joel stepped into the doorway behind them, and he accelerated again, heading on down the street. Phyllis had gotten a good look at his face, though, and recognized him as Lane Erskine, Kirk's friend.

Obviously, if Joel wasn't supposed to know about what Kirk was keeping in the shed, Lane couldn't stop and get it while Joel was here. So he had driven on, probably planning to come back later.

Sam opened the pickup door for her, then went around to get in on the driver's side. As he slid behind the wheel, he said in a quiet voice, "Something happened in there, didn't it?"

She nodded as he started the engine. "Yes, it did."

"I've got to tell you, I don't think that poor fella had a clue in the world that his ex-wife was tryin' to get his buddy Russ to sleep with her."

"No, he didn't. I agree with you about that."

Sam looked around to check the traffic, which was light on this residential street, then pulled out from the curb. "And if Dunston didn't know about that," he went on, "I don't see that he would have had any reason to want to kill anybody."

"No, I'm convinced that he didn't."

"Then what happened? You were different when you came back from the kitchen with that glass of water. You figured something out, didn't you?"

"Maybe." Phyllis wasn't sure whether she wanted to say anything else or not. Her brain was still whirling from the realization that had come to her. She didn't have all the answers. In fact, the ideas spinning around inside her head now might be completely wrong. But every instinct she possessed told her that they weren't.

"You know who killed Shannon Dunston, don't you?" Sam asked grimly.

Phyllis shook her head. "No, I don't," she said honestly, "but I have a pretty good idea *why* she was killed." Her eyes widened as she realized something else. "And we have to go back there, or the murderer will get away!"

Chapter 27

Sam hit the brakes, slowing the pickup, but doing it smoothly enough so that the tires didn't squeal on the pavement. He looked over at her and said, "Phyllis, no offense, but what in blazes are you talkin' about?"

"Make a block," she said, "and circle back around. We have to find a place at least a block away from the Dunston house, but close enough so that we can keep an eye on it after Joel and Becca and Kirk leave."

"And why would we want to do that?" Sam wanted to know. "Seems to me like what you ought to be doin' if you've figured this out is to call Mike and tell him."

"I'll call him, but he might not be able to get here in time. Please, Sam."

He sighed. "All right. I hope you know what you're doin'."

Phyllis hoped so, too.

As Sam turned onto a cross street and began circling back in the direction they had come from, Phyllis opened her purse and took out her cell phone.

"Callin' Mike?" Sam asked.

"Not just yet. I'm not sure about things. I need to find out a little more."

He muttered and shook his head but kept driving.

Phyllis called her house and was relieved when Carolyn

answered on the second ring. "Carolyn, I need the number of Loving Elementary."

"What's wrong?" Carolyn asked. "You sound upset about something, Phyllis."

"I just need to ask Frances Hickson a question or two."

"All right, hang on. I'll have to look it up." Carolyn put down the phone, and although she was back quickly with the number, the time seemed longer to Phyllis. She repeated back the number that Carolyn gave her, fixing it in her brain, since writing it down would have been awkward at the moment.

"Thanks," she said, then broke the connection and dialed again before Carolyn could ask her again what was wrong.

Katherine Felton, the school secretary, answered the phone at Loving Elementary and put Phyllis through to the principal right away when Phyllis said it was an emergency. Frances Hickson picked up the phone and said, "Mrs. Newsom, what is it? What's wrong? Someone else hasn't been arrested, have they?"

"Not yet," Phyllis said. "I need some information. Shannon Dunston had a key to the school, didn't she?"

Frances sighed. "Yes, she did. Normally, I wouldn't give one to someone who wasn't a member of the faculty or staff, but she said that she might need to get in to work on PTO projects when no one was here. To be honest, she nagged me about it until I gave in and let her have one."

"When was that?"

"Oh, goodness, a month or so ago, at least."

"Did she have a key to the secretary's desk?"

"Yes, she and Marie Tyler both did, but I just gave those keys to them at the carnival so they could lock up the cash box." Frances gasped. "Oh, my goodness. Marie gave her key back to me, but Shannon never did, of course. I never even thought about it until now. Surely the sheriff has it, don't you think?"

"I don't know," Phyllis told her, "but I intend to find out."

She hung up again and looked around. "What street are we on?"

"I don't know the name of it," Sam said, "but we're about to get back to the one where the Dunstons live. By my reckonin', we're a couple of blocks past their house."

Phyllis nodded. "That should do. Can you find a place to stop where we won't be too obvious?"

"I'll try."

Sam made the turn and a second later pulled the pickup to the curb in front of a large, two-story house that was still under construction. It appeared that no one was working on the place at the moment.

"Anybody notices the truck, they'll likely think it belongs to one of the contractors," he said.

Phyllis nodded. "This is perfect. I can see the Dunston house from here."

"While we're keepin' an eye on it, how about tellin' me just what's got you in such a tizzy?"

"In a minute." She made one more call, this time to Mike's cell phone number. As she waited for it to go through, she saw Joel Dunston's car back out of the driveway into the street. Joel was behind the wheel, and someone—probably Becca—was in the front seat beside him. The backseat was occupied, too. That had to be Kirk, who was probably accompanying his half sister and stepfather to lunch reluctantly. The car headed the other way along the street, away from where Phyllis and Sam were parked.

Mike answered promptly. "Yeah, Mom?"

"I'm not interrupting you, am I?"

"No, I'm out on patrol, but I was just about to stop for some lunch. What do you need?"

"Can you call in and get the records for Kirk Warren?"

Mike sounded puzzled. "We've already checked on him. He's clean since he turned eighteen."

"What about before that?"

"Juvenile records are usually sealed and sometimes even

expunged. Nothing showed up on Kirk. That means he either never got in trouble with the law or his parents were able to get his record wiped clean."

Phyllis nodded, a little disappointed but still convinced she was on the right track. "Find out what you can about a man named Lane Erskine, and meet me at Shannon Dunston's house as soon as possible."

There was a note of alarm in Mike's voice as he asked, "Mom, what are you doing? Have you found out something?"

Phyllis's fingers tightened on the phone as she spotted a familiar pickup several blocks away, coming toward them. "Just get here as fast as you can," she said, then closed the phone as the other pickup swung over toward the curb and then pulled into the driveway of the Dunston house. Just as she had figured, Lane Erskine had been parked somewhere close by, too, watching and waiting for Joel, Becca, and Kirk to drive by so that he would know the coast was clear. Phyllis saw him get out of his truck and go to the side of the garage, where there was probably a gate leading into the backyard. Erskine disappeared around the corner.

"Who's that?" Sam asked tensely.

"His name is Lane Erskine. He's the one who burglarized Loving Elementary a while back, along with Kirk Warren. Shannon had a key to the school, and Kirk must have gotten his hands on it and had a copy made. Then they hid what they stole in the shed in Kirk's backyard until they could dispose of it."

She glanced over to see that Sam was staring at her. "You know all this for a fact, do you?" he said.

"I'm convinced it's true. They may have been burglarizing places for years. When Kirk was sixteen, he was running with an older, rougher crowd. Lane was part of that crowd. Kirk got sent away to military school. But when he came back, he was still friends with Lane, who had supposedly straightened up after he got some girl pregnant and she had his baby. That baby grew up to be Nicole, Becca's little friend. Lane took her to the carnival. I saw them there in the cafeteria. Nicole was wearing a T-shirt with Elmo on it."

"Elmo who?"

Phyllis frowned at him.

"Oh, the Muppet," he went on. "Yeah, even I know about *Sesame Street*. But what's Elmo got to do with anything?"

Before Phyllis could answer, Lane Erskine reappeared, rounding the corner of the Dunston garage. He was carrying a fairly large cardboard box. He placed it in the back of the pickup, turned around, and went back around the garage.

"He's loading up the loot," Phyllis said. "I saw Lane here the other day and thought he looked familiar, but I didn't connect him with the carnival because he was alone. If I'd seen the little girl with him, I would have known him right away because I remembered her so well. Like Becca said, she's really cute."

"Back to Elmo . . . ?" Sam said hopefully.

"Yesterday at the school, Lindsey Gonzales said the only other person she saw while she was arguing with Shannon was a little girl who came out of the boy's restroom. The girl was wearing an Elmo T-shirt. I didn't make the connection, then, either, but I should have. I knew it instinctively."

"There could have been other little girls at the carnival wearing T-shirts like that," Sam pointed out.

"Yes, of course. But we *know* Nicole Erskine was, and we know the girl Lindsey saw came out of the boy's bathroom."

"So?"

"When a little girl who's out in a public place with her father needs to go to the bathroom, if he doesn't want to send her into the ladies room by herself, he'll check the men's room and if it's empty he'll take her in there. And that end of the school wasn't busy, so the boy's restroom probably *was* empty."

Sam nodded slowly. "Maybe. You think Erskine was inside that bathroom while Ms. Gonzales and Ms. Dunston were yellin' at each other?"

"I think it's possible. I think he was the witness who told the sheriff about it, too, hoping to throw more suspicion on Lindsey when a couple of days had gone by without the sheriff making a good case against anyone else."

"You're sayin' Erskine's the killer." Sam's voice was flat, the words a statement rather than a question.

Now that Phyllis had talked out some of the theory that had formed in her head, she was better able to draw conclusions from it. She nodded and said, "I think so. I suppose Kirk could have killed his mother, but I really think it was Erskine. I never saw Kirk in the cafeteria, but I know Lane was there with his little girl. He could have picked up that knife then."

"But why?" Sam asked. "Why would he do that?"

Erskine carried another box out to the pickup and returned to the backyard. Phyllis said, "Shannon must have found out that he and Kirk were responsible for the burglary at the school. She sent Kirk away to military school when he was sixteen. If she found out he was still breaking the law, I can see her threatening to turn him in."

"And she didn't say anything about that to her friend Marie or anybody else?"

"She was a proud woman," Phyllis said with a sigh, "and she regarded Kirk as one of her failures. I imagine she would have kept it to herself as long as possible. She could have even given him an ultimatum and told him to turn himself in and testify against his friend Lane, whom she probably blamed for getting Kirk mixed up in crime to start with."

Erskine added another box to the load in the pickup and went back around the garage again.

"So if Erskine knew that Kirk had been busted by his mama," Sam mused, "he was probably smart enough to know that the kid wouldn't go down by himself. Kirk would turn on him and try to save himself."

Phyllis nodded. She was getting worried now that Mike wouldn't arrive in time to stop Erskine from getting away.

And once the loot from the burglary was gone, there wouldn't be a bit of proof against Kirk or Erskine, only the theory that Phyllis had worked out. That wouldn't be worth a stale cupcake in court.

"So when Erskine heard Shannon and Lindsey arguing, he realized he could kill Shannon and someone else might get the blame for it," she went on. "He went to the cafeteria and got the knife, knowing that no one would ever connect him with it if he wiped his prints off it. Then, while his daughter was outside on the playground, he found Shannon and somehow decoyed her back down to that end of the hall. It was isolated there, and he wanted the body to be found near where Shannon and Lindsey had argued, just to make the case against Lindsey stronger."

"What about Gary Oakley?" Sam wanted to know.

"I don't think he had anything to do with any of it," Phyllis said. "It was just a lucky break for Lane that Gary had a record and the sheriff pounced on him as a suspect. If Sheriff Haney had been able to make a case against Gary, even though Gary was innocent, Lane probably wouldn't have tried to implicate Lindsey. He would have been satisfied with anyone getting the blame for the murder, as long as it wasn't him."

Sam nodded again. "The whole thing makes sense, but I don't see how you're gonna prove any of it."

"The stolen property from the school will prove that Kirk and Lane were behind the burglary. That'll give the sheriff something to hold them on while he tries to find more evidence and works on them for a confession."

"But without that stuff . . ."

"I know." Phyllis's voice rose in desperation, because Lane had just reappeared with yet another box. He placed it in the back of the pickup and turned. "Is he about to leave?" Phyllis asked.

She heaved a sigh of relief when Erskine went around the garage yet again.

"We can't take a chance on waiting," Phyllis went on. "Drive down there and block the driveway so he can't get out with the stolen property."

Sam glanced sharply at her. "He's liable not to take kindly to that."

"Please, Sam. He's not going to do anything in the middle of a residential neighborhood in broad daylight. At the worst, he'll run off and try to get away on foot. And Mike should be here any minute."

"Get out," Sam said.

"What?"

"Get out of the truck. I'll go block him in there, but I'm not takin' you with me where you can get hurt, Phyllis."

"But, Sam—"

"Up to you. Get out or I'm stayin' right here."

She reached for the door handle. "All right, but hurry."

She stepped out onto the street in front of the unfinished house and shut the door as Sam started the pickup. He put it in gear and hit the gas, sending it rolling quickly down the street. It didn't take him long to cover the two blocks. He brought the truck to a halt across the Dunston driveway just as Lane Erskine came around the corner of the garage. Erskine stopped short and set the box he was carrying on the ground as Sam got out of the pickup. Phyllis started walking quickly toward them. Sam had made her get out of the pickup, but he couldn't make her stay here.

Then Sam started up the driveway and Erskine moved quickly to meet him. Phyllis screamed, "Sam!", then broke into a run as she saw something glittering in Erskine's hand and knew that it was a knife.

Chapter 28

With a screech of tires, a sheriff's department cruiser slid around a corner into the street, the lights on its roof flashing. The car fishtailed for a second, then gained traction and sped forward.

At the same time, Lane Erskine slashed at Sam with the knife in his hand. Sam jerked his body backward so that the blade missed, then lunged at Erskine while the young man was off balance. He wrapped his fingers around the wrist of the hand holding the knife, and the two men grappled on the driveway.

Phyllis ran as hard as she could along the street, but she seemed to move with maddening slowness. Her heart thudded from fear and exertion as she watched Sam struggling with Erskine.

Then the sheriff's car slewed to a halt in front of the Dunston house and Mike leaped out, his service revolver in his hand. "Sam, get out of the way!" he shouted.

Sam gave Erskine a shove to put some distance between them and let go of the younger man's wrist. He dropped to the ground and rolled, putting himself out of the line of fire. Mike leveled his revolver at Erskine, but didn't fire.

"Drop it!" he yelled. "Drop the knife!"

Phyllis had almost reached the house by now. She was close enough to see the indecision on Erskine's face. She knew he was thinking about attacking Mike, and even though Phyllis didn't want to see anyone else get hurt, even Erskine, she hoped that Mike would shoot him before taking a chance on getting injured himself.

Then as Phyllis slowed to a stop and stood there trying to catch her breath, Erskine muttered an obscenity and opened his hand. The knife clattered to the concrete driveway.

"On the ground!" Mike ordered as he approached Erskine slowly and carefully. "Get on the ground now!"

Sam climbed to his feet and hurried over to Phyllis. He took hold of her arm and asked anxiously, "Are you all right?"

"Me? You're the one who . . . got attacked," she said, still out of breath. "Did he . . . cut you?"

Sam shook his head. "That knife never touched me. It came a mite too close for comfort, though."

"Hands behind your back," Mike told Erskine. The young man complied with the order, and Mike deftly snapped handcuffs on him, performing the task one-handed while the other hand still held his service revolver ready for use if need be. He didn't holster the gun until the cuffs were in place. Then he grabbed hold of Erskine's arm and hauled the prisoner to his feet.

"I don't know what the hell's going on here, but you've got it all wrong, Deputy," Erskine said. "I was just defending myself. That old geezer jumped me! He's the one who ought to be in handcuffs!"

"You're the one who had the knife," Mike said. "That looks like assault with a deadly weapon to me, maybe even attempted murder."

"But he attacked me!"

Phyllis said, "That's a lie. He pulled the knife and came at Sam with it before Sam did anything except block the driveway."

Erskine glared darkly at her. "You nosey old bitch! You don't know what you're talking about."

"That lady is my mother," Mike said in a hard, dangerous

voice, "and I'm having a hard time right now remembering that I'm an officer of the law."

"Yeah, but I'm a civilian," Sam said as he turned toward Erskine and his big, knobby-knuckled hands clenched into fists.

Mike lifted a hand to motion Sam back, and Phyllis took hold of his arm. "It's all right," she said. "It doesn't matter what he says now. Now it's just a matter of evidence."

"Evidence of what?" Erskine demanded. "I didn't do anything."

"You should look in those boxes in the back of his pickup," Phyllis told Mike. "I believe you'll find the things that were stolen from Loving Elementary in that burglary a while back."

Mike frowned in thought, then shook his head. "I'm not touching a thing in that pickup until the sheriff gets here with a search warrant."

"We saw him loadin' the boxes," Sam said. "He took 'em out of a shed in the Dunstons' backyard."

Mike nodded. "Yeah, and that's suspicious enough a judge might allow a search to stand up, but he might not, too. And I'm not taking a chance with this one." He still had a hard stare fixed on the prisoner. "I take it this is Lane Erskine?"

"That's right," Phyllis said.

"I checked him out. He was arrested when he was eighteen on suspicion of heading up a burglary ring made up of other teenagers. One of the bunch was going to testify against him. But then the witness recanted, and the charges were eventually dropped due to lack of evidence."

"Kirk Warren," Phyllis said. "He must have been the witness. But he decided not to testify, and Shannon sent him off to military school."

"And then later this one and Kirk picked up where they'd left off, robbin' folks," Sam put in.

"Until Shannon found out and threatened to turn them both in. That's why Lane killed her."

Erskine stared at her for a second, then howled, "I didn't kill anybody! Damn it, this is all a lie!"

"We'll sort it out," Mike said grimly, "but in the meanwhile, shut up." He grasped Erskine's arm and steered the young man toward the cruiser that was stopped at the curb, its lights still flashing.

While Mike secured Erskine in the backseat of the car and read him his rights, Phyllis and Sam climbed into the cab of Sam's pickup to get out of the chilly November wind. They waited there for the sheriff and the rest of the backup Mike called for to arrive.

"I thought he was going to kill you," Phyllis said quietly.

"He made a good stab at it, so to speak," Sam replied with a dry chuckle.

"It's not funny," Phyllis insisted. "My meddling in this case almost got you killed."

"Your meddlin', as you call it, uncovered a murderer. The way I see it, that's worth a few risks."

Phyllis didn't say anything, but she wasn't sure it was worth risking Sam Fletcher's life. She wasn't sure about that at all.

More police cars converged on the neighborhood, this time with sirens blaring as well as lights flashing. Not many people were home at this time of day during the week, but the few who were came out of their houses to see what was going on. Between the lawmen, the bystanders, and Phyllis and Sam, who got out of the pickup to join Mike, there was actually quite a crowd.

Sheriff Haney had moved quickly to get a search warrant. He had the document with him, so after being filled in by Mike, the sheriff opened one of the cardboard boxes in the back of Lane Erskine's pickup. Phyllis lifted herself on her toes to get a better view of what was inside the box and saw a couple of computer towers.

"The serial numbers have been scratched off the outside," Haney said, "but I bet we'll be able to identify them. The school district etches ID numbers on the inside of the cases."

Erskine had been taken out of the back of Mike's car to observe the search, and from the pained look that passed briefly over his face at the sheriff's words, Phyllis would have been willing to bet that he hadn't done anything to try to obliterate those hidden ID numbers. He probably hadn't even known about them.

Opening the rest of the boxes revealed more computers, monitors, printers, some digital cameras and cordless phones, and other assorted electronic equipment. Haney grinned at Erskine and commented, "Not a bad haul for small-time crooks. It would have netted them a thousand dollars, maybe fifteen hundred if they were lucky."

"And a woman died for that," Phyllis said.

Mike reached into another of the boxes. "And this," he said as he lifted out a metal cash box. "He must've taken the key to the school secretary's desk off of Ms. Dunston after he killed her. Just couldn't pass up the opportunity to steal something else, even after he'd committed murder."

Erskine didn't say anything now. He just stared down sullenly at the ground. Phyllis had a hunch he wouldn't say anything, but rather as soon as possible would get lawyered up.

A car drove fast down the street and stopped with a squeal of tires. Joel Dunston jumped out of the vehicle, obviously upset and frightened by the sight of so many official cars parked in front of his house.

"What's going on here?" he demanded. "What is all this?"

Behind him, Becca and Kirk got out of the car more slowly. Phyllis watched Kirk, saw him go stiff with fear at the sight of Lane Erskine in handcuffs.

"You're Dunston, aren't you?" the sheriff said to Joel. "It looks like the prisoner here had some stolen property stashed in your backyard shed. He was trying to move it while you were gone."

Mike added, "There's also a good chance that he's the one who murdered your ex-wife."

Joel stared at Erskine for a second, then turned to look at Kirk. "Did you know anything about this?"

Kirk had gone pale at Mike's accusation of Erskine. He came up the driveway, shaking his head. "I didn't," he said hollowly. "I swear I didn't."

"He's a damned liar!" Erskine burst out. "He knew the stuff was back there. He helped me steal it. We got in the school with a key that *he* had!"

Breath hissed between Kirk's teeth. "You killed my mother, man? You killed my *mother*?"

Mike grabbed him as he leaped at Erskine, his hands out-stretched and reaching for the prisoner's throat. As Mike and another deputy wrestled him to the ground, Kirk sobbed, "You bastard! You bastard! You didn't have to *do* that! I told you I could handle her!"

"Like you did a few years ago when she almost got both of us sent to jail? You're a wimp, Warren. You've always been a wimp."

"Save it all for your official statements," Haney told them. He pointed at Kirk. "Put him in cuffs, too. We're tak-ing both of them in." He looked at Joel and added, "Sorry, Mr. Dunston."

Joel just stood there, an arm around Becca's shoulders. He looked so stunned that he was barely able to comprehend what was going on. It had been one shock after another for him, for a good while now. Phyllis didn't blame him for feel-ing overwhelmed.

Mike stepped up beside her and said quietly, "You and Sam will have to come in, too, Mom, so we can get state-ments from the two of you. You'll need to run through the whole thing for us."

She nodded. "Whatever I can do to help."

"Looks to me like you already did more than help," Sam said. "You solved the whole darn case."

Yes, Phyllis thought, the truth had come out.

But as usual, the truth was less than completely satisfying.

"I don't know if you want this anymore," Mike said that evening as he handed a big plastic cake box to Phyllis. Inside the box was the jack-o'-lantern cake from the carnival. "It's been sitting in the evidence room at the sheriff's department for the past few days," Mike went on. "It's probably a little stale by now."

"Thanks for bringing it back. It should still be all right." Phyllis backed away from the front door. "Can you come in and sit down for a few minutes?"

Mike took off his hat as he stepped into the house. "Yeah, I figured you and Mr. Fletcher would want to hear how everything turned out."

"The others are in the living room. I'll put this cake in the kitchen and be right back."

When she returned to the living room, she found Mike and Sam sitting in armchairs while Carolyn and Eve were on the sofa. Phyllis took the other armchair and asked, "What else have you found out?"

"Kirk Warren's been talking all day, spilling everything he knows," Mike said. "That's not much of a surprise. He wants to cut a deal with the DA, of course, and he probably will. But he's confessed to getting his mother's key to the school and making a copy of it so that he and Erskine could burglarize the place. He said they still had the loot because the fence that Erskine usually used got busted a while back, and they were having trouble finding somebody else to take the stuff off their hands." Mike shook his head. "They really weren't very good criminals. If they hadn't gotten caught this time, they would have sooner or later."

"What about Shannon's murder?" Phyllis asked.

"According to Kirk, she found the key he had, recognized

it, and figured out that he and Erskine were responsible for the burglary. She wanted Kirk to turn himself in and testify against Erskine, just like you thought, Mom. Kirk was dumb enough to tell Erskine that his mother was on to them, and Erskine threatened to kill her then and there. But Kirk talked him out of it and promised Erskine that he could handle the problem. I guess Erskine didn't trust him, though. When he saw a chance to get rid of Mrs. Dunston, he took it."

Sam asked, "Are you gonna be able to prove that?"

"We've got Kirk's testimony that Erskine threatened to kill her, as well as the stolen property," Mike said, "and our crime scene people recovered some tissue from under Mrs. Dunston's fingernails that must have gotten there when she clawed at the killer as she was dying. I'm betting Erskine will be a DNA match for that tissue, and that ought to be all we need to tie him up nice and tight."

"Goodness, I hope so," Eve said. "It's terrible to think that people like that are running around loose."

"What about Nicole?" Phyllis asked.

"Who?"

"Lane Erskine's daughter."

Mike made a face. "Oh, yeah. He had shared custody with the mother, who's been in and out of jail several times for possession and solicitation. What a pair to have for parents. Anyway, I think Child Protective Services will probably try to place her in foster care. The mother doesn't need to have sole custody, that's for sure, and there's a real good chance Erskine won't be out of jail any time soon, if ever."

"I hope it all works out," Phyllis said with a sigh. "The poor child certainly wasn't to blame for any of it."

Carolyn asked, "What about the money that was stolen from the PTO? Was any of it recovered?"

"Most of it was still in the cash box," Mike replied. "So that's one good thing that came out of this, anyway."

"That's right," Carolyn said. "Now they won't have to

have a bake sale or something to try to make up for what they lost!"

It was late when Sam came into the kitchen as Phyllis was closing the refrigerator. She had just poured herself a small glass of milk. The house was quiet, Carolyn and Eve having already turned in for the night.

Sam wore pajamas and a bathrobe, as did Phyllis. He smiled at the glass of milk in her hand and said, "Ah. Great minds work alike."

"You're thirsty, too?"

"A little." He got a glass from the cabinet and opened the refrigerator. "I'm more of an orange juice man, myself, though."

When he had poured his juice they stood there, leaning against the counter on either side of the sink and sipping from their glasses. After a moment he asked, "What are you gonna do about Marie Tyler?"

"I thought you had something on your mind," Phyllis said. "Do you mean, am I going to tell her about Russ and Shannon?"

"Yep."

Phyllis didn't answer for a moment. Then she said, "I don't think so. What would be the point?"

"Might save Marie from some trouble down the road. I don't have too high an opinion of her husband."

Phyllis finished her milk, washed the glass, and put it in the drainer next to the sink. "Neither do I, but she probably knows him a lot better than we do. Maybe he'll keep that wandering eye of his under control from now on."

Sam didn't look convinced of that, but he nodded. "I guess folks have enough trouble making a go of life these days without lookin' for problems." He drank the rest of his orange juice, turned to the sink to wash out the glass, and put it in the drainer next to hers. That brought him close enough to her so that he could reach over to where she had a hand resting on the counter. He laid his hand on top of hers, but left it there only for a second before he patted it and said, "Good night, Phyllis."

"Good night, Sam," she said. He smiled at her and left the kitchen. She heard the stairs creaking a little as he climbed them. The autumn wind brushed a branch against a window somewhere.

She was smiling, too, as she turned out the light.

Peanut-Butter-and-Banana Cookies

¼ cup sugar
¼ cup firmly packed
    brown sugar
½ cup margarine or butter,
    softened
1 egg
1 cup all purpose flour

½ teaspoon baking powder
½ teaspoon baking soda
1 cup quick-cooking oats
½ cup peanut butter
⅓ cup applesauce
1 medium banana, mashed

Preheat oven to 375° F. In a large bowl, combine the sugar, brown sugar, margarine, and egg; beat well. Add the flour, baking powder, baking soda, and salt; mix well. Stir in the oats, peanut butter, applesauce, and mashed banana. Drop the dough by heaping teaspoonfuls 2 inches apart onto cookie sheets covered with parchment paper, or lightly greased. Bake for 12 to 14 minutes or until light golden brown. Remove from cookie sheets and cool completely.

Carolyn's Low-Fat Pizza Rolls

*1 package Pillsbury
    low-fat croissants*
4 tablespoons pizza sauce
*4 tablespoons grated
    mozzarella cheese*

*2 tablespoons grated
    parmesan cheese*
*4 tablespoons diced
    turkey pepperoni*

Preheat oven to 375° F. Carefully open and unroll the croissant dough until you have a rectangle. Be careful not to separate the dough at the perforations. If it does separate, just pinch it back together. Spread the pizza sauce evenly over the dough; then sprinkle the cheeses and pepperoni on the sauce. Reroll the dough like it was before. Cut the roll into 8 even slices. Lay the slices about 2 inches apart on a lightly greased cookie sheet. Bake for 18 to 20 minutes or until light golden brown. Remove from cookie sheet and serve warm.

Jack-O'-Lantern Cake

3 cups granulated sugar
1½ cups butter
6 eggs
2 tablespoons vanilla extract
4½ cups all-purpose flour

2 tablespoons baking powder
1½ cups milk
2 drops red food coloring
4 drops yellow food coloring

Preheat oven to 350° F for metal or glass pans, 325° F for dark or coated pans. Grease and flour 2 12-cup Bundt pans and 1 individual muffin tin. In a large bowl, cream the sugar and butter; then beat in the eggs one at a time. Stir in the vanilla. In a medium bowl, combine flour and baking powder, then add to the creamed mixture and blend well. Add the milk and food coloring, mixing until batter is smooth and a light creamy orange. Fill the 2 muffin tins ⅔ full. Split the rest of the mixture between the 2 Bundt pans. Bake muffins for 12–18 minutes and the Bundt cakes 35–40 minutes, or until a toothpick inserted comes out clean. Cool completely.

Orange and Green Frosting

8 cups powdered sugar
1 cup (2 sticks) softened
    butter or margarine
1 cup shortening
¼ cup milk

2 teaspoons vanilla extract
8 drops red food coloring
16 drops yellow food coloring
6 drops green food coloring

In a large bowl, beat the powdered sugar, butter, and shortening at low speed until blended. Beat in the milk and vanilla on medium speed until smooth. If necessary, stir in the milk a few drops at a time. Remove and reserve ⅓ cup of the frosting. Add red and yellow food coloring to the remaining frosting; blend well to make orange frosting.

To make pumpkin shape, place 1 cake, rounded side down, on a serving plate. If necessary, before assembling, trim cakes to form flat surfaces. Spread the top with some of the orange frosting. Place second cake, rounded side up, on top of first cake. Frost cakes with orange frosting. Add green food coloring to the reserved frosting. Blend green frosting well. Frost the bottom of the cupcake and position on top, forming the stem of the pumpkin.

Chocolate Frosting for Face

1 square (1 ounce) unsweetened chocolate, chopped
1 teaspoon butter or margarine

1 cup powdered sugar
1–2 tablespoons boiling water

Heat the chocolate and butter in a small saucepan over low heat until melted, stirring constantly. Blend in powdered sugar and 1 tablespoon water. Beat until smooth. Add additional water, a teaspoon at a time until it's the proper spreading consistency. Cool until less than body temperature while planning face details. Use a toothpick to make light indentions into the orange frosting to sketch out the face. Fill a plain-tipped pastry bag with the frosting. Create your own unique jack-o'-lantern face with the chocolate frosting.

Carolyn's Giant Hostess Cupcake

2 dark chocolate
    cake mixes

1 jar (7 ounces)
    marshmallow creme

Preheat oven to 350° F for metal or glass pans, 325° F for dark or coated pans. Grease the sides and bottom of a 10-inch angel food cake pan and a 10-inch springform pan. Prepare cake mixes using instructions on backs of boxes. After beating the batter, pour ¾ of the batter into the angel food cake pan. Pour the remaining ¼ into the springform pan. Bake cake in springform pan 15 minutes. Cake is done when a toothpick inserted in the center comes out clean. Bake cake in angel food cake pan for 45–50 minutes. Again check with toothpick. (Dark or coated pans may take 3–5 minutes longer.) Cool in pan on wire rack for 15 minutes. Cool completely before frosting.

Trim tops of both cakes to make completely flat surfaces. Place cake from angel food cake pan on plate with trimmed top up. Fill the center hole with marshmallow creme. Use some of the excess creme to ice the top, being careful to not get too close to the edge. The layers should stick together, but you don't want to be able to see any of the creme once the top layer is on. The cake from the springform pan goes on top, bottom up. This should be a thin layer to give a good, flat surface for the icing and to cover the marshmallow creme.

Ganache Chocolate Icing

4 squares (4 ounces) semisweet chocolate, chopped
½ cup whipping cream
¼ cup powdered sugar

Place the chopped chocolate in a medium bowl. In a small saucepan, bring whipping cream to a boil. Pour the cream into chocolate and stir until chocolate is completely melted. Let frosting cool until it doesn't feel warm to the touch. Pour icing on top of cake, covering the top completely and letting it run off the edges. Spread some along the edges, covering where the small top layer joins the main cake. If too much icing has drizzled onto the edges of the cake, just wipe off the excess with a paper towel. You want the icing just along the top like a Hostess cupcake. Put the cake in the refrigerator until the icing is firm.

White Icing

⅓ cup powdered sugar   *1 teaspoon milk*

Mix powdered sugar and milk in a small bowl until smooth. Add drops of milk if needed to get the right consistency. Fill a plain-tipped pastry bag with the white frosting and decorate with a squiggle across the top of the cake.

Note: Freeze leftover cake trimmed from the top of cakes to use later, crumbled on ice cream or pudding.

Don't miss the next
Fresh-Baked Mystery!

Christmastime is coming to Weatherford,
Texas, and Phyllis Newsom has a few
new holiday recipes to try out—and a
murder case to stir up trouble. . . .

Read on for an excerpt from
The Christmas Cookie Killer
by Livia J. Washburn

Coming from Obsidian
in December 2008

There were probably things in the world that smelled better than freshly baked cookies, but for the life of her, Phyllis Newsom couldn't think of what they might be.

Throw in the scent of pine from the Christmas tree in the corner of the living room, and this had to be what Heaven smelled like, Phyllis thought. The only thing that might improve it would be if she asked Sam Fletcher to start a fire in the big stone fireplace. Since this was Texas, where the winters were mild except for the occasional blue norther that came roaring down out of the panhandle, the fireplace didn't get much use. Phyllis's late husband, Kenny, had gotten a fire going in it once or twice a year, but it hadn't been used since he passed away.

Phyllis felt a mental twinge and wondered if it would be disloyal to Kenny's memory to have Sam build a fire. She decided that it wouldn't. The hearth was there to be used, after all. And with a cold front blowing through, by tonight the heat from some flames would feel awfully good in this drafty old house.

Of course, there was a central heating and cooling unit humming away, but that wasn't the same thing. It just wasn't the same thing at all.

Phyllis stood in the big arched opening between the living room and dining room and watched with a smile as most of her neighbors milled around the dining table, which was covered with platters of cookies. All kinds of cookies. Plain, fancy, some with frosting, some not. Holiday decorations abounded. Phyllis was sure the cookies tasted as good as they looked, too, but for now, no one was sampling—this was the time to just admire them.

On a day like today, with so many guests, having a big house came in handy. Quite a few people lived in this neighborhood of older homes a few blocks from the downtown square of Weatherford, Texas, and most of them had come over for the annual Christmas cookie exchange. As busy and hectic as life was these days, folks didn't see their neighbors as much as they used to. It was good to catch up on what had been going on in everybody's life. The get together also served as an unofficial welcome party for people who had moved into the neighborhood since the previous Christmas.

Sam Fletcher moved up beside Phyllis and asked in a quiet voice, "Is there always this big a turnout?"

That reminded Phyllis this was Sam's first Christmas in the house. He was a relative newcomer, too. He had only moved in during the summer, although he fit in so well with Phyllis and her other boarders that it seemed as if he had always been there. Even Carolyn Wilbarger, who had been leery of the idea of having a man living in the house with three women, had accepted him.

Phyllis had started taking in boarders after Kenny's death, when it became obvious that the house was too big for her alone. It wasn't so much a matter of money—it was more that she couldn't stand rattling around by herself in it. As a retired teacher, she had extended the offer to friends of hers who were also longtime educators and found themselves in need of a place to live. There had been other boarders along the way, but at the moment the inhabitants of the house consisted of herself; Carolyn Wilbarger, who was widowed like Phyllis; Eve Turner, who was divorced—or between marriages, as she liked to put it; and Sam Fletcher, who had lost his wife to cancer a few years earlier. All former teachers, and now all good friends. One of the rooms upstairs was vacant, but Phyllis hadn't gone out of her way to look for another boarder. She didn't want to disrupt the chemistry that had developed in the house. She knew from the years she had spent in a classroom that once a group of people got along well, you didn't want to go messing with it too much.

"Yes, there's usually a big crowd," she said to Sam, tilting her head back a little so she could look up at the lanky, rawboned former basketball coach and history teacher. Phyllis had taught eighth-grade history, so she had a love of the past in common with Sam. "People like to socialize at this time of year, and they'll always come out for cookies, even on a chilly afternoon like this."

A grin creased Sam's rugged face. "Can't argue with that. I'm a mite fond of cookies myself. When can we dig in?"

"In a little while. Just be patient."

Sam shook his head. "I'll try. But it won't be easy." He paused, then added, "When are you supposed to find out who won the contest?"

"The winner will be announced in the paper next week, a couple of days before Christmas."

"Think you've got a shot at winnin'?"

"I *always* think I have a chance to win. Otherwise I wouldn't enter."

Carolyn had come up behind Phyllis in time to hear that comment. She said, "Yes, you have to get credit for perserverance. It's a shame it hasn't paid off for you very often."

Phyllis turned her head to glare over her shoulder, but she didn't really mean it. It was true that she and Carolyn had a long history of competing against each other in various baking contests, and it was also true that Carolyn won considerably more often than she lost, but Phyllis didn't take the rivalry all that seriously. She didn't really care who won as long as she had a good time coming up with exciting new foods.

At least, that was what she tried to believe. . . .

"We'll see what the judges think next week."

Phyllis and Carolyn had both entered recipes in the local newspaper's annual Christmas cookie contest. The rules were simple: Bake a batch of cookies, take them to the newspaper office along with the recipe, and a panel of expert judges would select the best cookies. The recipe would be published in the paper. Phyllis wasn't exactly sure who those "expert" judges were—she suspected they were all the people who worked at the newspaper, and that the contest was at least partially a way to get people to give them cookies—but she didn't care. What she enjoyed was creating the recipes and actually baking the cookies.

This year she had baked lime sugar cookies sprinkled with powdered sugar and cut with a special set of snowflake cookie cutters that made each cookie's shape a little bit different than all the others. The cookies were unusual, looked good, and tasted great, so Phyllis thought she had at least a decent shot at winning.

Eve joined Phyllis, Carolyn, and Sam in the archway and scanned the crowd with avid interest, reminding Phyllis a little of a hunting falcon.

"If you're looking for eligible men who have moved in since last year, you're out of luck," Carolyn said. "You'll have to find husband number five—or is it six?—somewhere else."

Eve smiled and took Sam's arm. "Why, the most eligible man in the neighborhood is right here, don't you think, dear?"

Carolyn snorted and Sam looked uncomfortable, and to change the subject Phyllis said, "I suppose I'd better put a plate of cookies together for Agnes."

"I hadn't noticed that she's not here," Eve said. "She's always so quiet, you hardly notice when she's there, let alone when she's not."

"She called and said she wasn't coming," Phyllis explained. "She's getting around a little better these days, but she still has to use a walker and it's not easy for her. I walked over earlier and picked up her plate of ginger cookies, and I promised her I'd bring her a sampler of everyone else's."

Agnes Simmons had lived next door to Phyllis for more than thirty years. They were friends, but had never been close. Agnes was in her late eighties, more than twenty years older than Phyllis, and they had little in common.

A month earlier, when Agnes had fallen and broken her hip, Phyllis had pitched in to help her because that was what neighbors did, whether they were close friends or not. Once Agnes returned home from the rehab hospital, Phyllis visited often, bringing food, cleaning up around the place, and running any errands that needed to be done. Sam had gone with her a time or two to help with some of the heavy work like turning the mattresses.

Phyllis went into the kitchen and got a large plate from the cabinet. She had made a big bowl of punch and had it sitting on the kitchen counter along with a stack of plastic cups so that people could help themselves. Young people would probably be horrified at the thought of visitors—some of them almost strangers—milling around unattended in their houses. But Phyllis had been raised in a more hospitable time, a more innocent time, she supposed, and despite her own brushes with violent crime over the past half year, she liked to think that she maintained some of that bygone innocence. Mixed with a healthy dose of reasonable caution, of course.

She returned to the dining room and filled the plate with cookies from the various platters, taking one or two of each kind for Agnes Simmons. Catching Carolyn's eye, she said, "I'll be right back."

"Would you like some company?"

"No, that's all right. I'll be fine." It would take only a couple of minutes to walk next door.

Phyllis felt the chilly wind on her face as she stepped out onto the porch. The front that had come through wasn't strong enough to be considered a blue norther, but it would drop temperatures to a respectable December level. The sky was thick with clouds.

She followed the path to the sidewalk and turned right, preferring to follow the concrete path rather than cutting across her own lawn and Agnes's yard. That was another vestige of her upbringing. You didn't walk on the grass if you could avoid it.

Agnes's two-story house had a large front porch like Phyllis's, but there was no hanging swing on it. The porch had a rather bare look to it, in fact. Agnes had been widowed for fifteen years. She had children and grandchildren, but they seldom visited. Knowing that made Phyllis's heart go out to the older woman. She had only one son, herself, but Mike stopped by frequently, and Phyllis saw her daughter-in-law, Sarah, and her grandson, Bobby, fairly often, too. Whenever she stopped to think about it, although she missed Kenny, she still considered herself to be a lucky woman, surrounded by family and friends.

Phyllis rang the bell, and a moment later she heard the clumping of Agnes's walker as the woman approached the door. "It's just me, Agnes," she called.

The clumping stopped as Agnes replied, "Come on in."

Phyllis opened the screen door and then the wooden door and stepped into the house. Heat rolled out at her in waves. Agnes liked to keep the place warm. More than warm, actually. It was stifling in there a lot of the time. Phyllis had learned to put up with it, though. She herself was more prone to getting chilled than she had once been, and Agnes was considerably older. Age thinned the blood, one of many drawbacks to getting older.

If only the alternative wasn't so much worse.

Phyllis saw that Agnes had sat down in an armchair in the living room, but the woman grasped her walker and pushed herself to her feet again as her gaze landed on the plate of cookies. Her eyes lit up.

"Oh, my," Agnes said. "Don't those look good! You're a dear to bring them over to me like this, Phyllis."

"I just wish you felt well enough to attend the cookie exchange," Phyllis said. "Maybe next year."

"Yes, next year," Agnes said with that dry irony of the elderly, as if the thought of her still being around next year was almost too far-fetched to contemplate.

"Would you like me to put them in the kitchen for you?"

"Bring them over here first. I'd like to take a look at them and maybe try one."

Agnes was a small woman. Not birdlike and frail, as so many elderly women are, but compact, rather, with no wasted flesh on her. She wore a quilted, pale blue robe.

Phyllis held the plate where Agnes could see all the cookies. The woman's face, which bore the marks of the strain she had been under since her injury, lit up with a smile.

"They all look wonderful," she said. "I'm sure my grandchildren will love them."

"Oh? Your grandchildren are coming for a visit?"

"They're already here," Agnes said. "Well, not *here*, exactly. Not right at the moment. Frank and Ted and Billie, and all their families, came in earlier today. I'm not surprised you didn't notice, since you were busy getting ready for the cookie exchange and all."

"Where are they now?" Phyllis asked.

"They drove over to Fort Worth to go to the mall. They'll be back later."

Phyllis nodded. She wasn't convinced that Agnes's sons and daughter and their families had actually arrived to visit her. Agnes might be saying that just so Phyllis wouldn't think she was going to be alone again for the holidays. But questioning her wouldn't serve any purpose.

"Well, I hope everyone enjoys the cookies."

"I'm sure they will." Agnes took one hand off the walker and reached for the plate. "Look at these snowflakes! They're so pretty!"

"I made those," Phyllis said, not trying to keep the pride out of her voice. When it came to baking, she didn't believe in false modesty.

Agnes took a bite of the cookie and exclaimed how good it was. "How in the world did you find a cookie cutter shaped like this?"

"I have a special set of snowflake cookie cutters that allow you to cut several different designs," Phyllis explained.

"Would you mind if I borrowed them, dear? I plan to do baking with my granddaughters while they're here, and I'd love to make some cookies like that."

"Of course," Phyllis said. "I'll run next door and get them."

"You're sure you don't mind?"

"Not at all."

"Thank you. That's awfully nice of you, Phyllis."

Phyllis set the plate of cookies on an end table. "I'll be right back."

She left the house and headed back toward her own, tugging her thick sweater tighter around her as she went. She cut across the yards this time, not wanting to be away from her house and the cookie exchange any longer than she had to. Being neighborly to Agnes was one thing, but she had a houseful of guests and it wasn't right to make Carolyn and Eve look after them for any longer than necessary.

"How's Agnes?" Carolyn asked when Phyllis went inside.

"All right. I'm going to loan my snowflake cookie cutters to her."

Carolyn frowned. "Right now?"

"Her grandchildren are visiting and she wants to do some baking with them."

Carolyn's eyebrows rose. She was as surprised as Phyllis had been by the idea that Agnes's family had come to spend even part of the Christmas holiday with her.

Phyllis got the set of cookie cutters from a drawer in the kitchen and went out the back door this time, walking between the houses to the front. A hedge divided the properties, and she heard a door shut somewhere on the other side of it, at Agnes's house. Maybe the kids and grandkids were back from the mall.

No strange cars were in the driveway, though, Phyllis noted as she reached the front of the house and climbed the steps. She planned to just knock and go on in, since Agnes was expecting her back, but she noticed that the wooden door was ajar behind the screen. She felt the heat coming out of the house before she even reached the door. That was odd, to say the least. Agnes never liked to let the cold air in.

Phyllis pulled the screen door open and leaned toward the wooden door. "Agnes?" she called. "It's just me again. I've got the cookie cutters."

No response came from inside. Phyllis supposed that Agnes could have gone into the kitchen or somewhere else in the rear of the house. She had heard that door shut, after all.

"Agnes?" Phyllis stepped inside. "Are you still here?"

She looked toward the living room, and the first thing she noticed was that the cookies she had left on the end table were now scattered across the floor. Some of them were crushed as if they had been stepped on. The plate lay upside down on the floor next to the table.

Phyllis gasped in surprise at the sight. She took an instinctive step backward, then stopped as she saw a couple of feet in fuzzy slippers sticking out between the sofa and a coffee table. She spotted one of the legs of the walker, too, and she could tell from its position that it was overturned.

She knew in that moment what had happened. Agnes,

none too steady even on the walker, had fallen again. She had probably reached out as she was toppling over, trying to catch herself, and hit the plate of cookies with a hand, sending it flying. Those slippered feet weren't moving, so it was likely Agnes had either passed out or knocked herself out when she fell.

With her heart pounding, Phyllis rushed into the living room, crying out, "Agnes!" She came around the sofa and saw the elderly woman lying on her side, not moving. Her robe had fallen open, revealing a pink flannel nightgown under it.

Phyllis recoiled as she realized why the robe was open. The belt that had been around Agnes's waist was no longer there to hold it closed.

That was because the belt was now wrapped around Agnes's neck and pulled so tight it was sunk into the flesh. Agnes's eyes were wide-open, staring sightlessly from her twisted, lifeless face.

A PEACH OF A MURDER:

A Fresh Baked Mystery
LIVIA J. WASHBURN

*Fresh out of the oven: the first in a new series
of baking mysteries. Includes recipes!*

All year round, retired schoolteacher Phyllis
Newsom is as sweet as peach pie—except during
the Peach Festival, whose blue ribbon has slipped
through Phyllis's fingers more than once...

Everyone's a little shook up when the corpse of a
no-good local turns up underneath a car in a local
garage. But even as Phyllis engages in some
amateur sleuthing, she won't let it distract her from
out-baking her rivals and winning the upcoming
Peach Festival contest.

With her unusual Spicy Peach Cobbler, Phyllis
hopes to knock 'em dead. But that's just an
expression—never in her wildest dreams did she
think her cobbler would actually kill a judge. Now,
she's suspected of murder—and she's got to bake
this case wide open.

**Available wherever books are sold or
at penguin.com**